D1827678

ONE A MINUTE

ONE A MINUTE

John Delaney

UNITED WRITERS
Cornwall

UNITED WRITERS PUBLICATIONS LTD
Ailsa, Castle Gate, Penzance, Cornwall.

*All Rights Reserved. No part of this publica-
tion may be reproduced, stored in a retrieval
system, or transmitted, in any form or by any
means, electronic, mechanical, photocopying,
recording or otherwise, without the prior
permission of the Copyright owner.*

British Library Cataloguing in Publication Data
Delaney, John
One a minute.
I. Title
823'.914[F]   PR6054.E39/

ISBN 1 85200 007 4

Copyright (c) 1987 John Delaney

Printed in Great Britain by
United Writers Publications Ltd
Cornwall

For Mam and Dad

Love John

To Mam and Dad
and all at Halewood.
Thanks Mike.

Chapter One

The rain eased and the sun barged its way through the billowed greyness like an overworked doctor through a crowd, fragile, irritable but conscientious. Called out in the middle of the night to administer life-saving light to a premature day.

Exploratory fingers ran cautiously over an oblivious horizon, touching and probing and carefully drawing the day from its dark and close confinement. Then it came more quickly, stretching and pushing itself up into the black-browed sky.

It showed no promise of being a particularly notable day, but it had arrived and that was the main thing. The sun's old hands were cold but thorough. It seemed the day would survive.

Halliwell and Worth had decided to forgo the second of their nightly patrols. The mellow tones of Sinatra rendering a medley of his greatest hits on the radio proved infinitely more preferable to dutiful, pneumonia-including vigilance.

As Worth had once illogically observed on a previous and similarly bleak night: "No one in their right mind would be mad enough to be up to no good on a night like this." Everyone laughed, but no one argued.

The internal line telephone rang. It had an irritating over enthusiasm about it for that hour and Halliwell was quick to silence it. He did not bother with his official: 'Security, number three gate' slogan. The plant was deserted but for his strategically dispersed colleagues.

"Good morning, campers," he yawned.

"Morning, Robert," chirped a voice. It was Terry Cummings at number two gate. "What's the weather like over there? It's been pissing down all night here," he called. His voice was piled with unnecessary emphasis, like an inexperienced user speaking to someone on the other side of the world.

Halliwell squinted through the rain-smeared window. He blinked, his eyelids felt like flaps of coarse canvas. "Bit better, Terence, it's trying to brighten up a bit now. Oh look there's the sun!"

It was fatuous conversation they knew, but it passed the night away.

There was a short pause then Cummings said: "I didn't see any of you guys patrolling your area at the usual time this morning."

"Come to think of it, we didn't see any of you lot, either."

"Dead right you didn't, mate! The first one was bad enough. Burt got soaked. He's been hanging around here in his undies all night and it's not a pretty sight, I can tell you. His trousers have been steaming in front of our electric fire for hours."

"Fancy being scared of a drop of rain," taunted Halliwell harmlessly.

"Drop of rain! More like a bloody monsoon!"

"Okay, okay, keep your hat on. You started it."

"I could do with keeping my hat on," said Cummings, considering the suggestion. "We've got a leak in our roof. It's been drip, drip into the bucket like a bloody Chinese water torture all night."

"Well, God help us if anyone has broken in and pinched all the motors, that's all I can say."

"Not much chance of that," sniffed Cummings. "They'd have to get the buggering things started first. Anyway, at least we stay awake all night. Which is more than can be said for the sleeping uglies at number six. That reminds me, they're due for their alarm call in five minutes so we'd better not natter for too long, we don't want them to over-sleep, do we?"

"Those buggers, how do they get away with it?" said Halliwell. He glanced towards his third partner, Security Guard Atkin. Only his broad upper quarter was visible above the table, his head was tucked into his folded arms, his

8

shoulders rose and fell like a gentle sea.

"It's a well known fact," sighed Cummings. "The cheekier you are the more you get away with. I reckon it's only a matter of time before they turn up at the start of the shift with three dummies from Burton's window dressed up in their uniforms so they can stand them in the middle of the lodge and bugger off home for the rest of the night."

"You haven't suggested that to them have you?" asked Halliwell with a tinge of alarm.

"No, not yet."

"Well I wouldn't go putting ideas into their heads if I were you."

A thoughtful pause followed, then Cummings said: "Perhaps you're right. Oh, by the way, did you hear about that bloke who collapsed going through their gate last Friday?"

"No."

"Well there was this scrawny little bloke walking out with the crowd at the end of the shift and just before he got through the gate he just collapsed like a ton of bricks. Then when two of the guards went to help him he started yelling at them to leave him alone and tried to get up by himself, but he couldn't hardly budge off the ground. Then one of them noticed this square bulge under his mac and it turned out he had these two heavy duty batteries hanging from a rope around his neck."

Halliwell smiled. The story did not surprise him. He had been witness to too many similar incidents for that. "So much for your theory that the cheekier you are the more you get away with."

"No, that was where he went wrong," corrected Cummings. "He should have said they were for his digital watch or something. Dear me, can you hear that row?"

Burt Ryder had caused the sudden change of subject. He was faint in the background but none the more endurable for that as he groaned murderously through the opening lyrics of *My Way*.

"Ol' knobbly knees is back," mumbled Cummings. "He's been like this ever since he heard it on the radio before. You should see the silly old sod, he's doing all the actions, you

9

know. Standing here on legs like hairy milk bottles, using a rolled up Express for a microphone."

"You've got to admit though, it is an original interpretation."

"I don't know how he does it." Cummings was genuinely perplexed. "My dog didn't make a noise half as bad as that when he woke up at the vet's and found out he'd had his goolies whipped off. The disc jockey said it's Mick Jagger tomorrow. The mind boggles. Bloody hell, is that the time, I'd better give the other shower a tinkle. See you tonight . . . if it's not piddlin' down again."

The Fuhrer sat eclipsed. His strident voice, awesome and inspiring scaled the huge mound of unopened envelopes and tumbled down onto the long table beyond.

"Dis fan mail iz getting too much for me."

The remark was greeted with an uneasy silence by his ministers. He toppled the mound onto the floor with a long graceful sweep of his arm.

Eva 'Daffy' Braun, poured nakedly over the Fuhrer's lap, chewed passionately at his neck. He fondled her small right breast absently.

"Vell, do you sinc zay are too much for me?"

"Ya, ya, Mine Fuhrer!" responded the ministers in harmony.

"Zo, you sinc I can't cope, uh?"

"Ya, ya, Mine Fuhrer!" responded the ministers in harmony.

"Vot!" he roared ferociously. His ministers cringed. Then his voice dropped to a lover's whisper as he turned to Eva 'Daffy' Braun. "Now der ear you German Shepherd bitch." He returned to his ministers. "YOU SINC YOUR FUHRER CANNOT COPE MIT A FEW LETTERS!"

"Nine, nine, Mine Fuhrer!"

'Vot do you mean nine? Der are thousands here!" His hand left her breast and ran down her bare stomach. She gasped.

"Ve mean dat our Fuhrer could be addressing der troops," pointed out Joachim Von Ribbentrop obsequiously.

10

"You mean instead of addressing der envelopes, uh, hee, hee, hee."

The pun was greeted with an uneasy silence by the ministers.

"VY ARE YOU NOT LAUGHING?"

The ministers responded with instant, uproarious howls. The Fuhrer studied them with jutting chin and half closed eyes. "Hey, Himler," he called. "You are not trying. Look at Goring over der going purple unt rolling on der floor telling der Stormtrooper to beat him on der head mitt der rifle butt. Ya, ya! Dats more like it Himler, baby! I like der vay you slam der drawer mitt your head in it. Oh, look, everybody! Now he is viddling himself!"

Eva "Daffy" Braun gasped: "Oh, Adolf. I'm coming!"

"But now Rosenburg has told der Stormtrooper to shoot him in der privates! Okay, kviete everyone. Albie Steep is jumping out of der window. I like it, I like it! Vell done, Albieeeeee . . . !"

Steep woke with a start. Fighting the sensation of falling he scrambled to the surface of the blankets. The room stopped spinning.

A thin, diffident morning light hid behind the closed curtains allowing the murkiness within the room to attempt to coax him back to sleep. Somewhere in the distance it was thundering. He closed his eyes, blissfully, warmly remote, then opened one and searched for the alarm clock with it. Its luminous hands glowed dimly and only now did he become aware of its busy tick.

It told him that the time was twenty-three minutes to six but as it gained one and a half minutes every two and a quarter hours and the last time he put it right was eleven-thirty p.m. two days ago that made the correct time . . . sod it.

With an effort he raised his head from the pillow and peered over the candy-striped plain to the remote white feet on the horizon's edge, shivering, cold and unsheltered like homeless waifs. He pulled them charitably under cover, although it took some compromised splaying of his legs to accommodate them. He would have to get shorter legs or a longer bed.

11

His icy feet touched Daffy's legs and she pulled them away, drawing them up to her stomach like a hedgehog at a sign of danger. Her left knee rested on his hip. His hand found the knee and slid up her warm thigh, stopping at the top. He rolled his head over the pillow to look at her.

Her hair fell in dull greasy streaks across her face. It always looked greasy no matter how often she washed it, and her ears always poked through like two halves of a digestive biscuit. Her mouth was hung open and her lips were dry and flaky white. A little waterfall of saliva ran from a corner into a spreading pool on the pillow. An ingratiating half memory whispered to him of some faraway liaison she had taken with Adolf Hitler. He did not listen.

He turned to the ceiling. To the comforting flakes and cracks. The shapes and patterns they made were indistinct and unfamiliar in the half light, as though they moved about during the night and had not got back into their proper positions in time for his unexpectedly early awakening.

But there was something else disquieting about the gloom. A nebulous feeling of uneasiness hovered just out of arms reach. It worried him that he did not know what he was worrying about.

He was wide awake now. He slid a hand behind his head.

Daffy had been spending her weekends in his home and his bed for five months. She usually went home on Sunday evenings but last night they had been watching television and she had fallen asleep and he had neglected to wake her until the last bus had gone. He had suggested a taxi but she yawningly declined on account of taxi drivers being 'robin' swines', especially after midnight.

It was a similar situation which had begun their sleeping together. Again they had been watching television until late and had both fallen asleep. They eventually woke at half past two on a Sunday morning and crawled, dim-eyed into the same bed. Neither of them suggested it. Neither of them had gone with the flimsiest sexual stirring or design. It just seemed the obvious thing to do.

They woke later that morning and found two cups of steaming hot tea on his bedside table. Auntie Aggie had left them there. Auntie Aggie was the most broad-minded

12

seventy-one-year-old that Steep had ever known.

From then it had become a welcome weekend ritual. During the early months it was exciting; mid-week thoughts of what the weekend held in store would burst little puffs of anticipation in his stomach.

He had always thought that if you slept and had sex with a woman on a regular basis then it would not be long before you loved her and you began to feel sort of domesticated and cosy inside. He looked across at Daffy. A secondary little salivafall ran from the pool on the pillow down onto the sheet covering the mattress and he wondered why he couldn't live with a normal seventy-one-year-old aunt; one with conventionally boring, stolid, stick-in-the-mud Victorian principles.

Halliwell moved to the door, opened it just wide enough and poked his head out. The rain had gone altogether now but the air still hung in that damp weary way so expected of it when mingled with northern industry.

"I'll open the gates," he said to Worth. "Admit the madding throng," he added unenthusiastically. He lifted his cap from the window ledge and let it drop carelessly onto his head.

Worth called after him: "Don't be long, the kettle's nearly boiling."

Predictably, Atkin let go a rasping snore, which, Halliwell knew, meant he was not asleep.

A couple of paces took him to the locked gates. He unlocked them, folded them back and stepped through.

To his right the pavement began a cautious upward slope. The sun beyond was having difficulty in impressing itself any further on the day and it clung to the pale cliff of sky like an exhausted mountain climber.

Somebody was half way down the slope, crossing the road from the other side. It was a maintenance man who had been on the night shift for the past week, resulting in his biological functions being out of synchronisation to antipodean proportions: Back on the day shift now, he had woken early from a restless sleep on this soggy non-event of a Monday morning, his senses tingling with misplaced and pre-doomed passion.

His wife, regrettably being firmly in tune with local time had remained inert and unresponsive despite substantial and contorted efforts aimed at inducing some degree of mutual stimulation, and he had dismally dressed and wandered from the house, aching with a badly damaged pride and a sense of anti-climax that he would have to endure for the entire, interminable day.

He shuffled sullenly along. His shoulders hunched inside a grubby blue anorak and his hands sunk and sulky in deep pockets. He splashed mercilessly through any of the murky pavement pools that got in his way.

"Morning. You're an early bird," nodded Halliwell as the maintenance man reached him.

The maintenance man passed beneath Halliwell like a bellicose beetle beneath a size twelve boot. He did not speak but in response to Halliwell's greeting, flashed a quick insolent glare from below his eyelids as though the words had been virulent expletives. Halliwell shrugged and returned to the lodge.

That was a rather pretentious title for a one roomed hut measuring twenty feet by twelve, he had always thought. Inside was a table and four padded tubular steel chairs; one of which was currently being amply filled with Atkin pretending to be asleep. The yellow Formica table top was strewn with curling Sunday supplements, chewed *Playboys* and a pristine *Numismatics Monthly*; along with a locally scattered pack of fifty-one playing cards that had lost its seven of diamonds.

On the window ledge, next to a fine burgeoning specimen of Geranium Red Express, sat the radio; or the wireless as Halliwell pedantically called it in deference to its age which was believed to be something pre-Marconi. To Halliwell anything post-Guy Lombardo and His Royal Canadians wafting from its battered wooden cabinet seemed positively precocious.

To the left of the door were two telephones, the internal line fixed to the wall, the external on the window ledge lower down. In the middle of the opposite wall was a second door opening onto a narrow pavement and then the roadway; barred by a hefty steel gate.

The remainder of the compact early morning hut belonged

14

to Worth. Like a latter-day sorcerer surrounded by cupboards, mugs, teapots, electric kettles, large plastic water containers, sundry items of cutlery and numerous neatly labled tins all thoughtfully laid out in a paragon of ergonomics, he performed.

"Just in time," said Worth, lifting the teapot and sending a curving column of steaming amber liquid spinning into Halliwell's mug. Atkin snored. "Tea's up, Fred," said Worth, then: "Still cold out?" to Halliwell, holding his hands up to the glowing red bar of the electric fire above the door.

"Not too bad," shrugged Halliwell. "At least the rain's stopped."

Worth opened two of his tins and spooned out the requisite measures of powdered milk and sugar. "Don't like the look of it, though," he opined, rubbing a rough little port hole in the window's steamy condensation and peering through it.

"It can do what it likes today," yawned Halliwell, taking the mug from Worth. "I'll be well away." He blew gently across the surface of the brew, dispersing the hypnotic wraith of steam which returned impudently immediately he stopped.

Atkin snored again. The bastard was rubbing it in, Halliwell knew, gloating!

He took an investigative sip, like a man tentatively sampling some unfamiliar concoction. He held it for an appraisive moment, then as it began to burn hurriedly gulped it down his throat.

It tasted exactly the same as it always did. And not for the first time did Halliwell wonder how the blending of such mundane ingredients which, when left to the devices of anyone else would invariably result in a mere brew of tea, could, when allied to a little flair and ingenuity be made to assume to such a devastating degree all the subtle characteristics and nuances of boiled giraffe piss.

Halliwell had grown quite used to his partner's diabolical brews. He had not developed an immunity to its appalling taste but he could almost control any outward signs of revulsion and he had learned to swallow the stuff without hardly making a face: Whenever the opportunity presented itself he would dispose of it in the plastic plant pot on the window ledge. Curiously the Geranium Red Express domiciled therein thrived on the vile concoctions and Halliwell had always half expected to turn up for work one day and discover the lodge demolished and the Geranium Red Express, now two hundred feet tall, lumbering off in the distance to have a go at the Eiffel Tower or the Empire State Building. People made science fiction films about the likes of Worth's tea. One day, Halliwell feared it would conquer the world.

"Come on, Fred, nice cuppa," said Worth.

Atkin snored.

Halliwell looked at his watch, synchronising it with the man on the wireless. It was twelve minutes after seven.

"He's got it right for a change," he said with mock surprise. "He must have been practising." He observed Worth from a secret corner of his eye, hoping for a sudden resumption of some back-turned activity which might allow him a furtive lunge for the Geranium.

Worth sipped contentedly at his tea and smacked his lips with quiet relish.

Halliwell stared down resignedly into his mug and the evil brown eye stared back. He braced himself for another sip. Then someone knocked on the door. "I'll go," he said quickly, putting down his mug so hurriedly that several mouthfuls slopped over the side.

It was a small man in a large green jacket. He wore obvious dentures and a haggard but willing expression.

"I'm new," he said, and as though in response to his own cue he sent a volunteer hand down into the dark reaches of some sinister bottomless inside pocket.

Halliwell wondered what he might retrieve. A lawn mower? A twenty-six inch colour television? A stuffed ostrich?

"I've got a letter here somewhere," said the man. His entire arm followed the fingers into the heavy clown-like excesses of the jacket. The garment wriggled and billowed as though he was struggling with a concealed live python.

"They don't start until eight, you know," pointed out Halliwell.

"Ah, *eight*, is it." The man nodded as though he had suspected as much and continued his tunnelling. "My youngest beat me to the envelope when it arrived." His

16

eyes turned up towards Halliwell, they were weary but plucky eyes. "He thinks he's a dog," he explained simply. "He keeps chewing all the letters up before we can get to him. He sits by the front door and waits, you see. I stuck all the bits together again but he must've swallowed some of it because the bit with the time on was missing."

Halliwell nodded as though that sort of thing happened to him all the time.

The man continued. He seemed to be enjoying himself just standing there chatting, as though it was a luxury seldom permitted him at home. "He took a lump out of the postman's arse once," he went on conversationally. "Latched on like a bleedin' doberman, he did."

"How did you get him off?" asked Halliwell with genuine and amused interest.

"We had to bring the third youngest out to him. He's the only one my youngest will take any notice of."

"Got a way with dogs, has he?" smiled Halliwell.

"You could say that," conceded the man. "He thinks he's a yeti. Hang on a minute. I think it's fallen down into the lining."

With that the man's head began to nose, then burrow into the jacket. He looked like some shabby green budgerigar settling down to sleep. "I can see it!" he called with sudden and muffled excitement. " 'ello, there's a couple of cheese butties down here as well. Pooo, they don't half pong."

For some moments the man became motionless. Then his submerged head began to jerk and tug inside the jacket.

"I'm sorry about this," he eventually called from inside the jacket. It was a saintly patient and well practised statement. One, it seemed, that he carried everywhere with him and always portrayed with the same harassed expression and tone. Halliwell imagined he must use it a lot when he took the kids out.

"You couldn't give me a hand, could you," asked the man helplessly. "Only I think I've got me head stuck."

The fading rain splashed against the muddy window, making little pearly globules that raced each other down the glass.

Steep enjoyed bus rides through the rain and he regretted its departure. The bus was almost full. It smelled of wet hair and damp clothes and implicit defeat. A humming heater under Steep's seat blew paradoxically cold air up his trouser legs. His ankles were freezing.

The girl who always boarded three stops after Steep had sat next to him. She had been travelling with him — when he was on the day shift — on that same bus for some seven or eight months now but this was the first time that their thighs had ever lain at such an excruciating proximity to each other.

She was wearing a blue patterned skirt to just below her knees and when she sat they pushed themselves free like inquisitive bald brown baby heads. He felt the closeness of her covered and undiscovered thighs through the seat and caught the immediate soft sweetness of her perfume amid the dampness and the mustiness. Her hair was a silky blonde that splashed into loose curls about her shoulders and she had a friendly natural smile that made her blue-grey eyes sparkle. They were the sort of eyes that washed all over you and made your stomach tingle when they looked at you: not that she had ever looked at him but if she ever did he was sure they would.

She wore no rings. Some mornings he allowed himself to feel encouraged by the fact, but more often all he could manage was an unseemly and lascivious frustration. He groaned a lusty, slightly whimpering, private groan: there was not an inch of her body that he did not crave to touch and to run his tongue over.

The bus left Nybs Lane and entered Hackets Hill, like Nybs Lane a dun and weary district of the city, but with its own brooding personality imputable to an incurable summer stink which came from an ill-disposed chemical factory lodged deep within its heart that manufactured deodorants and soap that cured body odour.

Now, with the clawing dregs of winter hanging on until late March the smell remained subdued.

The little old Hackets Hill houses stood sombre and joyless and huddled tightly together as though searching for some common warmth. Their cracked ledges and gutters dripped like runny noses. It seemed to Steep that if you looked at them for long enough you would catch one of them sniffing or shivering.

Her name was Sarah. He knew because she sometimes travelled with a friend called Carol and on suitable occasions he eavesdropped on their conversations. As far as he could deduce she worked in an office with two middle-aged men called Mr Walsh, who was fat and bald with greasy skin and always stood too close when he was speaking to her, and Mr Samson who was strange and quiet and hardly ever spoke to her at all. Sometimes she would glance at Mr Samson and he would be weeping while he worked; spilling real tears and choked sobs onto his blotter and trying to pretend that nothing was the matter and that nobody had noticed.

She was going to Corfu for a fortnight in July. She was left handed. Her favourite yoghurt was almond flavour. She hated semolina. And she kept something that was brown and white and called 'Chloe'.

The bus encountered its first thick traffic of the morning at Cambletown Avenue — Hackets Hill's only dual carriageway. Its length was plagued with traffic lights and pedestrian crossings which made the journey tedious at that hour: But this morning, with his best girl by his side, Steep did not mind.

Parasitic shops perched in motley rows gathered along the clogged road, their faces too tightly shut as though in childish attempts to feign sleep. The bus stopped outside a heavily armoured Tesco's. A slim, gum chewing, hard faced teenage girl wearing clomping heavy black boots and an indecorously brief and impractically draughty skirt clattered upstairs. Irresistible curiosity sent Steep's furtive eyes scurrying up after her. She was wearing the most deliciously black silky knickers and suspenders and he felt a sudden guilty surge through his loins.

The bus moved away and the engine began to moan and groan again. The girls delightful undergarments disappeared up the stairs. Steep wondered what she gave her boyfriend for his birthday.

Beyond Hackets Hill the bus cut directly through the centre of the Lellerscroft Industrial Estate. It was a large sprawled place but quite modern with some grass and young trees and limp but colourful flags: Sarah would leave him at the next stop, outside the Sunbug Radiator Company. She always walked back in the opposite direction to the bus and he watched her slyly in case she cast a hopeful parting glance or bashful 'bye-bye' smile up at him. But she hadn't bothered. She walked straight past him in the direction of the greasy, bulky Mr Walsh and the secretly sobbing Mr Samson. Poor old Mr Samson. What makes you cry?

Is it inside everyone, wondered Steep. A concealed compartment brimming with its own specially allocated emotion that can only be triggered by some carefully hidden lever marked, 'For Emergency Use Only'. Perhaps most people never discover what's inside their compartment because nobody ever gets inside them deeply enough to trigger their lever. Steep wondered who had triggered Mr Samson's lever?

He began to scan the headlines in the *Sun* over the shoulder of the man seated in front of him but they held his attention only fleetingly.

Without logical or definable reason his apparently aimless worry began to fog his head and blur his thoughts again. What the hell was he worried about? He couldn't think of anything and that worried him. You're better off knowing that there's something to worry about, he thought. Then you don't feel so worried. But when you worry and you don't know what you're worrying about, that really makes you worry.

Isn't it funny the way a word loses its meaning when you think it enough times. Perhaps if he thought 'worry' enough times it would lose its meaning and there would be nothing to worry about. Worry worry worry worry worry worry . . .

Bellend was a slow and grudging riser at the start of a week. As though aware that it would not rest again for five days and nights it awoke only to its own routine and reluctant pace. It did not like stirring itself, and it was never cheerful.

A trickle of torpid motor cars coughed around the perimeter road. They contained mostly foremen who were paid

20

to arrive early to prepare paperwork and to place the clocking-on machines in their racks in readiness for the incoming shift. The machines were always removed from their racks and locked away when not required by shifts clocking on or off, because if they were left out they would most certainly have had their innards filled with glue or been struck fatal blows by heavy metal objects, or in some other way rendered permanently inoperative.

Beneath the broad covering 'span between the lodge at number three gate and its storeroom a few yards opposite a group of twenty-one men sheltered from a sky that was not raining. There was a coolness between them and several had retreated unsociably behind newspapers upon the instant of their arrival and seemed quite prepared to remain there indefinitely. Some appeared uncertain, quietly confused. They stared blankly at their feet as though convinced that that very night they had been exchanged for someone else's while they slept.

The gathering of a new intake was a rare occurrence these days. A few years earlier more than twice that number would have occupied that same ground *every* Monday morning. But now there was nowhere else for the operators to work and so they did not leave in the numbers they used to.

Inside the lodge two day shift security guards were politely refusing cups of Worth's tea. They, like Halliwell and Atkin — who had gone out for a quick patrol because it looked as though the rain would hold off — lived in real dread of Worth's brews, yet none of them had ever been capable of summoning the necessary heartlessness to tell him so. He waved away their refusals in a gesture of honest kindliness and moved in amongst his equipment; quickly returning with two of the evil beverages.

The guards slurped noisily, like dubious suicides over mugs of poison. Worth turned back to tidy his steamy apparatus and the guards scowled and twisted their faces into the most hideous contortions, in the manner of rival, on-form gurners, then pulled and pushed at each other like quarrelling children behind teacher's back. Forcibly restraining each other in their selfish attempts to make the first break for the geranium.

*　　*　　*　　*

21

The rain did not stay away for long. The first fresh blobs spattered against the still damp ground. Some dribbled icily down the back of Billy Suggs' neck. He peddled faster, grateful for the slight downward incline.

Suggs, when the mood took him, would choose to ride his bicycle on the pavement once within the factory grounds, for no other reason than after seventeen years company service he felt entitled to a few exclusive privileges. Usually, if the pavement was cluttered he would use the road except when in a particularly ornery state of mind when he liked to ring his bell and shout obscenity laden warnings at the pedestrians. Sometimes, with the pavement to himself he would push his legs out far astride of his bicycle and freewheel down the slope.

But this morning was no time for such games. His hands were wet and cold, his thick stub fingers stiffened in the dank air. The rain hammered with increasing violence on his bowed back. His nose was running.

He let himself drift out towards the edge of the pavement so as to negotiate the ample curve which would bring him to the bicycle shed. He swept skilfully around the familiar corner applying the rear brake, at first moderately and then with a greater and mildly concerned force when the bicycle did not slow.

The bicycle shed stood this side of the security storeroom, adjacent to it the twenty-one new men sheltered from the rain. For a few desperately inadequate moments Billy Suggs debated the respective implications of colliding with a hard, impassive, cast iron bicycle shed or a soft, but potentially hostile new intake. He had no other options, and even now as his normally languid brain raced as fast as his runaway bicycle, one of those options was being removed.

The men at the threatened edge of the group maintained an unflinching stance in the face of the onrushing Suggs, induced rather by dull incredulity than some secret Matador daring, each of them now more wise to the extent of knowing what empty, doomed expression claws at the face of the kamikaze pilot just seconds before his inevitably fatal impact.

Suggs squeezed as hard as he could on his rear brake lever, at last the wheel locked and suddenly began to weave wildly beneath him like a frantically waved warning. There was no hope of avoiding them now, Suggs knew. So did the two men on the outskirts of the group for whom Suggs was directly headed and it seemed as though a starter's gun had just fired as both of them almost fell headlong as they scrambled clear.

Suggs and his bicycle flew through at an oblique angle into the peaceful, thickly populated and totally unsuspecting interior. A sudden stupefied chaos fell about them. Bodies were crashed and sprawled over the ground. Instinctive cries of: "Ow, gerroff me 'and!" and "Can't breathe, yer foot's on me belly!" And, most popularly: "Ahhhhh!" rose like escaping birds from the grovelling pandemonium.

One man who had been privately reliving last night's slow and sensual undressing of his wife, and was down to her scant frilly knickers and one suspendered black nylon when some-how thrust into this intruding madness, stared disbelievingly at a bicycle wheel and rusting red mudguard lodged between his legs, then at some grimy handle-bars pressed into his lower stomach, and finally at a sallow, crumpled dripping face hardly a nose breadth from his own. The face was vacant, so confused as to what expression it should wear that it could not even look confused. Its mouth was moving, repeating flatly. "Couldn't be 'elped, lads, couldn't be 'elped." But to this man the words were no more than empty noises among the enveloping bedlam.

Suddenly, in a tantrum of pique and delayed shock the man grabbed Suggs' handle-bars and began a curious esoteric tussle with them.

"Come on, steady on, now," said Suggs, his voice and expression now settling on an uneasy, half requesting, half threatening stance.

But the man either did not hear or did not heed the words and battled blindly on, the beginnings of a snarl now tugging at a corner of his mouth.

"Leggo, you!" growled Suggs, thumping his open palm squarely into the man's chest, knocking him a staggered step backwards.

Then, with all the lightning dexterity of a pony express rider about to change steeds Suggs dismounted and removed his pump from the crossbar. He drew it back, in doing so

23

poking a neutral man behind him in the ear.

"Aye-aye, pal," came the protest as Suggs swung the hard white plastic in a vicious arc without making contact with anyone, but causing two men just stumbling to their feet to hurl themselves back groundwards as the pump slashed inches above their heads.

Inside the lodge Halliwell enlarged Worth's weather forecasting port hole and looked through it to find the commotion. "What the sodding hell's going on," he grumbled, being joined at the window by his partners.

The two new guards were still off duty and readily ignored the disturbance. Instead, with Worth's attentions distracted they both, in a sensibly devised spirit of co-operation, crept like fugitives to the geranium, ditched the contents of their mugs into its soil and returned to their seats. Only now did they offer some spectatorial interest in what was going on outside.

"Aye-aye, pal!" The man with the throbbing ear indignantly reaffirmed his protest. Suggs whipped back the pump for another swipe, poking the man with the throbbing ear in his eye. "Aye-aye, pal!" he objected as another swing flashed above the heads of the two men embracing each other on the ground.

A stupid realisation of where he was and what he was trying to do seemed to be dawning on the man whose apparent intention it had once been to tear Suggs' handlebars from their frame. He stood making minutely ineffectual movements from side to side, driven on now only by ragged instincts of pride and honour.

Suggs reloaded his arm for a third time, cracking the man with the throbbing ear and the stinging eye cleanly in the mouth.

"WILL YOU FUCK OFF!" roared the man with the throbbing ear, the stinging eye and the bleeding gums. He snatched the pump from Suggs' hand and smashed it onto the top of his head.

"Ow, me 'ead, me 'ead!"

"I warned him, I warned him!" cried the man, then suddenly dropping the pump with a brief cry as though it were a hot steel bar.

Suggs, dancing in a tight circle, clasping his hands on top of his head and grunting like an Indian witch doctor let the bicycle fall away from him. The two men embracing each other on the ground tried to scramble clear but their intertwined limbs were too intricately bound to afford them the required manoeuvrability.

Halliwell sighed and hurried, muttering from the lodge. Worth and Atkin went with him as far as the doorway where they stopped and leaned against its frame, stretching their necks like nosey neighbours.

"Okay, okay, what's going on?" demanded Halliwell, pushing his way into the maw of the rumpus. Impressions of an indigestion tablet sinking into a rumbling gut came to him.

Suggs had stopped rotating by now, he just stood with his legs astride and his hands clasped on top of his head as though waiting for some retaining glue to set. His body rocked gently up and down. At his feet lay a chinese puzzle of limbs and bicycle steelwork.

"Bloody hell," breathed Halliwell, then turning to Suggs' apparent dance, guessed: "Don't tell me, Billy . . . the hootchy-kootchy?"

"Some bastard hit me," groaned Suggs miserably. "With me own pump! I've gone all dizzy." He began to sway precariously, his eyes fluttered as though attempting some comical seduction, before he tipped forward onto the two men underneath the bicycle who did not seem all that bothered anymore. But one of them grumbled with muffled peevishness: "Oh shit."

It took several seconds for Aubrey Cranby to recognise the approaching vehicle as an ambulance. The perimeter road was choked by that hour and it could only move in short darts and dodges. The urgent spinning lamp distorted and sharpened through his windscreen as the wipers brushed aside the splotches of rain. It was indicating left and it turned in at the junction of number three gate.

"What the hell's going on?" mouthed Cranby to himself. He reached down to the radio and switched off the 'Today' programme. He was at the junction himself now, dithering

25

b

impatiently, waiting to turn right. At a space in the traffic he swung across and through the gate.

The two ambulance men had hurried over to a group of men compressed beneath the shelter between the lodge and the storeroom. Cranby gave a short toot on his horn, aimed at Halliwell who glanced testily over his shoulder and, seeing who it was, turned and came soggily to the plant manager's car. Cranby lowered his window, his car filled with wet splashing sounds and chilled air.

"Morning, Mister Cranby."

Whatever happened to the salute, lamented Cranby, as he did most working mornings. Halliwell's hands were lost deep in the pockets of his uniform mackintosh. The peak of his cap was acting as a springboard for the fat raindrops and as he bent forward they dived gymnastically through the opening. Cranby raised the window to a four inch gap, thinking with some vexation that you don't even get a full '*good* morning' these days.

"What the devil's happened, Bob?" he asked.

"It's old Bill Suggs, the janitor. Had a bit of a dizzy spell, that's all. I thought it best to take no chances," Halliwell explained. Deep in his pockets his fingers were crossed.

"Hmmm. Fair enough," said Cranby absently, observing the stretcher bound janitor emerging from the ruck. "Why is he shaking his fist at those men like that?"

"Oh, er, the ambulance man told him to do that to get his circulation going," offered Halliwell. "Everything's under control," he assured.

"Hmmm," Cranby seemed satisfied. He slid the automatic gearbox into drive. But then he noticed Worth wheeling the bicycle out a few feet behind the stetcher. Halliwell prayed that Cranby would not notice the chain.

Cranby was a big, hefty man with a body of almost neanderthal hairiness. When he frowned his luxuriant eyebrows kissed like besotted caterpillars, as they did when he said: "Is he chained to that bicycle?"

Halliwell attempted a hearty laugh that came out thinly undernourished. "Yes, that's right. He's not the most trusting of souls, is he? He refused to leave it behind, can't imagine why. So he took the chain he uses to lock it up, and sort

26

of . . . chained himself to it."

Cranby watched in puzzled silence as the recumbent janitor and his attached bicycle, like some bizarre life support equipment were loaded aboard the ambulance and the doors closed.

Again the plant manager made to move off, until he heard the enraged cries from within the departing ambulance.

"Which one of you bastards've pinched me sarnies outta me saddle-bag, yer thievin' shower of cunts. Wait'll I get me hands on . . . " The words faded as the distance they had to travel increased.

Cranby looked up at Halliwell through the open slot in his window. He summoned the security guard closer with a wagged finger. His eyebrows smooched tenderly on the bridge of his nose. "You know, Bob," he confided. "There are times when I wonder what kind of lunatics I'm employing in this place."

The sign said: 'DRAM WELCOMES YOU TO BELLEND'. Steep hated that sign for its dumb smugness and its perfidious sincerity. It limply shook his hand while firmly bringing its knee up into his groin.

The sign stood at the top of the short connecting road between the public highway and Dram's plant perimeter road. The traffic had bottle-necked there now, as it always did at that hour and the coughing cars stood stubbornly motionless, seemingly happy to make do with what part of the road they held.

Exhaust fumes, pinned down by the heavy rain were thick in the air. Those on foot traipsed damply in a common direction like vanquished infantry retreating from battle.

Beyond the perimeter road loomed the factory. From here only its expansive flat back could be seen as at that end the modest hill had been hewn into and the factory lurked in its dugout, camouflaged in corrugated grey and brown brick like some giant predatory creature couched in its lair.

Encircling the plant was a high chain link fence topped with barbed wire. At certain points holes big enough for a man to get through had been cut in the fence, when discovered

27

these were blocked by nasty, excessively spiralling rolls of barbed wire. In places the fence looked as though it belonged to a prisoner of war camp rather than a motor car factory.

On the other side of the fence was a wedge shaped, abrupt grassy bank, levelling out onto a car storage area in the foreground of the factory. This was where cars — frequently hundreds at a time — requiring repair or attention which could not be handled in the normal way were kept until such time that the work could be carried out; invariably at double-timed weekends. By Monday morning the area was normally cleared and ready for the officially prohibited, lunchtime football matches.

Steep's stomach had developed that bottomless quality it sometimes did and a cold despondency plummeted through him. The word 'worry' had by now lost its meaning but there were too many surrogate words queueing up to take its place.

Now he was frought, anxious, apprehensive, distressed, perturbed, troubled, tormented, disturbed and vexed. He had felt better being just plain worried.

At the top of the hill now he could see the small figures entering the plant. He wanted to shout down to them. "Don't go in, it's a trap!" But it was as though he was looking through a powerful telescope at a past existence on some far distant planet. What he could see had already happened and he could only stand and watch. And what was worse, in a couple of minutes time he would be down there on that far distant planet himself. It was all Daffy's fault, he decided with childish arbitrariness. Silly cow.

They had first met in a Southport bar two years earlier. Both were with friends and nervous and unsure of each other and themselves, which meant that they were more or less dumped together. Steep drank more than he normally did that night, so, he guessed, did Daffy. But it did help, together with the bar's dusky lighting which he could hide behind, to dull his nerves.

He did not remember noticing her sticky-out ears or her greasy hair at all that first night. Any imperfections she possessed he was blinded to by the oncoming of drunkenness and standard lustful intent. He could hardly remember anything at all they had talked about either. He remembered them exchanging names and somewhere along the way she had told him that she was twenty-seven, a year older than himself, but that was all.

The next thing he recalled they were wandering the post midnight town centre streets on the feeble pretext that he knew of an Italian restaurant that would still be open and the owner, Pierre (at the time he could not think of a single Italian name) was an old friend and would give them the table of honour and play a romantic violin at their shoulder. In truth Steep knew nothing of the geography of Southport and they walked, probably in circles, for almost an hour with Steep feverishly straining his eyes and poking his head into dark shop doorways and mysterious alleys like a man with little time to discover and defuse an imminently exploding bomb. They had not talked much and Daffy had begun yawning and her pace had slackened. In desperation he decided that the next black hole they came across would have to do.

It was between two shops. A shuttered butcher's and a men's boutique. They fumbled through the blackness, Steep leading the way like a classic sleepwalker.

The alley came to a T junction some yards in. There were a few dabs of light from the rear of the boutique spilling over its backyard wall. He chose that way, telling Daffy that it was a short cut and they were nearly there.

His eyes were becoming accustomed to the darkness now and on the wall above him he made out two cats well on their way to making some new little kittens. Daffy yawned again, Steep wanted to shoo the cats away but thought it too unsporting, besides, he might not have much time. He turned and faced her. She stood a few steps away, silent and indistinct. Her perfume came to him through the darkness. He was trembling, becoming tighter and tighter inside until he thought he might explode. "Don't . . . " he whispered. Don't what? He thought. "Don't be frightened," he croaked. "Don't run away or scream. Please." She said nothing.

He stepped forwards and bent to her, his mouth searching her face and quickly connecting with her lips. Their tongues collided like panicked pink snakes, squirming and searching blindly inside dark wet caves. His shaking hand dipped hungrily below her dress and up to the top elastic lip of her pants. He felt as though his trousers were bursting and thankfully her small fingers began to tug zealously at his zip. His fingers were now fully down in front of her, working and probing for an entry and she gave off those strangely deceitful moans that could equally have signified anguish or pleasure. With his other hand he fumbled with hectic clumsiness at her tights. "Tear them off," she moaned suddenly. "Rip them, tear them." Gasping he pulled wildly at the smooth nylon, it came apart deliciously, a staggering lustful violence flowing through him. His breaths were heavy and rapid, he felt as though he had been running for miles but wanted to run more. His forehead was wet and cold. She helped him as he lowered her pants around the shreds of her tights. She stepped out of one leg and in a reckless display of liberation kicked them from her, in so doing cracking him precisely in mid-shin. The raw pain tried his ardour to its limit and he felt a whirling ambivalence of sensations as he hopped on one leg with Daffy whispering apologies and frantically peeling his trousers away from him with one hand while holding him like a frying pan handle with the other. He was dimly aware of a ceasing of activity on the wall above him, he managed a glance up. The cats had finished and were gazing down on him and his partner like people puzzling over a joke they did not understand.

"I'm sorry, Albert. I'm sorry," she whispered.

His shin stung like hell. "It's okay, honest," he lied. He stopped hopping and eased the weight of the leg on to his toes. "You can do it again if you like," he joked.

"Let me rub it," she offered solicitously. She bent to the shin and began to rub it vigorously with her spare hand while maintaining firm purchase on his tenaciously unwilting member with the other. "How's that now?" she asked as she rubbed.

"It's fine. It's okay now." Indeed the pain was beginning to dissolve.

"You're sure?" she enquired, turning her shadowy, mo
pale face up towards him.

Oh, God! Her mouth was hardly two inches away from it!

"Yes, yes," he gasped. He could not restrain himself. He thrust himself forward but at the same moment she straightened abruptly and the back of her head caught his lasciviously loose chin with a clean and jolting upper cut. His head snapped back against his neck and his teeth crashed together like sprung jaws in a trap. But now he was determined. He interrupted her at the breathless beginnings of some more apologies. "Forget it. How's your head?" he whispered gently.

"Okay. How's your chin?"

"Okay."

As though satisfied that some curious preliminary ritual had been successfully completed she half turned and pressed her back to the wall. With her free hand she hoisted the front of her dress and pulled him to her. She lifted herself accommodatingly onto tiptoe for him, this was clearly not the first time for her, there had been other walls. In the formal manner of a dance teacher she positioned his hands at her armpits and he pressed his chest to hers in order to maintain her elevated position. But even then their union, once achieved was not the most comfortable or secure. He found it difficult to sustain any strong rhythm in case they might part, and already his arms were tiring. He struggled for what seemed like an age, on two occasions when the exhilaration of the moment instilled an impetuous over-fluidity in his movement they almost parted, forcing him to check and return to his previous ineffectual constraints.

At first he thought it was because his arms were tired that Daffy was becoming heavier, but then he noticed how silent and still she had become. He let her drop onto the flat of her feet but even they seemed reluctant to support her. He pressed his chest more tightly to her to ease the strain on his failing arms, her head fell like a cabbage onto his shoulder. It was hopeless now, they stood together like tired boxers in a clinch, their union and mutual desires dissolved. The chilled air brushed his legs and sweating bare backside. The cats squatted complacently above him, one mewed seductively to its mate. He let her slide slowly to the ground and then looked down at himself through the literal and mental gloom. He had never felt so ridiculous in all of his life, and that was *saying* something. Dejectedly he dragged up his trousers.

On the wall, with tactless arrogance the cats were at it again. "You little bastards," he growled, searching the dark ground for some hurlable missile. He found a segment of brick and lashed it with inaccurate rage. It missed its target completely and briefly met with some unseen window. The sound of shattering glass was buried almost instantly by the shrill panic of an alarm bell. The cats squealed and took off along the wall, Steep made to run off also, but what about the girl, he couldn't just leave her lying there. Hurriedly he crouched down, the alarm hammering at his ears and lightly slapped her face, her heavy head did not move.

He shook her shoulders vigorously. "Come on, you stupid cow. Wake up." For some extraordinary reason among all that din he was whispering. Then it occurred to him that the alarm might be connected to a police station. They could be here at any minute!

There was nothing else for it, he grabbed her beneath her arms, fear now revitalising his drained reserves of strength, and manoeuvring her into a scrappy fireman's lift he hauled her off, knickerless, into the night.

The rain had not abated when a short, dark personnel officer stepped from the plant's administration block. He turned up the collar on his jacket, clasping it at the front, and made a crouched dash towards the sheltering new men fifty yards away. Half way there he stopped and waved an arm at them and called: "Morning, gents. Follow me, please." Then he turned and scurried back towards another door.

The men followed with varying degrees of urgency, some strolled fearlessly through the rain as if to prove that they were made of sterner stuff than anyone who wore a suit for a living. Others ran, seemingly deciding that anyone who wore a suit for a living must have brains and know best.

The door led directly into the factory. The personnel

officer held it open as the ragged, damp file passed through.

The day shift's start was still two minutes away and the factory was calm and remarkably quiet. The air inside smelled of oil and paint and plastic. It was parched and bone dry and draped in an instantly uncomfortable soporific warmth that made it somehow thin and heavy at the same time.

Cars were everywhere. Far away to the right just naked silver-grey shells. A similar distance to the left, in multi-colours, cars on wheels queued as though in a forgotten traffic jam where all the drivers had got out and walked. Everywhere assembly lines stretched out of, then double backed and ran away parallel into, the same distant haze. Some were at ground level, others hung in the air, their cars held like culprits by thick metal grabs.

Staircases reached up beyond regimented neon rows and lost themselves in tangles of pipes and ducts and girders.

Few human beings were evident to the casual glance. Only the keener or more probing eye would detect them, gathered at wooden benches around improvised tables, hunched over newspapers and cigarettes and languid conversation. It was not that they were in any way hidden or particularly obscured, but that they were almost imperceptibly fused into the vastly overpowering impersonality of the place. Only that keen or probing eye would consciously recognise the fine, fuzzy boundaries between where people started and the factory left off.

Near the doorway was a metallic green five door 'Khan' peppered with stick-on arrows each apparently highlighting some fault in workmanship. A sign on its roof said: YOU BUILT IT – WOULD YOU BUY IT?

The new intake was being taken to one of the lecture rooms in the administration block for the introductory briefing that all new employees received. The talk was normally given by four men; a personnel officer, a union official and the chief safety and fire officers. Today however the latter two would not be available, as earlier that morning the fire officer had accidentally set the safety officer's eyelashes ablaze while giving him a light for his cigarette with a carelessly adjusted gas lighter. The safety officer had been taken to hospital and the fire officer had driven home, his confidence in his ability to deliver effective comment on the perils of conflagration, for today at least, as painfully shrivelled and charred as the safety officer's eyelashes.

Bellend's 'trim' lines consisted of two independent production systems, one built 'Khan' five door saloons and commercial vans, the second system built 'Khan' three doors and the 'Kama' coupe. During an average shift, free from disputes or breakdowns, finished cars rolled off the final assembly lines at a rate of thirty per line per hour.

The lines kicked into life promptly with the sound of the eight o'clock hooter. Operators shuffled from their benches alongside the lines to collect tool boxes from lockers. Although the lockers were always opened earlier by the foremen, few operators collected their tools and brought them to their work stations until they were being paid to do so. Such actions were not always evidence of a meanness of spirit. As often they were induced by honest pride or cynical principle. It offered those operators a hint of independence from the despotic commands of the line. They were insignificant and futile gestures. But it made them feel better.

The first hour of the shift was always a hectic time, particularly for those whose jobs entailed some sub-assembly operation prior to the finished component being fitted to the car, as during this time as much sub-assembled stock as possible — in some instances enough to last for the whole shift — would be made up, while feeding and working on the line at the same time. It was also a bad time for quality as men on jobs where a 'welt' could be worked dashed about performing two or three of four men's jobs single-handed. The 'welt' was a widely employed practice where, for instance on a three man job, instead of each man working on every third car, one man would 'hold' the line by himself for an agreed number of cars, perhaps half an hour or an hour's worth. Early in the shift the others would be assembling stock where required, but later on they had it easy while they were off the line.

It seemed to be a psychological thing as much as anything. Later in the shift that same man could handle a three man job with ease, but for now he struggled, and there was

34

something grossly indecent about sweating at a quarter past eight on a Monday morning.

The new men's introductory talk had been somewhat short-ened in the absence of available deputies for the fire and safety officers. The Personnel Manager, Nicholas Sloan had attempted to impart what little he knew of such matters, and now all that remained was for someone from the union to turn up and do his bit before they were all taken down onto the lines, where, for the first day only, they were ominously informed, they would be entitled to terminate their contract of employment at one hour's notice.

Sloan wished them good luck and a good morning and set off back towards his office. Usually one of his personnel officers would handle a new intake but on occasion he would deal with them himself, partly because he liked to keep his hand in, and partly because the expressions of defenceless boredom they returned in response to explanations of 'uncertificated absence' and 'Disciplinary Action Reports' always amused him. And this morning, God knows, he needed amusing. Sometimes, during particularly low ebbs in the discourse he would inject some moderately earthy terminology into a sentence, such as 'pissed as a handcart' or 'get your arse kicked', which would snatch them back for a few subsequent sentences before they began to drift away from him again. Often he wanted to say to them: 'If you think this is bad, just wait until they get you onto that arseholing line'.

At six feet one and a half inches he was the tallest senior manager at Bellend. His tall frame was well preserved and supple for its age, his hair was dark and his eyes, though normally clear and alert were duller today because he had been thinking about Helen again. Actually she was always vaguely present somewhere in his head, but of late those wilfully specific, everyday domestic images of her preparing a meal or busying through housework or working at her sewing machine or smiling 'good morning' from the next pillow would again stray cruelly and without warning before his mind's eye.

Although nobody had ever actually said as much he could tell that they considered what had happened a foregone conclusion. Twenty-one years difference in ages promised nothing but eventual calamity from the outset. Forty-seven plus twenty-six equalled two people divided by a generation. That little equation he had formulated himself and its awful, blundering, quasi-profoundness would bring the corners of a rueful smile to his face whenever he recalled it.

Somebody said: "Good morning." He blinked after them and returned the greeting.

The offices were still full of yawning morning post weekend chatter. Through open doors and passing conversations he caught brief excerpts of private weekend adventures. He felt terribly alone, as though somehow trapped in a remote and untouchable orbit around ordinary people and their ordinary cosiness. Somehow locked out of an unseeing and totally preoccupied world.

She had been gone for five months now. To love and live with something in sanitaryware called Douglas who drove a 1973 Ferrari Dino 246 GT finished in white with chianti rosso interior. He was, explained Helen, gentle and kind and thoughtful and understanding and twenty-seven years of age and Helen had cried when she broke the news, and said she was *so* sorry.

Five minutes before the morning break, four of the new intake stood uncomfortably at Rex McBean's battered and initial inscribed desk. He was on the telephone, holding a hand over his other ear as a man two yards away drove a fearsome metal spike into the nearside wing of a yellow Kama with a two pound hammer. Like a lead musician in a clueless orchestra he hammered to an amorphous backing of squeals and screeches from compressed air power tools, from subordinate hammers and mallets and from blurred shouts and ragged singing.

McBean glanced up at them upon their arrival, waved curt acknowledgement to the man who had brought them, and returned to his telephone conversation. That was several minutes ago; he glowered at the man with the hammer and the spike, slipping away on the moving line. The man, apparently without noticing McBean's look, broke into a clumsy but glowing rendition of *The Sun has got His Hat On*, and continued his hammering with a subtly increased vitality.

"You still here?" McBean mumbled listlessly, when he had at last finished on the telephone. "Look, it's break-time now, go and sit down over there and come back when it's over." He waved towards 'a bench next to a row of vending machines across the line, then opened a drawer and took out a newspaper which he raised before him in an almost defensive fashion, as though he was trying to hide behind it.

The four wandered over to the bench and sat in a shift-less, isolated silence. The lines had stopped now and the place was quiet but for the distant threatening rumble of the press shop three hundred yards away. Presently a short, ungainly man in a dark grubby bib and brace overall and large, dazzlingly white plimsolls stopped at the tea and coffee machine. He seemed quite unperturbed by the Monday morning and he sang jollily: "Zipadee-dooda zipadee-a, my oh my what a wonderful day." Jiggling some coins rhyth-mically in his hand. He took two of the coins and dropped them into the slot. He pushed the button indicating: TEA — NO SUGAR, and waited, now only whistling his tune but with no less abandon. His right leg danced an extravagant freestyle. After some seconds of inactivity within the machine he pulled a lever, but to no avail. He ceased his tune and rattled the machine lightly with the palm of his hand, then thumped it hard with the side of his fist, both without result. The man shrugged his shoulders and turned unconcernedly away. Then suddenly he spun back to the machine and smashed his forehead with a sickening crack into its metal casing. Undazed and still unruffled he stepped an easy pace back. The dent in the machine was the size of half a large potato. After a moment a plastic cup dropped fawningly onto its tray and the machine filled it to the brim. Calmly the man bent and took the cup. He sipped his tea and turned away from the machine and winked amiably at the four new men as he passed them, singing: "If you want my

37

body and you think I'm sexy."

Rex McBean had been a foreman or general foreman for thirteen of his nineteen years at Bellend and there were strong suspicions that the job had made him mad. People sometimes heard him saying 'thank you' to the cigarette machine which he would visit two or three times a day. And he had also been seen talking to his waste paper basket, a packet of Polo mints and a ball point pen. Once, it was rumoured, he chatted for ten minutes with a large red fire extinguisher.

At the end of the twenty minutes break the four new men returned to McBean's desk. He made no immediate acknowledgement of their return, he remained hidden in his newspaper for some seconds, then he folded it twice and placed it in his desk drawer.

At first a slightly warily puzzled look came to him. He leaned cautiously away from them in his bursting wobbling swivel chair. For several moments he seemed to be pondering over some difficult problem. His brow creased into bloodhoundish folds, his eyes half closed in concentration. "Names!" he announced suddenly and with a real sense of achievement, and he acrobatically hoisted himself on the arms of his wobbly swivel chair. "Right, what's your name?"

"Way'll howdy, pardner. Harold Melrose is m'name, but you can call me Hank if it makes you feel more at home."

Steep went for a walk at lunchtime because he thought the cool air might help to clear his mind. And because the rest of the friendly card school had gone to look at the barmaid with the big tits at the nearby 'Dog's Dinner' – thus renamed from the Prince Edward Vaults after rumours that the landlord's comprehensive and suspiciously inexpensive range of pies and pasties were filled with Bounce, Pal and Pedigree Chum.

Steep had not gone because the others drank too fast for him. They might easily down five or six pints while Steep would be struggling to finish two which he would not enjoy because he was not partial to lunchtime drinking anyway.

Once he had tried to keep up with them pint for pint, and managed successfully until half way through his fourth when he had had to slip away and be quietly sick down the toilet.

Apart from those who were clients of one of the plant's resident bookmakers, card games were probably the least strenuous, if most costly indoor pastimes to be found on an excursion through Bellend at lunchtimes. Few schools played for serious stakes however, the' majority played frivolously for nominal amounts; Steep had lost forty-three pence last Friday, and that was a bad day.

Makeshift badminton, table tennis, darts and miniature snooker were also played alongside the lines or in the avenues between them. They were played generally without any great proficiency but always with genuine and at times ruthless enthusiasm. Many participants formed teams and hence leagues with engraved medals and dinky silver plated cups for the victors: With such prestigious trophies at stake occasional outbursts of unpleasantness were inevitable, particularly in crunch matches or during fleeting moments of high tension when some stroke, pot or throw might mean victory and an opponent would employ a distracting act of gamesmanship such as breaking into an abrupt whistle or coughing at the crucial second. Hand to hand combat with badminton rackets was not unheard of, nor was a swash-buckling duel with snooker cues.

Steep had walked the length of the line and now made towards the swing doors that led outside. Away to his left a large white board with red cross marked the entrance to the medical centre. The memories returned with lingering, taunting embarrassment. He shuddered.

He sat with a dozen others from his intake on the thinly padded benches in the small waiting room. The walls were a cold blue and dotted with unimaginative medical posters. Dilute disinfectant lightly peppered the air. The label on his new underpants rubbed irritatingly against the small of his back.

The surgery door opened and the doctor, a tired, middle-aged man with gold rimmed bifocals poked his balding head around. In the manner of a brusque bus conductor he said: "First six inside."

Steep and another five trooped in. The doctor took their names and told them to go into a cubicle and strip to the waist and to give a urine sample in the container provided. Steep drew the purple curtain behind him; inside was a small bench with the stainless steel container beneath it and a hook on one of the partition walls. He took off his coat and shirt. He shivered, even though the air was warm that chilling edge of disinfectant possessed a distinctly unnerving quality.

After he had given his sample he sat on the bench and placed the container next to him. A wispy trail of steam rose from its bottle-neck up to his eye level and he decided, in the interests of propriety to replace it beneath the bench. He took hold of the container and made a funny face at his distorted reflection in its bulbous bottom. Then he heard a whispered voice from the next cubicle, very low and almost too faint for him to make out.

"Fuck off," came a growled reply from what was presumably the occupant of the next cubicle but one.

"It's just that . . ."

"Fuck off," repeated the second voice. "Or you'll get this can of piss across your fucking head."

"Right. Sorry to have bothered you," whispered the first voice obsequiously.

There were some slight shuffling sounds and Steep could see the man's shadow moving about beneath the narrow space at the bottom of the partition.

"Excuse me. Have you been yet?" the voice whispered again, this time closer to their shared partition.

Steep ignored it but then there was some more shuffling and a face, stretched and straining crammed itself into the six inch gap below the partition. One eye was forced shut and the other could hardly see past the overhang of the nose above it. The mouth had been pushed into a tight, skeletal smile. Steep stared in astonishment, it seemed surrealistically as though the man was going to squeeze his entire head through the narrow slot.

"Only I can't go," explained the face, its taut lips working like some hideous ventriloquist's dummy. "I only went before I came out. It was only supposed to be a shit but I forgot."

"Yeah," nodded Steep uncertainly.

"Can I borrow a drop of yours, then?" enquired the face hopefully.

Steep looked bemusedly at the quietly steaming container he still held. "Borrow," he murmured. It seemed such a curious choice of words.

"I'll pass it over the top, then," said the face optimistically. It began to pull away but then stopped and spoke again: "Er, it's good stuff is it, by the way?" it questioned suspiciously. "Nothing wrong with it, like?"

"No, don't think so," answered Steep. He was beginning to wonder if all this was really happening.

"Okay, fair enough," conceded the face. It withdrew and moments later the steel container crept cautiously over the top of the partition.

Steep accepted it with the worried resignation of someone who was fairly certain that they were probably going insane. He weighed the vessels against each other and tipped one into the other like a scientist with his test tubes. Then the curtain swished open.

"Can I have . . . " began the doctor.

Instantly Steep felt his face begin to boil. He stared, horrified at a gold pen top in the doctor's breast pocket. An explanation! He wants an explanation! Oh God!

"Er, one's the bloke next doors," he offered feebly.

"I see," said the doctor flatly.

"Er, we were having a competition to see who could do the most."

"Good God," sighed the doctor. He looked tired and aggrieved, like a man who had been unjustly sentenced to a lifetime of constant association with simpletons and half-wits. Without further comment he took the containers and collected the rest from the other cubicles. There was some clanking and sounds of running water from a small side room in the surgery. Then he instructed: "When I come to you drop your trousers, turn your head to one side and cough."

Steep listened anxiously as the coughs became louder

41

and closer. Some other ineffable disaster was about to befall him. He just knew it.

Three coughs gone. Two more before it was his turn. He could smell the sweat rising from his bare torso. Another cough. Now the doctor was next door. The close cubicle walls seemed to press in on him. The fifth cough. He itched all over. The curtain slid aside. He looked up sheepishly at the doctor and tugged at his trousers and his new underpants, exposing to himself and the doctor his credentials of manhood all horrifically shrivelled and whithered like so much rotten pink fruit. He remembered to turn his head and coughed dryly. "They're not usually like this. I don't know what's come over them." He desperately wanted to explain.

"That's fine, just fine," said the doctor, suddenly warm and sympathetic. Similar tones, Steep imagined to those of a specialist who is about to inform a patient that he has contracted some incurably fatal disease. He leaned into the cubicle and patted Steep's forearm and whispered with genuine solace: "Never mind, old son, never mind."

He pushed the incident to the back of his mind. It was getting pretty crowded back there now, so crowded that past catastrophies seemed to be forced forward to be re-endured with frighteningly increasing regularity.

He was outside now. The sky was like grey canvas and the air was cool. Over on the empty storage area a football match was going on. It was a typically intense and dishonourable affair full of flailing feet, brutal challenges, bad language and, in the absence of arbitration and proper goalposts, contention as to the actual score-line.

Warily Steep kept to the edge of the vaguely defined pitch, knowing too well that football matches supplied the plant's medical staff with more broken limbs and injuries than the plant itself did. So should the ball happen to come his way and he did not quickly disclaim responsibility for it he might easily be mistaken for a member of the opposition and suffer a severe kicking.

Football was the dominant outdoor activity all year round

at Bellend. Any reasonably level and uncluttered areas of ground within the vicinity of the plant being commandeered for use as pitches. Only at the height of summer did cricket prise back the odd finger on football's firm stranglehold, and even then most games would only proceed at an apathetic, staccatoed pace due to artless sloggers constantly smashing the ball great distances onto roofs or into unkempt grass or tight formations of new cars. Despite rigorous searches the balls were often lost forever. ˙

One hot August day the previous summer someone had rashly brought in a real leather cricket ball. The outfit was completed by a bat 'to suit eight to eleven year old', which someone else had borrowed from his son, and a cardboard box for the wickets.

The bowler had taken his time. Pacing out his run up meticulously then rubbing the ball professionally against the top of his leg as he turned to face the dry mouthed batsman. The fielders were poised.

His run up was a long and intimidating one. He reached his mark with measured precision and let the ball fly with a powerful ferocity. The batsman's first blind, brutish swipe had sent the ball crashing through the rear window of one of a line of Kamas parked thirty yards away and the players had scattered in giggling panic.

Sometimes Steep tried to look as though he had some secrets to keep. Cunningly utilising his subtle double-bluff technique he would appear to prefer to leave the world eternally ignorant of erstwhile episodes of courage, misfortune and conquest in his life: Standing in a queue at the Post Office he might look as though he was an ex-secret agent whose former feats of supreme heroism and bravado would forever be known only to a few faceless men in Whitehall. And oh boy, that Svetlana! Travelling on a bus people could only guess that *he* was the unnamed party in the notorious scandal involving the millionaire industrialist's beautiful young wife. He had ended it because he knew it could never be. They were from different worlds. She was heart broken. The gossip columnist's claims of a six figure pay off were totally untrue.

At the moment he was looking as though he was football's

most sensational discovery since Pele; snatched from the obscurity of non-league football he had been signed up by Everton. But his promise was never fulfilled. A heavy fall sustained going up for a fifty-fifty ball in his first practice match had torn his knee ligaments to shreds. Howard Kendall was heart broken. He would never kick a ball again.

He took a short cut back through 'receiving' because some light drizzle had begun to fall.

There were seven bays, four empty and two filled with long trailered lorries. The seventh bay held a muddy green van, buried like a child in a man's overcoat, with only its roof peeping out over the deep, wide slot.

One driver slept peacefully across his cab with heavy booted legs dangling through the window. Work-a-day sparrows flew freely in and out through the gaping doors and hopped and twittered about the high girders. A man grasping an orange coloured piece of paper shuffled distractedly up and down alongside the bay holding the small green van. He tipped occasional glances over its edge like a potential suicide.

"Just a minute," he shouted over the cold concrete in a robust Scottish accent.

Steep continued walking and pretended not to hear.

"Hang on. Oy!" he called again, and Steep could hear the man running after him. Reluctantly he looked back over his shoulder. The man was middle aged with a bloated belly and he puffed from the exertion, his frequent breath redolent of stale tobacco and beer. Steep stepped back, hopefully out of range as the man held out his piece of paper.

"Here, sign this, will you," he wheezed.

"Er, I don't think I can," said Steep doubtfully.

The man stepped forward, nullifying Steep's retreat. "Look, I've got to get back to Bootle by one o'clock," he said as though the disclosure somehow constrained Steep to sign the paper.

"Is there no one else about," suggested Steep, taking a step back.

"Not now. I only got here a minute ago. As soon as they saw me backing in they all vanished," said the Scotsman cancelling out Steep's withdrawal. They were like two novice ballroom dancers attempting some revolutionary new tango.

44

"It's dinner time, you see," explained Steep, stepping back. "They've probably all rushed off for their dinner."

"Dinner. There's no dinner for me today. I'll be lucky to get back before closing time at this rate."

"It's not my job, you see. I don't work over here. I'm not authorised."

"Oh, that's it, is it." The Scotsman began to nod large knowing nods. "I suppose they'd all go out on strike just because someone who wasn't authorised scribbled a name on a piece of paper. Listen," he confided, leaning towards Steep and making him want to retch with the stench of his breath. "All I want.is a signature. You can sign the buggering thing Rob Roy for all I care, d'you know what I mean?" He produced a chewed plastic ballpoint. "Just sign there, any old thing'll do." He winked and smiled at their secret.

Why did he always give in to these people? Why had he been cursed with this unerring ability of landing himself in exactly the wrong places at exactly the wrong times? Was the former an inevitable consequence of the latter, or vice versa?

He took the paper and the savaged ballpoint. He noticed now that they were some ten yards away from their starting point. He signed a name, not his own but the first appropriate name that came to him. He offered the pen and paper back.

"That's your copy," said the Scotsman. "These are ours." He pulled from a pocket a wad of green, blue, pink, yellow, white and purple papers and spread them like a fan. "Sign there and there on each one, I'll go and get the boxes out."

By the time Steep had signed all the papers with the same fictitious name the Scotsman had unloaded twelve cardboard cartons and arranged them at the side of the bay.

"They're all yours now," he said, reaching up to take the papers and pen from Steep, then going around to the driver's door of his van.

"What do I do with this?" asked Steep waving the orange paper.

The Scotsman shrugged and opened the door of his van. He was half way in when some private amusement seemed to occur to him. Over the van's roof he laughed: "You could try wiping your arse on it, ha!" And he was gone. Bootle bound.

45

Steep began to stamp erratically about at the side of the empty bay, boiling up to a futile, blustering anger. "Haggis-faced bastard!" he shouted. "Look, this is what I think of your poxy piece of paper." He tore the receipt into pieces and threw them pointlessly after the van. "And your stupid bleedin' boxes!" He kicked one and it skidded several feet across the hard floor. Then he kicked another and another. Around him and his tantrum torn scraps of paper fell like gentle orange snow.

"Er, if you don't mind." The voice came nastily from behind. Steep turned, feeling his stomach tighten and freeze. It was the lorry driver, his leaden boots still hung through the window, hauled up by his steering wheel. "If you don't mind there are people trying to sleep around here." He smiled sourly, then fell back into his cab, but Steep heard him mutter: "Bloody nutcase."

There was still twenty minutes break left when Steep got back to his work station. Two of the new intake who had started on his section that morning were already seated at the stolen table: The stolen table had been stolen during a daring daylight raid on the east canteen several months earlier. Its acquisition became necessary after a discussion between two operators concerning the sturdiness of the previous table, which comprised of some metal storage bins and a sheet of hardboard, had culminated in a fifty pence wager being placed, the point to be proved being whether it would or would not withstand the combined weight of both men jumping up and down on it.

One of the new men appeared to be barely into his twenties. He had a dumpy frame with smooth child's skin and red cheeks. He sat with his hands between his thighs and chewed resolutely at his lower lip, his wide naive eyes flitting anxiously around him. The second, older man was skipping through a copy of the *Sun*. He looked to be in his forties, wiry and evidently quite tall. His hair was slicked back with thick sideburns. Perhaps he had once been a teddy boy.

When Steep sat down the man folded the newspaper

and offered it to him.

"I read it on the bus this morning, thanks," he said.

"Not much in it anyway," shrugged the man. "It's all adverts and tits. Want the paper, son?"

The younger man looked surprised. "Er, okay, thanks," he almost whispered. He took the paper and placed it on the table in front of him. He seemed relieved to at last have something upon which he could anchor his eyes.

"They have to make their money, I suppose," said Steep. "What have they put you on?"

"I'm hammering those rubber things on around the boot."

"Ah, weather strips," said Steep as though translating the man's words from a foreign language. "Got any blisters yet?"

The man turned his hands upwards on the stolen table and looked down at them. His palms were like grimy white leather, the pads of his fingers just thick calloused lumps. He lifted them close to his face and examined them carefully. Steep thought he was probably taking the piss. "No, no blisters," he announced finally. "Not yet."

"What do you think of it so far? The place overall I mean," inquired Steep, deliberately changing the subject.

"I've worked in worse places." He looked around him as though he was basing his opinion on his surroundings at that moment. Then he straightened his back and turned to Steep, leaning slightly in the manner of someone about to pass a secret message. "That General Foreman thinks I'm mad, you know."

Steep was shocked. "Who, Rex McBean, why?"

"Because as far as I'm concerned he's an American called Tex McQueen."

"Of course, I should have realised," said Steep, bemused.

"I didn't like the look of him you see, so I thought, 'this bugger's not going to shit all over Harry Melrose.' I've got these bad ears you see." He pointed at his ears as though his fingers were guns held to his head. "We had a gas explosion at a place I used to work, it made a bastard of a bang. It's got its advantages though, it's great for knocking gobshites like him down a peg or two. When they start acting smart I just pretend I can't hear them, or get things

wrong. It doesn't half take the wind out of their sails."
He smiled roguishly. "Sometimes I pretend I can't hear
the missus when the tele's on. We have to have the sound on
loud you see, really I have it on louder than I need, but
she doesn't know that. It's bloody marvellous, I just sit
there and ignore her, drives her round the bend," he beamed.
Then he sighed, like a man coming to the end of a long,
enjoyable holiday. "It's my birthday next month, the old
cow said she's buying me a new battery for my hearing
aid. Mind you, don't get me wrong, sometimes I *really*
can't hear what people are saying, but after twenty-odd
years in places like this you realise it helps to keep a few
tricks up your sleeve."

"Twenty-odd years, God," breathed Steep. "How have
you stuck it that long?"

"Oh I don't mind it. You've got to not mind it whether
you mind it or not, if you see what I mean. I mean there are
only two types of job for the likes of us." Steep did not like
the sound of the 'likes of us' bit. "Shitty ones that pay
a living wage and shitty ones that don't. Answer me this.
Did you come here to earn enough money to feed the wife
and kids, or for the sheer ecstatic delight of screwing a million
fucking nuts onto a million fucking bolts every day?"

"Well, for the money," conceded Steep. "I'm not married
though," he added.

"Courting then?"

"Well, yes I suppose so."

"You don't sound very enthusiastic about it," remarked
Melrose frankly. "Don't tell me, she's started pointing out
three piece suites and coffee tables in the shops," he guessed
confidently.

"No," answered Steep shaking his head. He felt reassured
by the firmness of his reply.

"Oh," muttered Melrose with a trace of disappointment.
"Well don't worry, she will."

Steep looked at him questioningly.

"And when she does it's all systems go for you, matey. A
hundred miles an hour and no stopping until she gets you
there."

"Where?" asked Steep worriedly.

"The altar, Walter," grinned Melrose.

"Oh God, don't be saying things like that."

The section began to gather in its operators for the commencement of the Monday afternoon stint. Some returned richer or poorer from two subsidised courses and after lunch brag in the canteens, or flushed from a bruising football match. Others merely stirred themselves from some position of slovenly but comfortable repose, folding newspapers, closing tattered books or opening shattered eyes. There was Parkes, who kept two women in precarious ignorance of each other in houses only three quarters of a mile apart, and who took everywhere with him the skulking, harassed look of a hotly pursued escaped convict. There was Fishwick, a trained barber who cut operator's hair and aroused frequent suspicions behind locked toilet doors; Littler, who had exactly enough children to field a football team and then a vasectomy because his wife had finally baulked at the thought of a substitute. It was still a source of some amusement on the lines how, on the same day as his operation, he had ridden in for the night shift on his bicycle and then spent the entire shift perched, spread-legged on the corner of a bench in a state of paralysed agony. There was Weller, an introspective, softly spoken nineteen-year-old who took three obscure left wing newspapers and dreamt quietly of civil insurrection and gutters red with capitalist blood; Randolf, who spent all of his spare time assiduously assembling realistic replicas of the Cadbury's Smash spacemen out of bits of Dram motor cars; Ernie Barlow, cursed with the painful obstinacies of constipation; and Graeme Leatherbarrow, a congenial gay with pale Nordic features who accepted the ribald references to his homosexuality with a generous and resilient spirit. He would often return from his lunchbreaks smelling of and occasionally lightly dabbed with custard powder because he had become involved with the east canteen's dessert chef, a runtish, ferret-faced Welshman called Emlyn.

Another six operators, red-faced and boisterous with drink made their way along the broad avenue between

49

two stationary lines. In the lead was Henry Chong the man from Hong Kong, who had a poor moustache which consisted of an almost countable number of half inch long hairs. He was apparently demonstrating a movement of a particular martial art to George Spivak, a slight – and in some people's opinion, unbalanced – man of unjustly shifty looks and large duck feet that he kept permanently enshrined in immaculately blancoed plimsolls. On this day he bore a tight, round ruby-red blotch on his forehead after an earlier altercation with a vending machine.

Following at a respectful distance were Steve Sproat and Derek Kettle, two similarly short, dull men in their thirties who would bicker between themselves for sometimes hours at a time propounding the most ludicrous cases in the most hopeless arguments; topics so far today had included; where Einstein had got it wrong about black holes in his Theory of Relativity, digressing slightly to consider the specific biological function and anti-social ramifications in an alien ambience of Mr Spock's pointed ears; do sparrows urinate; and how Christ had walked on the water – Kettle arguing that he had once seen David Nixon do it just as good on television.

The final pair in the group were the sections two utility men. They were called Sammy and Godfrey and their combined total of years served at Bellend amounted to more than a quarter of the combined total of the section's remaining twenty-seven operators.

Utility men were a pay grade up from the ordinary operator and their duties included standing in for operators who required toilet or medical reliefs and performing the section's non-specific tasks at the behest of their foremen. They were a foreman's lieutenants and they did possess some small authority although this was seldom exercised on, or recognised by, the operators.

Sammy walked with his feet splayed at slightly the wrong side of ten-to-two. He had a cheeky, resilient face with a youthful fringe running close to mischievous brown eyes; yet he was, in fact, the second oldest man on the section.

Godfrey was the oldest. He was not as tall as Sammy and his hair was greying, but in a quite dignified manner, mainly around the temples. He had eyes like an old spaniel and a quiet, ingenuous face which was not an entirely honest witness to his character; Godfrey claimed to have seen action as a conscript in Malaya during the Communist guerrilla war, and on occasions he liked to illustrate his claim by proudly displaying the inch long stub of an index finger on his left hand whilst eagerly telling the tale of how the missing remainder had been bitten off by a rabid Malay bandit during hand to hand combat somewhere in a far eastern jungle. Sometimes he liked to press the stub to his nostril and waggle it about vigorously, declaring with a long, enjoyable sucking in of breath: "God, my brain's not half itchy."

"No. No. Bleedin' lubbish," said Henry Chong in response to Spivak's ineffectual attempt at a neck high kick with the sole of his plimsoll. Spivak stood now with his hands clasped to his crotch, a look of mock, agonised surprise on his face.

"More like a friggin' Tiller Girl, that," laughed Sproat. His was not so much a laugh as a hard staccatoed bray fired like machine-gun bullets straight from the throat.

"My kid's little monkey do better, and it only got one leg," commented Henry.

"The other leg went in last night's soup, didn't it, Henry. Ha ha ha ha!"

Henry Chong, being the only ethnic element among the group took the brunt of the throwaway taunts and banter, he was used to it and it did not bother him.

"Monkey leg soup favolite food in Hong Kong," replied Henry. He often answered their jokey remarks in that matter of fact oriental tone. The others were never sure if he was having the last, secret laugh.

They reached the stolen table and Spivak sat and crumbled quietly onto it, positioning his arms on the large deluxe table so as to cradle his head. At that moment the hooter sounded and the lines jerked obediently into motion. With an effort Spivak raised his head. Like an insolent child answering back an adult he shouted: "Ah piss off." Then amiably to Steep: "Hello, Albert." And dropped his head back into his arms.

"Who's flashin' the ash, Spiv?" asked Kettle pointedly.

"Fuck off. You've been cadgin' off me all piggin' day," protested Spivak without attempting to raise his head. He went on, mumbling into the table: "Ask Henry if he's got any opium rollies left."

"Just finished last one," said Henry. "I far out, man."

"Ay, Spiv, you're going bald," Sammy nudged the new young lad who blushed vividly, coyly inspected the top of Spivak's head, smiled feebly and without comment hurried back to his newspaper.

"Told you," said Sammy seriously. "Look, Derek, just there."

"Ooo, yeah," confirmed Kettle.

"Friar Tuck, ha ha ha ha." said Sproat.

"Er, excuse me, Mister Spivak. If you could possibly spare me a moment from your peaceful slumbers during company time I'd be awfully grateful." The voice was unctuous and servile and thickly spread with sarcasm. It was Ted Slutswater, the section foreman.

Spivak hauled his chin onto his arms. "Hello, Ted, ol' buddy, ol' mate." He smiled broadly, keeping his thin lips pressed tightly together. Then, still smiling, buried his face in his arms again.

Slutswater had been a foreman for almost three years now, yet still he retained the bowed back and jutting head induced through too many years of stooping and bending into car boots to fit rear bumpers and petrol tanks. He was tall and stringy, features which exaggerated the condition to a point where when he walked he gave the impression of a man about to cross a finishing line in some curiously casual race.

"Look, Ted, Spiv's going bald," said Sammy.

The foreman ignored the remark. He sank his hands into the pockets of the royal blue overall jacket that denoted his rank and bent further towards Spivak until it seemed he might topple forward onto the table.

"Is that the Papermate you bought for your missus, Ted?" asked Sammy, peering into his foreman's breast pocket, sagging under the weight of several pencils and pens.

Slutswater ignored him again: "I was just wondering," he began.

"Because she was looking for more excitement in bed,"

52

pursued Sammy with quiet determination.

"What are you on about?" snapped Slutswater.

"I was just wondering if that was the aforementioned Papermate," explained Sammy.

Slutswater straightened. "What?" he snorted, squinting irritably down his nose into his breast pocket. "What?" he repeated.

"Now she does crosswords over your shoulder with it."

Contempt and confusion formed into a scowl on the foreman's face. He sniffed and returned his attentions to Spivak. "I was just wondering," he repeated, still following his line of overplayed sarcasm. "If you were having any problems with these boot locks. Only they keep coming away in the inspector's hands when they try to open the boot."

"I don't get paid to have problems, Ted, you should know that by now," mumbled Spivak. "Faulty materials," he shrugged. "Nothing to do with me."

"You're the only faulty material in here, mate." He paused suddenly, his nostrils twitching like a nervous antelopes. "You lot been drinking? Smells like a bloody dunnowhat around here."

"Us, drinking! That's a good'n, Ted. I like that, ha ha ha ha," said Sproat.

"Well fuck me with a big dick," endorsed Sammy. "Just as if."

"Bloody good example to set for these new blokes, I must say. You know a bloke in the press shop got sacked last week for coming in pissed, don't you?"

"You mean the one who ploughed his fork lift truck into the stock controller's office?" asked Godfrey.

"Yes well, that's not the point," sniffed Slutswater. "Don't say you haven't been warned, that's all. And Spiv, try and get the odd screw in the odd hole this afternoon will you. Pretend you're on the job or something."

"Don't say that or he'll never get one in," grunted Kettle.

Spivak raised his head and called after the foreman: "Faulty materials!"

Without turning Slutswater called back: "Faulty arseholes!"

*   *   *   *

At specific times during a shift a sudden infusion of activity far beyond the call of duty would erupt on Bellend's assembly lines. The phenomenon could be observed in a comparatively subdued form for approximately half an hour prior to lunch and tea breaks, but was most keenly demonstrated two hours or so before the end of the shift, when hundreds of operators laden like pack animals with toolboxes and airguns and long trailing air lines and as great a number of pieces of motor car as was practicable, would begin the ritual mass trudge, or gallop, depending upon the entailments of each operator's task, 'up the line'. The object of the exercise being that any operator who might complete his jobs thirty cars up from his work station would be finished one hour before the end of the shift. A greater or lesser number of cars would mean a proportionately longer or shorter 'finish'.

At such times a peacefully trundling car might suddenly be set upon by up to a dozen operators and their cumbersome impedementa, half of them leaping onto some region of its exterior, the rest crouching and cramming intimately inside. Air lines extended from its interior, its boot and its engine compartment like knotted and tangled arteries from a heart, while twenty-four relentless elbows all frantically hammered and screwed and glued and got in each other's way and dashed off to set upon the next one before the rest.

It was at this stage of a shift that those with a wavering sense of quality consciousness would submit, without much of a struggle, to the ways of slapdash indifference. They had committed themselves to working at a speed two or three times faster than was normally required, and so if a component did not fit properly at the first attempt it would perhaps be only half fitted or left off altogether, and many nuts and bolts and screws might not be fully tightened, even in areas of brakes and steering, as a matter of selfish expedience.

It was a hard, sweaty campaign and sometimes frustrating when a group of advancing operators came upon a colleague who, through ineptitude or indolence remained at his work station and could not be overtaken because he installed some vital component upon which the others were dependent.

Although the solitary operator always endeavoured to appear unruffled during such encounters it was never a comfortable situation for him; there were too many narrowed eyes, too many overheard grumbles for that. Eventually the altruist in him usually decided that it would be advisable to hurry things along a little.

Most were finished by the time thirty minutes of the shift remained. Gradually the din and the clatter of the assembly lines had thinned to a near reverent silence. The half built cars continued to roll by, oblivious of the fact that for most operators the day's work was done and interest in them had evaporated. The odd power tool still rattled or churned intermittently, its operator probably without the freedom afforded to most operators to move from his work station due to its location or the encumbrances of his job. He would plod on miserably until the end of the shift.

Many cars showed glaring signs of a lack of detail finish that would not have been so prevalent earlier that day. The inspectors would detect most of them, but often write a lesser number on the car's fault sheet. An over zealous inspector was not a popular character among the repair men who followed him. Nor among foremen who were ultimately responsible for their sections build quality record. Sometimes, during bad production weeks, inspectors would be instructed to let go some defects which they would otherwise have detailed on the fault sheet. The following week, when production targets were being met, previous quality control standards would resume and such instructions rescinded. 'Cars through the gate', was the ultimate and overriding priority.

Steep dipped his hand into the liquid soap container in the middle of the large circular, stained enamel basin. As usual the soap bit into the countless tiny cuts that he had accumulated during the day. The fascia pads he sub-assembled and fitted were riddled with sharp tinny edges behind their smooth vinyl exteriors and the nicks and scratches were unavoidable. But then most jobs on the line brought about physical discomforts of some sort or another; in the past he had endured aching arms, legs, back and head, raw knuckles, bruised knees and blistered hands.

A busy janitor with thick glasses and a bristly grey chin made little dull islands around the feet of those who stood at the basin as he painted the red tiled floor with his soggy mop. Voices behind a row of lockers argued without much heat over a clandestine domino game. Steep moved from the basin to the paper towel dispenser. Beneath the only occupied toilet cubicle he noticed Ernie Barlow's unavoidably monstrous pair of old brown boots, cracked and curled and set huffily at right angles as though not on speaking terms. Suddenly the boots shuddered as though cold, this accompanied by a tortuous straining heave from behind the locked door. The janitor, noticing the direction of Steep's glance moved towards him still hunched over and diligently splashing his mop. "Half a bleedin' hour 'e's been in there. I'm waitin' to clean that one out," he said without raising his head and making another dry little island about Steep's feet. "If 'e doesn't get a move on 'e'll get this mop 'andle up 'is arse," he affirmed loudly. "That should cure 'im."

Chapter Two

A crisp, freshly laundered Tuesday morning hung drying in a spotlessly pale blue sky. A muscular yellow sun kicked its cold blinding light into Aubrey Cranby's face as he motored along Bellend's perimeter road. On his radio a particularly lugubrious trade union official was threatening that 'severely disruptive industrial action' would ensue should some company or other not withdraw plans to make thirty-two cod filleters in Grimsby redundant. Cranby had six and a half thousand potential problems of his own to worry about, each and every one of them quite capable of causing 'severely disruptive industrial action' should they put their minds to it without having to listen to the troubles of thirty-two cod filleters from Grimsby. He retuned to Radio Three joining a bustling, inflamed orchestra galloping at full tilt through what he guessed was probably a Rossini overture. Cranby's mouth moved in minute silence and his head made small tight movements as though he were a conductor with a stiff neck as the orchestra charged up to a frenzied crescendo. His own ascendence to the heights of Plant Manager had hardly been achieved with such exuberance or overwhelming gusto, but it had been steady and predictable; more at Wagner's pace than Rossini's, which he considered appropriate; Dram's roots being deeply Teutonic. Six years as Plant Manager at Bellend however, was an eternity in Stuttgart's scheme of things. The average plant manager's life span seldom exceeded three years before they were moved on, some never to be heard of again and some to achieve greater status within the company's hierarchy. But at least *something* happened to the others in one way or another:

57

He knew that all managerial performances were closely observed and recorded at Dram (Europe) Headquarters in Stuttgart and sometimes wondered whether his file had somehow become detached from those despotic and top secret 'traffic lights' dossiers and he had been forgotten about. Perhaps someone was using it to prop up a wonky table leg.

Cranby took the steps two at a time as he climbed the staircase to the third and top floor of the administration block. There was a lift of course but he had declined to use it this morning. He stopped at the top, stepping clear but gripping the bannister with one hand and listening to the thump thumping inside his head and waiting for the inky blackness to wash before his eyes. The thumping in his head was there all right, and he was rather out of breath, but otherwise he felt fine, hardly even giddy, let alone about to pass out at any second as had been the case earlier that morning. Nevertheless, he decided as he strode towards his office, black leather thigh boots or no black leather thigh boots, in future sex on an empty stomach was definitely out.

The lights were already on in Cranby's office. He always left them on when he went home at night because he liked to think that it gave an impression of constant diligence. He moved behind his desk and pulled open the venetian blinds. The supplementary sunlight splashed the morning onto the opposite wall upon which hung a large gold framed sepia photograph of the company founder – Gottlieb Dram 1862-1929. The pose was typical of those of that era, immaculately groomed but with a stiff and stilted expression. Portrayed in his late fifties it showed Gottlieb's hair was almost completely grey but still thick and complemented with the inevitably illustrious matching moustache. He seemed to have been a frail man, with thin face and narrow shoulders. And yet despite a rather unassuming overall appearance the photograph had a particularly disconcerting quality about it, in as much as its bold head-on angle made no attempt to disguise or soften Gottlieb's pronounced squint, which gave him the unnerving and yet somehow fiendishly economical ability to follow someone around the office using only one eye. The effect became doubly disquieting with several people in the office; then the eyes would seem to wander about completely independently, eerily inspecting each of the persons in their presence.

Cranby lowered himself into his chair and took his *Guardian* and *Times* from his brief-case, he dropped one on his desk and examined the front page of the other. As usual the only internal sounds at that hour were those of the cleaning women, rattling tongues and waste paper bins above the muted hum of the vacuum cleaner as they plodded through their regular mapped routine. They were in his secretary's — Mrs Spicer's — office now, which was more than could be said for Mrs Spicer who would not arrive for another half an hour. He could hear that unmistakable timbre of working class female gossip. They spoke as though they were participants in some highly competitive verbal relay race, each sprinting through their allocated distance before handing over, without falter to the next.

The adjoining door opened and in they trooped, their briskly wheeled apparatus giving the misleading impression of adroit janitorial expertise. It was the usual trio; the first armed with a powerful and lawless hoover that, once plugged in dragged her about like a pugnacious bulldog, indiscriminately picking fights with skirting boards, table and chair legs and filing cabinets; the next one trundled her trolley with a large cardboard box on it into which she would empty bins and ashtrays, and some cloths and an aerosol to polish the desks and cabinets; the third held a ragged chamois leather and a bottle of Windowlene.

The bin emptyer and furniture polisher was in her early forties, perhaps twenty years junior to her workmates, and was a woman possessing splendidly hefty thighs and large meaty buttocks which she flashed almost continually during the course of her bin emptying and furniture polishing activities. She padded pertly around to Cranby's side of the desk. "Morning," she said, adding cheekily. "Nice day for it." As she bent to remove the bin from beneath the desk, exposing as she did a vast expanse of dual globular yellow knicker. Cranby wanted to bite into those luscious shifting dunes but instead said politely:

59

"Good morning."

The two older women busied through their chores at a perfunctory, self-conscious silent dash, like burglars hastily removing some conspicuous, incriminating evidence. They shut up like clams when they did Cranby's office, at least when he was present. They had hardly spoken a word in his presence since the morning when the hoover had suddenly dived under Cranby's desk and grabbed hold of the trouser bottom of his left leg. The hoover's keeper had tugged with all her meagre elderly strength to remove it and the whole thing was plunging into heavy farce until the bin emptyer pulled the plug. She was the only one who had laughed about it.

The three women were finished inside a minute and a half — it always seemed to Cranby that the place was more presentable before they started on it — and they exited through Mrs Spicer's office. The gossip recommenced promptly and faded into the corridor.

Cranby put down the newspaper and unlocked and slid open a bottom drawer taking out a small mirror and a pair of small, sharp pointed scissors. He brought the mirror close to his nose, and then to such angles as to inspect each of his ears, but you really needed two mirrors for ears. He came back to his nose, holding the mirror at his right profile and carefully began to snip off the offending black spikey hairs further up his nostrils. He had almost finished when a sudden sharp rap came on the door and the shock made him jump in his chair and impale his right nostril on the small, needle-pointed scissors. He knew it was his Assistant Plant Manager, Cliff Fawcett, he recognised the knock. What the hell was he doing in this early? Hurriedly he bundled mirror and scissors back into the drawer. "Come in, Cliff," he called, brushing his nose with a handkerchief.

Gottlieb's left eye swivelled towards the door, while the right stared fixedly at Cranby.

"Morning, Aubrey."

"Morning, Cliff."

"Got a cold. Oh hell," said Fawcett, barely sympathetic.

"Oh, bit of a sniffler," lied Cranby, stuffing the handkerchief back into his pocket. "All this bloody rain I suppose."

60

"Brighter this morning though." Gottlieb's left eye followed Fawcett to the window. "Don't you think that a sunny morning after a rainy night always seems so . . . " He paused thoughtfully and composed a word. "Virginal," he said finally as though it were the title of a poem.

Fawcett was thirty-eight, quite tall, fair haired, unmarried and a bit too indulgent in the permissive age department as far as Cranby was concerned. He also had a habit of using dubious and suggestive adjectives to illustrate the most inconsequential points. Or perhaps it was just Cranby's imagination.

"You're in early this morning," said Cranby, making a conscious effort not to grumble the words.

"Had to drop a lady off at the airport, an air hostess." He glanced at his watch then gazed up at the morning blue sky and sighed: "Be on her way to Bombay by now. Fantastic Jumbos," he concluded in quiet and wistful admiration.

"Brotherston Avenue sank again last night. I had to go all over the show to get in this morning," said Cranby. "Every year as soon as we get a bit of rain the whole bloody thing falls apart. All those tanks I suppose."

"Tanks," said Fawcett without much interest.

"During the war they made tanks and half-tracks not far from here, used to run them along Brotherston Avenue to the station at Lellerscroft. Until they bombed the factory that is. Pity they didn't bomb Brotherston Avenue while they were at it . . . "

"How are the film shows going?" interrupted Fawcett. He seemed to have been mentally distracted for the past few moments, his concentration following his oblique sky-wards gaze.

"Don't ask," groaned Cranby, flapping an agitated hand. "They all sit there sniggering and making jokes. It's damned embarrassing, Cliff!"

A recently introduced company directive had decreed that in future all its employees should, at quarterly intervals, be made aware of both its own and its rivals production and sales performances for that period based on a comparative model versus model basis and also be kept in touch with company developments in general and its aspirations for the future, via the medium of video taped displays to be presented by the plant manager.

"One of them fell asleep yesterday morning. It wasn't until he started snoring that he woke himself up, and half the others probably."

"Perhaps they find the presentation a bit dull. Oh I don't mean to decry your efforts, Aubrey, you come across quite well considering."

"Considering?" frowned Cranby.

"Well let's face it, you're not exactly Panorama material, are you? I mean there's an art to holding people's attention, you've got it or you haven't," shrugged Fawcett.

"What should I have done then, come on wearing a red nose and a revolving bow tie?"

"That's it," enthused Fawcett. "And a curled up shirt front and an exploding bowler hat."

"It's not funny, Cliff," said Cranby seriously.

"Sorry, Aubrey," said Fawcett dejectedly, composing himself with a little dry cough.

"Nobody's even asked any questions yet. Except for one bloke who asked to be excused to go to the toilet. Then of course the rest of them fell about in hysterics, he probably only did it for a bet. They're just not interested, we're flogging a dead horse as far as I'm concerned."

"Flagellation! Now there's a thought, perhaps if you had two naked bits of crumpet whipping each other in the background."

"Cliff," said Cranby sternly.

"Sorry," said Fawcett. He turned from the window. Gottlieb's reproving eye followed him into the chair opposite Cranby. "Anyway you can only get better the next time — oh I didn't mean . . ."

"All right, all right, let's forget the sodding thing for heaven's sake."

"Right, sorry . . . Aubrey."

"Yes?"

"Your nose is bleeding."

Sloan always knew if Mrs Reginald had arrived before him

before he could open his outer office door more than a crack, because her perfume possessed all the subtle delicacy of a drunken buffalo. Strictly speaking it was not the fragrance, rather its over-generous application that caused the problem and he had never quite decided whether this was due simply to a dull sense of smell on her part, or whether it was a camouflaging tactic employed to smother some unmentionable problem of personal hygiene.

Mrs Reginald was a plump, middle-aged, matronly woman who also slightly overdid her make-up. She sat behind her desk, typewriter and this week's *Woman's Own*. "Oh, good morning, Mr Sloan," she said in that quirkily surprised and slightly relieved manner she had of greeting anyone who entered Sloan's outer office. It seemed to Sloan that she lived in constant expectation of some raving rapist bursting in upon her.

"Good morning, Mrs Reginald," he nodded.

"Lovely morning."

"Lovely," agreed Sloan.

"Oh, there was a call for you about five minutes ago," remembered Mrs Reginald.

Sloan stopped in the doorway to his office.

"It was from that chap, Joe Miggins. Remember him?"

"Miggins . . . Miggins," mused Sloan. "It rings a bell."

"You must remember him. He got five years for attacking his foreman."

"Not the bloke who threw George Cubley into the boot of a car and reversed it into a brick wall."

"Eight times so they said," confirmed Mrs Reginald. "Drunk as a lord apparently."

"Good grief! It's never five years since he was put away, is it?"

"He got eighteen months off for good behaviour. He wanted to know if we could put that in his reference by the way."

"His what!" spluttered Sloan.

"He's after a job in an abattoir apparently . . ."

"We can't go around handing out references to ex-convicts for goodness sakes!" interrupted Sloan. "Not favourable ones anyway. What am I supposed to say? 'To whom it may concern. Only once in the whole of his employment with this company did Mr Miggins batter his supervisor to within an inch of his life, causing him permanent psychological injury, and in the process demolish a waxing booth wall and write off a brand new motor car. We feel that such commendable restraint should be borne in mind by anyone who may be considering him for employment within their organisation'."

"I did try to explain that to him myself," said Mrs Reginald.

"Good show," nodded Sloan, pushing his shoulder into the door.

"But he insisted on calling back," hesitated Mrs Reginald. Her telephone began to ring and she pulled a face at the probable coincidence. "In five minutes."

"Put him through then," sighed Sloan. "Let's hope he doesn't bite."

He installed himself behind his desk and picked up his telephone. "Sloan speaking," he said crisply.

"Er, the name's Miggins, I'm ringing about a reference." His voice was thick and blunt, and, Sloan suspected, one wrong word's distance from aggressive.

"So I understand, Mr Miggins."

"For a job, see. Otherwise they won't take me on."

"Well to be perfectly honest, Mr Miggins, as my secretary has already explained to you, there's no way that the company can consider giving you a reference because of the circumstances in which you left us. I'm sure you can see that."

"Well 'ow about if there was a few quid in it for you to give me one and leave all that bit out," he suggested quite blatantly. "I 'aven't told them about going inside see, so . . ."

"Mr Miggins, I think we'd better leave it at that," interrupted Sloan. I don't believe it! I just don't believe it! He thought.

"But they won't give me the job . . ."

"I'm sorry but . . ."

"All right, you fuckin' bastard . . ."

Sloan snatched the telephone away from his ear, staring for several seconds at it, all the time gushing its yelled obscenities at him. He whistled silently and placed the

64

receiver gently back on its hook with Miggins still in full flow.

"That's just what I need," he sighed tiredly. "Cabaret, first thing on a Tuesday morning."

The presentation display room was actually an annexed corner of the vast east canteen that had been partitioned off and furnished with a close cropped grey carpet, two hundred plastic chairs, a small stage at one end and fourteen twenty-six inch colour television sets hired from the people who had produced the presentation, and mounted on tall strategically positioned stands.

Eight blue coated foremen sat, affectedly attentive in the front row like monitors at a school assembly, their shining faces upturned in anticipation towards Cranby, the headmaster.

Throughout the remainder of the audience ran a buzz of what Cranby had, for the first few sessions, optimistically construed as restless expectation, or at least modest curiosity. But in reality neither appraisal was an accurate one. It was not that they were not glad to be there, after all, it meant a break from the tedium of the line, and if a few operators asked some questions after the film the session might stretch until break-time. But it was merely the quaint novelty of the occasion that had occupied them in that animated fashion: And it had been a brief and frivolous occupation.

"Where's the tart with the raspberry ripples?" inquired Sammy, craning his neck over the heads around him.

"I've been looking out for her myself," responded Steep. "Looks like the place hasn't got one."

"Perhaps Rex McBean'll come round with them in the interval ha ha ha ha," put in Sproat.

"You could always nip through to the canteen and fetch back a plate of egg and chips," suggested Melrose.

"Naw, it's not the same as a raspberry ripple," sniffed Sammy. "Anyway, you can't find the yolk to dip your chips in in the dark."

"Some lousy picture house this is," commented Steep disgustedly. "No raspberry ripples, no Wurlitzer, plastic seats."

"Yeah," agreed Sammy. "And I bet the film's a load of shit as well."

On the stage with Cranby was Arthur Brain, the trim lines superintendent. He was a vain, turgid man who always wore houndstooth or large check sports jackets and smoked filthy little Turkish cheroots. He had virtually no memory for faces and a nastily suspicious nature and it was said that he always carried a picture of his wife to work with him so as to verify that the same woman was living in the house when he got home. He sat nonchalantly beneath a large circular 'No Smoking' symbol, his big bald head breaking into the lowest portion of it, so favouring the impression that he had been recently canonised and allocated the position of patron saint of smoking related diseases. He spoke privately with Cranby at the back of the stage, fumbling blindly in his pocket then pulling out the slim silver case containing his blasphemous, vile smelling cigars. He lit one as they spoke, immediately enveloping both he and Cranby in a billowing grey cloud.

"Look at him," complained Godfrey. "Puffing away on his stinking cheroots with a dirty big no smoking sign right behind him."

"Go and tell him, then," challenged Sammy.

"He's lit it now, hasn't he," shrugged Godfrey with hastily contrived resignation. "He's got nowhere to stub it out."

"Oh I'm sure we could think of somewhere," said Sammy.

Cranby emerged with stylish but unintentional elegance from the nebula, spoiling the effect only slightly by blinking with the smoke and briefly stifling a cough. He stopped at the lectern at the edge of the stage and leaned cautiously forward to speak into its microphone. "Good morning, gentlemen," he began. The operators became readily silent, like people at a party who were about to hear a good joke. "I don't want to say anything just yet," went on Cranby. "Other than to say that we have prepared a short film for you to watch. If there are any questions or anything you would like to discuss then we can do so later. Thank you, gentlemen." Cranby nodded to the video machine operator at the rear of the room and slid gracefully back into Arthur

Brain's spectral mists.

The lights were switched off and the room fell into a thick, close darkness. There was a short smattering of childish cheers, and a voice half hissed and half giggled: "Gerroff me arse, Spiv."

With a great dramatic enthusiasm, the Dram logo leapt onto the dispersed screens, immaculate in its cherry red and vivid gold livery and accompanied by a mercenary burst of rallying music that provoked an outbreak of embarrassed, screen-lit grins to permeate the audience, and Rex McBean to secretly shiver off a spontaneous attack of goose bumps induced by the moment's sheer inspirational uplift.

The scene then cut briefly to a ground level shot of the administration block and then to Cranby, seated rather stiffly at his desk, as though a mild electric current was flowing through him. Behind him was a tall bookcase that totally obscured the window behind it. Its shelves were neatly filled with richly bound red leather books with gold lettered spines which were really only dummy spines glued onto a balsa wood construction, and brought in by the film people in the fraudulent knowledge that impressions of erudition and sincerity are best nurtured by such a backcloth.

The camera began to close in. "Hello," said the fourteen strategically positioned Cranbys, each with the same slight tightness about their lips, the same minute agitation in their eyes that seemed, disquietingly, to be focused somewhere inside the audiences heads. "I'm Aubrey Cranby, Plant Manager, Bellend Operations," they went on in their uneasy unison, and as if to confirm that the statement was a legitimate one a caption appeared at the bottom of the screens, it read:

AUBREY CRANBY – PLANT MANAGER – BELLEND
OPERATIONS

Soon attentions began to drift, and despite the occasional urgent interjections of important coloured graphs and charts listing the last six months' production figures many were uncontrollably drawn to a greater, almost hypnotic fascination in the end of Arthur Brain's cigar. Its glowing red tip hovered, disembodied, like some sinister staring bloodshot eye.

Suddenly it would take off, scribbling darting abstract shapes on the blackness, then steady and glow a burning angry red.

Cranby knew already that it was going the way of the previous sessions. He could sense the lack of interest in them, the contented boredom from men who were bored for a living. They were experts at it, authorities on it, and they knew that this was a rare and precious boredom, a boredom to be coveted; they were being paid at the full hourly rate and yet asked to do no more than sit in a darkened room with just a few television sets containing nothing more than his own effulgent but paralysed countenance and diligent but droning commentary to entrammel their warm dark preoccupations. The feeling washed over him like weak little waves on an ebbing moonlit tide.

Suddenly his eyes were stung by another cloud of raiding smoke from Arthur Brain's cigar and his nostrils filled with its sly, foreign smell. He glanced irritably into the darkness and made to lean towards the trim lines superintendent but stopped himself, then he caught the smell again and tipped testily to his right. "What in God's name is in those things?"

Unfortunately the whisper was caught by the microphone and broadcast to the four corners of the room.

"Camel shit!" somebody instantly suggested.

"Sweaty socks!"

"Arabs undies, ha ha ha ha!"

The place was suddenly a dim, screen-lit riot of boisterous contagious laughter, of howls and hoots and claims and counterclaims as to the real ingredients of Arthur Brain's filthy cigars.

Throughout, the televised Cranby pressed on with an admirably professional disregard. He continued to speak seriously of the vital importance of 'productive efficiency' and 'co-operation at all levels', while the real Cranby held his head in his hands and groaned: And Ted Slutswater, who was immensely grateful for the camouflaging nature of the disturbance because he was being rapidly choked by Arthur Brain's cigar, but was too bashful to interrupt the proceedings by issuing the relevant distressful utterances, and was hence, by the second, becoming a more garish shade

of purple about the cheeks and temples, coughed himself
to an unheeded exhaustion in the roistering darkness.

"You know yesterday, when you said about the girlfriend,
that you reckon she's planning to get married and all that.
Were you just messing about?" ventured Steep hopefully.

He sat across a table from Melrose in the bustling west
canteen, bowls of muddy oxtail, the soup of the day — or if
the amended chalk lettering on the menu board was to be
believed, SLOP OF THE DAY — steaming gently between
them. Melrose pouted his lips and shook his large ageing
teddy boys head gravely. "Sounds like the classic modus
operandi to me, old son. I reckon you've got twelve months
at the outside, then . . . " Melrose ran his half full spoon
graphically across his throat causing a thin trail of blood-
brown oxtail soup to splash realistically across the yellow
topped table and trickle over the edge.

"Christ, you make it sound like an execution!"

"You could put it like that," nodded Melrose, wiping the
spilled soup with a single finger then noisily sucking off what
he had collected. "Marriage isn't a word you know, it's a
sentence. D'you like that, clever, eh," he winked and smiled
immodestly.

"Oh yes, dead poetic, I must say," grumbled Steep. "You
know, you've missed your calling in life, you should have
been a Samaritan."

"Bloody hell, this soup's hot," slurped Melrose. "A what?"

"Never mind. I just wouldn't fancy being on top of a
twenty storey building getting ready to jump with only you
up there to talk me out of it."

Melrose looked puzzled. "Why should you want somebody
to talk you out of it? I mean you don't go up to the top of
a building on the off chance that you might fancy jumping
off when you get there, do you. Surely you'd make up your
mind before you went. Premeditated like."

"Well I might land on somebody mightn't I," joked Steep
evasively. What the hell am I talking about? He wondered.

Suddenly the busy, hungry clatter around them became
strangely muted and thankfully the conversation lapsed

while everybody followed the tightly packaged rear of the redhead from the soft trim sewing room as it headed towards the dessert counter. She walked slowly, her buttocks rolling with a practiced and brassy deliberateness. She knew they were watching.

"If you're so right why do people keep doing it?" challenged Steep eventually, impulsively inspired by the sight of the redhead's wonderful backside.

"You've just seen why," pointed out Melrose, as the diners built up their momentum again around them. "Because all bloke's basically want is a handy cunt. I mean nobody really *enjoyed* ogling that piece of fluff just then. It just made them frustrated because all they wanted to do was to get stuck into it, but they can't so they'll all go home and get stuck into the missus instead, then, once they're on the job they won't care who it is because all they wanted was somewhere hot and sloppy to shove it. The Power of the Minge, you can't resist it. You spend your first nine months trying to get out of it and the rest of your life trying to get back in."

"That's a bit chauvinistic, isn't it?" smiled Steep uncertainly. "What about women. I don't think that theory seriously considers their aspirations on the matter, does it?"

"All women are whores," explained Melrose easily. "They use their bodies to get what they want from us. Why are they always tarting themselves up? So they'll look attractive to us, right? And what does 'looking attractive' mean to a bloke? Shagworthiness, that's all. They can buy anything they like with their bodies from a seat on a bus to a trip to the altar, and it's all down to the Power of the Minge, it's bloody frightening!"

"What about love?" inquired Steep. "Don't people get married for that?"

"Women don't. Women just want to get their claws into meal tickets. Blokes just succumb to the Power. So we're the mugs." He prodded his chest with the end of his spoon. "We're the ones who keep not winning the pools on Saturday afternoons and getting pissed on Saturday nights instead. We're the ones with the insatiable cocks. Don't worry about it though, there's nothing we can do," he shrugged. "Drink

70

your soup, it's going cold."

"I'd forget the Samaritans if I were you," advised Steep, skimming his spoon across the surface of his soup and raising it, brimming to his lips. "Marriage guidance, that's what you should go for."

"Wayll howdie, Tex!" called Melrose suddenly, in a loud and ridiculously thick, cowboy drawl that made Steep spray his oxtail soup all over the table.

Melrose was beaming and waving amiably over Steep's shoulder. He turned and saw Rex McBean and Ted Slutswater taking their usual short cut through the canteen to the supervisors' dining room. McBean stopped dead and then proceeded to shoo the puzzled and constantly toppling Slutswater in a direction away from their table.

"Yawl fixin' t' hayve yoursaylf a mess o' grits n' hog-jowls?" called Melrose, and McBean began to make agitated protestations at Slutswater's appropriately bent back as the pair of them scurried away.

"Rex isn't the only one who thinks you've got a screw loose now," said Steep, staring self-consciously into his oxtail soup and wiping some splashes off his chin with the back of his hand. "Half the bleeding canteen's looking."

"Sod 'em," shrugged Melrose, unconcerned.

"It's all very well you saying that," hissed Steep. "Carry on like this and you're gonna end up moseyin' on down to the li'lle ole looney bin."

As the Tuesday menu offered a largely vegetarian fare many of the sections' operators were reluctant to avail themselves of its services since the incident involving George Spivak, a lettuce leaf and something extant and hairy, both of which Spivak claimed to have eaten, with the latter, he insisted, roaming energetically around his stomach for several subsequent days.

"Can't stand salads, me," said Godfrey, curling his lip and shaking his head. He placed his packaged sandwiches on the stolen table.

"What's on yours?" asked Derek Kettle, nodding in agreement.

Godfrey opened his Mothers Pride wrapper and peeled back a layer of white medium-sliced bread. He peered at its filling like a dentist peering into a horribly diseased mouth. "Cucumber and tomato, she's a stupid twat, my missus. What've you got?"

"Beetroot and egg and little green things," replied Kettle, fussily picking off the water cress and flicking the bits at Steve Sproat.

"Fuck off," grunted Sproat, chivalrously brushing the cress off the picture of the naked lady in his newspaper.

"You should've saw the stripper at the club last night," said Spivak, admiring the lady in Sproat's paper. "Nipples like cigar stubs she had." His lips pouted and his mobile features distorted into creases and folds of imagined ecstasy.

"I was with this Chinese one once," mused Sammy. "Few years ago now, like." He turned to Henry Chong and offered a description. "Short piece, dark hair."

"With slanty eyes?" asked Henry.

"That's right, yeah."

"She my missus you bastard."

"Oh, nowt happened, mate, honest. It's just that she said she had this bed shaped like a cross because it goes the other way."

"Honest!" gasped Spivak. "Is that right, Henry?" he asked eagerly. "That Chinese tarts fannies go sideways?"

Henry paused, his round, yellow-tan, frying pan face composing itself into that spiritual thoughtfulness of which only the oriental countenance is capable. "It been long time," he said finally. "Can't lemember."

"My shoulder's killing me," piped a voice timidly.

"Who said that?" said Sproat, lifting his dull face from his newspaper and searching with stupid extravagance around and under the table.

Most sections employed a crude, unofficial promotional structure whereby new men would, in general, be given the most unpopular jobs to do; the criterion for inclusion being based upon the physical demands or excessive tedium involved in each operation. Andrew Bright had been given roof felts which fell principally into the former category and entailed painting a thick black glue onto the inside roof of

72

a car to which sections of flaky, smelly felt would then be fixed. To anyone who was not used to the job, it was a back-breaker.

Andrew Bright's soft young face grew red. He flashed a brief and uncomfortable smile around the table. Ugly blotches of dripped glue clung itself to the side of his hair. "My shoulder," he explained shyly. "I think my arm's going to drop off."

"You wanna stop pullin' your plonker, then," mumbled Kettle unfeelingly through an obscene mouthful of egg and beetroot sandwich.

"No, it's my *left* shoulder," said Andrew Bright a little less apprehensively.

At first he seemed pleased that the entire table had suddenly riveted their open faces to his. But then, after only an instant, the flat, vacant landscape that was his audience at once split and crumbled as though struck without warning by some violent earthquake. At the same time he seemed to realise the awful consequences of what he had said. He fought himself to his feet through the cruel uncontrollable howls and snorts, his tubby body trembled and he made podgy red fists with his hands, his eyes burned with a roaring yet somehow pathetically impotent rage. He saw that in the pandemonium Kettle's egg and beetroot sandwiches had been knocked to the floor so he jerked forward and stamped viciously on them.

This only served to fuel the uproar and Spivak actually fell off the end of the bench onto his knees, his hands kneading his aching belly and when Andrew Bright kicked the mushed egg and beetroot sandwiches at him he keeled over onto his back, hitting the floor with his hand like a wrestler in agony, his brilliant plimsolls kicking out like the paws of a convulsive white rabbit.

The young man's eyes were glazed now and a dampness in them had quenched their stillborn rage and made them lonely and afraid. "Fucking arseballs!" he screamed.

"Oh no!" choked Spivak. "He called us arseballs! Stop it, stop it!"

Andrew Bright's lower lip began to curl and tremble. His wet, child's eyes stared a moment longer then burst into

73

spectacular, infant tears. He was a five-year-old lost in a strange and frightening place. He wanted to go home. He wanted his Mummy. "I hate you!" he screamed through his sobs, and then, in the finest traditions of five-year-olds, he stamped his foot and ran away.

Chapter Three

A state of frosty and cautious tolerance was probably the best that could ever be hoped for in the relationship between Bellend's management and its workforce — as opposed to its union, which was not the same thing. They lived together in a sort of reluctant symbiosis, like a married couple both convinced of the others addiction to infidelity; enduring each other's presence beneath the same roof only because that presence was essential to the other's continued existence; both knowing only too well of the other's failings and failures of the past, of the black lies and conveniently forgotten promises. They seldom spoke directly to each other in any serious or constructive fashion.

Whenever they did converse the exchanges were almost inevitably a consequence of some rancorous, localised dispute and took place from behind freshly sharpened, wagged fingers of accusation and stubbornly entrenched positions, separated by a no-man's-land strewn with all the old jagged and poisoned prejudices. Neither sought to understand or respect the other's attitudes or aspirations, and as a result there would always be squabbling between them.

Cranby stood at his office window, the blinds tilted at a sufficiently obscuring angle. Outside, beyond the perimeter road on the open grassy space adjacent to the car park gathered eight hundred paint shop operators, an audience to seven shop stewards and a convener strung out like dowdy pigeons along a low partitioning wall.

Cranby looked at his watch, it was nine twenty-five in the morning. He raised his eyes to the morning's grey, lifeless sky and hoped mischievously for a sudden downpour.

e convener exchanged the cigarette in his mouth for a
ɹ hailer. "Testing, testing. One, two, three." The strident,
ɹnplified voice rung metallically over the heads of the
assembly. "Right, lads," he went on after a pause. "If you're
all here we can get started."

"We can't 'ear yer," came a barely audible voice from the
crowd.

"Take them funny masks off," called another.

There was a knock on Cranby's door and it opened behind
him. He half turned his head, it was Sloan. He joined Cranby
at the window and they stood silently and watched the
proceedings for some seconds. Sloan spoke first.

"He didn't waste much time getting them out there. I
was only talking to him . . . " He paused and consulted his
watch. "Seven minutes ago."

"Nicholas?"

"Aubrey?"

"I realise all this may be none of my business," said Cranby
quietly, almost absentmindedly, without turning. "What
with me only being the sodding plant manager and all, but
do you think somebody might take the trouble to sort of put
me in the picture as to what the hell's going on, exactly."

"You mean nobody's told you? No, I don't suppose they
would have, would they, what with everything happening
so quickly. Well." Sloan took a deep breath. "Apparently
they were minus one primer inspector this morning so they
borrowed this chap from underseal inspection. Now as you
know, primer inspectors are supposed to check the bodies
for pits and runs and things, and chalk a circle around any
faults they find. The snag was that this chap they got was
only five feet and a half an inch tall and he could hardly
reach any of the roofs on tip-toes, never mind inspect them.
But he was all they had to spare apparently so they told him
to manage as best he could . . . which he did until the other
inspectors realised what was going on, and then they all
refused to inspect their roofs as well."

Outside, in response to an unheard recommendation
by the convener, eight hundred hands rose as one, like a
giant classful of know-alls.

"Things weren't too bad up to that point," went on Sloan.

76

"They called for their shop steward and he persuaded them to carry on working while he discussed the matter with the foreman. It wasn't until the foreman allegedly and or inadvertently referred to the diminutive inspector as "that short-arsed little turd" that they all stopped work."

Both men continued their thoughtful watch over the congregation below them, disintegrating rapidly now like a huge cell exploding into separate hundreds.

"It's only a one day thing, though. A protest," said Sloan encouragingly. "They'll all be back tomorrow."

"Oh goody gumdrops," murmured Cranby.

Then came an interruption. The door to Mrs Spicer's office blew powerfully open as though it had been struck by some sudden, savage gale. Both men spun away from the window; crammed in the doorway stood a huge and hideous woman. She must have been something over six feet tall, but had her height been in average female proportion to her width then she would have measured nearer twice that. Her hair was black and crudely cut with a long fringe and a sudden short drop like curtains just behind her eyes. Her breasts were like cloaked boulders beneath the voluminous bulging square yards and yards of her brown bear coloured coat and they extended down, with a fearful overhang, almost to where a normal woman's waist would have been, but with her the sides of her body were still diverging at that point. She was a woman who would defy and defeat the most rampant imagination, even in its most strenuous attempts to project an image of what inexpressible horrors lay unexplored below her clothing.

The two men just stared, loose jawed at the woman. In return she eyed them individually as though casting a spell on them one at a time.

"Which one is it. 'im?" she eventually boomed into the office, and she nodded her head like the butt of a buffalo at Cranby. It was impossible to see at whom she spoke as she eclipsed everything behind her in the doorway, but as she lumbered closer they could see Mrs Spicer holding on with both hands to the belt of her coat, pulling hopelessly and leaning backwards, her sensible shoes gliding smoothly over the carpet in the manner of an ageing but expert water skier.

"Sorry, Mr Cranby," called Mrs Spicer still being towed along behind the woman. "I asked her to wait but she wouldn't."

"What 'ave you done to my Andrew? Sobbed 'is 'eart out all night 'e 'as," she boomed again, stopping at the edge of Cranby's desk.

"Good morning, Madam," smiled Cranby nervously. His voice was choked with polite self-preservation. Had he not known better he could have sworn that Gottlieb's eyes had actually uncrossed and were *both* gazing in wild disbelief at the woman's enormous bulk.

"Good for you, per'aps. You 'aven't seen 'is poor little face."

"No, that's true," conceded Cranby meekly. "Er, what appears to be the lady's problem, Mrs Spicer?" He leaned alternately to one side and the other to try to locate his secretary behind the woman.

"I'm afraid she wouldn't speak to me, Mr Cranby," said Mrs Spicer breathlessly. Her tightly curled, bleached blonde head peeked carefully around the woman's broad trunk. "She just said her name was Mrs Bright and she wanted to see the Plant Manager."

"Chief Ponce," she corrected.

"Quite," gulped Cranby. "Please, Mrs Bright, take a seat." He barely stopped himself from adding. "Take a *couple* of seats."

"I'll see you later, then," said Sloan, edging away from Cranby.

"I just want a word that's all, no need to rush off." She made it sound like a command for Sloan to stay where he was, which he did.

She bent forward and gripped the rim of the table with her big white paws. She looked as though she might break off a chunk. She glared with terrible black eyes directly at Cranby — he noticed that she had a juvenile moustache and sparse whiskers on her chin — her large grey face moved as though it was formed of half set concrete. "But if I ever find out what 'appened to 'im in 'ere, and it's anythin' to do with you, Mister. I'll be back 'ere." Then at last she allowed

78

some hidden vestige of wanton femininity to drift carelessly to the surface. "To 'ave someone's bollocks for earrings."

Less than an hour later the entire assembly plant was, but for pockets of gossiping foremen, silent and still and empty of its workers. As was usual when such situations arose shop stewards would, from the outset, display an uncannily swift conspicuous absence about the place. The few to be caught napping would, when accosted, claim to be unaware of any sort of official situation as yet — indeed they were at that very moment on their way to determine whether one existed. Whereupon they vanished.

Each man then, in his ignorance, nurtured his own private rumour or toyed with one until it bored him and he exchanged it for somebody else's. Some would collect several until they found the one which best suited their own individual requirements and then acted upon it. Some, therefore, were on strike, others were laid off, some did not care either way, the pubs would soon be open.

Many held their ground until the cause became hopeless, while others wandered about restlessly like a ship's crew uncertain as to whether or not they were sinking: They drifted out in dribs, in resigned and confused clusters, knowing for certain only that they would report as normal tomorrow and the whole thing would be forgotten. On leaving, Sammy called across the line to Graeme Leatherbarrow: "I'll tell you what, Graeme. These stewards want fucking."

Graeme smiled quietly and replied: "Line 'em up, Sam."

Steep's bus roamed unhurriedly among the monotonous, blurred-edged suburbs at the fringe of the city. It left Bellend behind and cut through Lellerscroft, coming upon the prematurely moribund, concrete-grey shopping centre on the far side of that district. Many of its shops that had not already died and been hurriedly shuttered, chained and pad-locked away, cringed in their sickly light behind heavy wire screens as though in the hope that such protection might render them immune to the endemic disease and its fatal

79

consequences. People mingled loosely among the scarred and hideously tattooed pillars like lost amnesiacs. Housewives, their hair eternally and optimistically trapped and tortured in curlers in anticipation of perpetually forthcoming celebrations met and rehashed yesterday's conversation or was it the day before's? Others pushed squeaking prams and squawking children blindly past the sprayed missives of hate and violence, the cowardly esoteric nicknames and the vilest obscenities. Their action seemed motivated by a desire merely to exist — which is no desire at all — without any of the garnitures which upgrade an existence to a life. Only the swashbuckling and cosmopolitan population of mongrel dogs, with their brisk trot and hungry eye seemed to have any purpose about their lives.

There were only eight other people downstairs on the bus and five of them had boarded with Steep outside the plant. The other passengers comprised of an elderly man who, upon boarding revealed his free pass to the driver as though he were a secret agent furtively identifying himself to a colleague before infiltrating a nest of enemy spies; a blind man with dead staring eyes and a handsome golden guide dog; and an acne cursed school boy anxiously transscribbling notes into an exercise book from a frazzled text book called 'Multiple Choice Questions in Electro-Magnetics' by E.E. Handford.

It seemed as though everyone in the world with somewhere to go had already got there and the buses were left to the devices of the late and the lost and the lunatic.

The bus pulled up at some traffic lights and a smart metallic green Mini stopped alongside it. Steep immediately noticed a woman's thighs, flattened and spread like lumps of dough against the seat as she worked the pedals. He could not see her face because of reflections in the windscreen but her thighs were very presentable and if he leaned forward a fraction he could probably see right up the inside of her skirt. He began to tilt slowly, and slyly lower his head. Then the traffic lights changed and the rude tug of the bus moving away threw his delicate balance and made him appear to start as if suddenly awakened. The thighs in the Mini had gone and he felt a certain relief trickle

80

through him, as though some wicked, whispering temptation had been snatched away from him in the nick of time. Was it *normal* to want to look up womens' skirts, he wondered? This was the second time this week he had caught himself at it. Good God, he wasn't turning into a pervert on top of everything else, was he?

The Nybs Lane housing estate was enjoying its mid-morning nap. Its habitual housewives had shopped for the day and retreated indoors to womanly chores or a black and white Spencer Tracey on television. Its children were locked up, yawning blamelessly in airless classrooms. The whereabouts of its menfolk were less predictable. Some were at their places of work, or sleeping — their day's work done the previous night — through what they would never have guessed could have turned into such a pleasant spring morning. Some were equally safe and oblivious in their local public houses, others crushed and inglorious at their local Social Security office, or browsing around their Job Centre in the manner of indignant browsers in an exclusive and expensive department store.

Occasional gas board or television repair vans dawdled unnoticed along its tight, vacuous streets, as did the death defying, scabby kneed infants who pedalled at scaled down great speed over its cracked pavements on evenly matched plastic tractors and formula one racing cars.

The air was light and fresh where the sun could reach and what little clingings of council approved colour the estate possessed seemed to stand out like vividly painted flags. But in the long-hanging, razor-edged shadows the air chilled instantly and the colours were withered and weak.

Steep always used the back door of 38 Blenheim Street because Auntie Agnes always kept the chain on the front. Even before he reached the garden gate he could smell she was burning something again. He lifted the latch but knew it would be locked so he agilely scaled it as he had done ever since he had been tall enough to jump up and reach the top. He heard Mr Neeves' voice the instant the gate rattled under his weight.

"She's burning something again," he called, his voice was rough and raw but characteristically tremulous. Mr Neeves was a short, heavy redundant docker who took Valium for his nerves.

As Steep dropped down into the little patch of weedy garden Mr Neeves repeated himself: "She's burning something again. Can't you do something about her, Albert? Mrs Neeves is a bag of nerves."

Mr Neeves was perfectly positioned as usual, with just a head and no neck on top of the dividing wall. Today, all week in fact, he had been a weight-lifter with bulging muscles and a leopard skin leotard. Steep changed Mr Neeves' identity quite frequently simply by rubbing out the chalked-in torso and limbs and replacing it with another. Some days Mr Neeves would be a grotesquely big bosomed lady, other days a petite female ballet dancer, a dribbling footballer, a skeleton or a kangaroo.

Thin fingers of smoke squeezed out around the kitchen window. Steep unlocked the kitchen door and opened it. The grey nebula rolled out like an unwrapped cloud.

"It's okay now, Mr Neeves," assured Steep, putting his handkerchief over his mouth and nose and stepping into the foggy kitchen. He made immediately for the gas cooker, checking through the haze the dials along the front; the middle one was turned on, the grill: Four blackened, shrivelled shapes lay there smouldering. He took the tray outside.

"Toast," he confirmed, showing the charred remnants to Mr Neeves who examined them with a certain sombre satisfaction, as though they were small sick animals that had just been put out of their misery. He nodded slowly and called in to Mrs Neeves: "Toast, Doris. You win." Then he turned back to Steep. "I said it was the ironing," he said in the manner of a doctor who had mis-diagnosed the illness of a dead patient. "She gets the stirrup pump on her side of the bed tonight."

Steep smiled at the joke but then realised from Mr Neeves' sober expression that he was being serious and quickly smothered it. "It's only good for the birds now," said Steep, throwing them onto the bit of garden.

Mr Neeves nodded again at the sad and indisputable fact of life. Only now did he turn his attention to why Steep should be home in the middle of the day. "How come you're so early?"

"We're on strike, or laid off, or something."

"Oh God," mumbled Mr Neeves non-committally. He looked anxiously back into the kitchen, the smoke had mostly gone but the worry did not leave him. "Oh well, I'll see you, then," he said unenthusiastically and went back indoors, decapitating the strong man in the leopard skin leotard.

Steep went back into the kitchen, half filled the sink and placed the scorched tray into it. The cold water hissed on contact. He could hear voices coming from the front room. He knew it was a radio play because Auntie Agnes did not know anyone who spoke with a bad southern United States negroid accent. He went into the hall to hang his coat up and then into the front room.

The front rooms of Blenheim Street were packed and dull. Only a sliver of sun ever ventured through the tightly boxed windows for perhaps an hour or so each day.

Auntie Agnes was asleep in her old armchair. She looked so peaceful when she was asleep, so much so that sometimes he found himself creeping right up to her and intently watching her crumpled, kindly face for a sign of breath or a sleepy sigh. Her grey head lolled on her bony shoulder, the old fashioned lacey antimacassar had fallen about her head like a badly placed veil. Her thin white hands were gathered on her lap and her legs crossed at the ankles before a single bar of the electric fire. She looked nothing at all like the raving pyromaniac that the Neeves' were convinced she was. It was true enough she burnt things quite often but not deliberately, she would just forget and fall asleep.

He warned her frequently of the dangers but she seemed neither interested nor concerned; she would tell him not to worry and say that his mother and father and his Uncle Stan would make sure nothing happened to them.

He switched off the radio. It was on the sideboard flanked by two framed photographs on little stands. One was a sepia tinted picture taken forty-two years ago and showing Uncle

Stan and Auntie Agnes posing woodenly, obviously under management but with genuinely happy smiles, on their wedding day. In the background of the picture, between the couple and the church doors was a woman crouching slightly to hold a toddler's hand, scurrying to get out of the shot. The dragged toddler's free hand had a finger tunnelling up his nose and the woman smiled at the camera as she hurried by: The other picture, in dwindling colours was of Steep's parents taken during their honeymoon on the beach at Rhyl. They were sitting together on the sand in their bare feet, his father with his trousers rolled up to his knees. His mother wore one of those loose airy skirts that flew out like a rosette when you danced rock and roll in them. She had her head on his shoulder and he had his arm around her waist.

They all looked so cosily happy, so full of each other in a way that Steep could never envisage *he* could be with Daffy.

On the coffee table next to Auntie Agnes' armchair was a tea cup. She hardly ever drank her hot chocolate which was a pity when she had managed to make it without burning a hole in anything. Steep picked it up, cupping one hand around and sniffing at it. It was drinkably warm. He took a sip and moved to the old two seater settee, lowering himself carefully onto it — the springs were treacherous. He did not ask her any more to get rid of the sagging, slowly disintegrating three piece suite. It was the last thing that her husband had bought for her before he died.

Daffy was coming round later. He had not seen her since last Monday night when a spring came through the cushion on the settee and cut her thigh in the middle of Panorama.

Steep raised the cup to his mouth again, absently rolling the rim on his lower lip. He peered in quiet and frought, anxious, distressed, perturbed, troubled, tormented, disturbed and vexed thought down into the dark liquid chocolate and tipped it forward taking a slow slurp. Then, as the level went down a hideous smirk began to emerge from the depths of the cup, pink and white and horrific. Instantly he pushed the cup away from him. The shock of the encounter shot through him like an electric charge, causing him to cry out and jolt in his seat. The cup lay unbroken and the carpet thirstily soaked up the hot chocolate while Auntie Agnes'

84

top set of dentures grinned broadly and disembodiedly at him from the floor.

Auntie Agnes rolled her head across to her other shoulder and whispered a thin, elderly sigh. Steep closed his eyes for a few seconds to compose himself then rose from the settee, picked up the cup and scooped Auntie Agnes' dentures into it.

He went out to the kitchen to get some paper towels to mop the carpet. Through the kitchen window he noticed a lone sparrow hopping agitatedly between the four pieces of burnt toast, its game little beak setting about the offerings with all the vitality of a champion woodpecker, but making no impression. Then two bullying starlings fluttered down and chased the sparrow. They tried a few half-hearted pecks but the going was too tough for them and they flew off. The sparrow was back instantly.

Steep filled the cup with water and left it on the draining board. He tore a couple of towels from the roll and went back into the front room, mopping the carpet and returning to the kitchen. In the garden the charred relics remained intact and the sparrow had gone. He opened the door to take the soggy towels to the dustbin and as he stepped outside a tiny white action painting splattered on his upper arm. He looked up towards the guttering from where an impish sparrow made its escape. Steep tutted to himself and began to wipe his arm with a dry corner of the towels. Had that been just any old sparrow impersonally performing a normal sparrow-like act, he wondered? Or was it the sparrow defeated and disgusted by Auntie Agnes' burnt toast, trying to tell him something?

Auntie Agnes and her sidekick, Mrs Wilks always left for their Wednesday night bingo at half past five despite the fact that the first session did not begin until seven o'clock and the church hall was only a ten minute walk away. The thing was; they liked to get there early and claim the front seats because they had the hots for Wayne Concorde — the caller and D.J.

There was a knock at the front door. It was Daffy. She had

her hair tied back behind her head in an unfortunate arrangement she sometimes adopted which placed undue emphasis on her prominent ears. She was wearing jeans and a long beige coat.

"Hello," they said together as she stepped in. She was holding the evening Echo. "The paper lad just gave it to me. The newspaper," she clarified tiredly in response to his quietly startled expression.

"I suppose he's gone tearing down the road, has he. Paper lad. Tearing down the road," he explained laboriously. "Oh, forget it."

"There's a bit about your place on the front page. Don't tell me you're on strike," she said rhetorically, taking her coat off and hanging it on the hall stand. She was wearing a red crew-neck sweater. Her small breasts looked tired and sloppy. She could do with a new bra, thought Steep.

"D'you want a cup of tea?" he asked. "The kettle's on."

"Okay," she shrugged, following him into the kitchen. "Auntie Aggie gone, has she?"

"Five minutes ago."

"So we're all alone for the evening," she said attempting the sort of sudden female suggestiveness that she had never quite mastered.

"There's a good film documentary I want to watch on tele tonight," he said quickly without immediately understanding why.

"Oh," she said curling her bottom lip and opening the newspaper at the television page. "What, you mean the one on BBC Two about the meta . . . mor . . . phose of the Amazonian Water Gnat?" She sounded hurt, like a woman who had been jilted for an Amazonian Water Gnat. "Bette Davis is on the other side — Whatever Happened to Baby Jane," she offered, as though trying to salvage what she could from an already collapsed evening.

"Even better," he enthused, lifting the cups and saucers and going into the front room.

They sat in two armchairs across the small dim room from each other. On the television a cordial but competitive round of 'It's a Knockout' between Teignmouth, Clacton and Bude was being emulously contested. They watched it because it was there.

Steep sipped his tea and witnessed the haunting spectre of Auntie Agnes' top set looming directly beneath his nose. He knew then that the memory would be unshakable.

"What are you on strike for?" asked Daffy after Bude had made a complete hash of the 'fil rouge'.

Steep shrugged. "I don't think we're on strike. I think we're laid off, but don't quote me on it."

"It's terrible, isn't it," she said with dilute indignity. "The way they can just chuck you out whenever they feel like it. Doesn't the union do anything about it?"

"Not a lot." It was a discussion he was not particularly keen to pursue in any serious fashion. "We could go on strike about being laid off, I suppose. But I think that's what they call being counter productive."

She nodded in serious agreement, seemingly not sensing the facetiousness in his voice. "It's not much use to men with responsibilities, is it. Being sent home like that. Losing all that money."

"It could have been worse," pointed out Steep. "We could have been sent home on nights. That causes more domestic upheavals than anything. Half of them are frightened to go home until they've given their wife a ring to tell them they're on their way home. You should see the queues at the phone boxes." She frowned at him obtusely. "Most blokes would rather not know." He was being deliberately circuitous now, enjoying his little tease.

"What are you on about? Not know what?"

"Whether or not the milkman's giving their missus a damn good seeing to," he explained simply.

"Charming!" she squeaked. "Oh, that reminds me," she went on quickly. A sudden unguarded surprise leapt to Steep's face. "You know that fella I told you about, who works in our office," she continued from behind her teacup.

"No," he answered blankly. He could tell straight away she was leading up to something.

"Yes you do. The one who keeps chatting me up."

"Oh, him." His surprise dissolved as quickly as it had formed, but he felt slightly confused for a moment, as though for those previous moments his life had almost spun

87

off on a dramatic new tangent, as though some ethereal administrative error had allowed him the briefest glimpse of a radical alternative version of the rest of his life that he was never meant to see.

"You mean the short-sighted one with one leg longer than the other and piles," he recalled without interest.

"Yes, well he asked me to go out again tonight."

"Why, is he staying in?"

"You know what I mean. He asked me to go out with *him*."

"Oh, yes," he said coolly. He tried a sip of tea with his eyes closed but still the demon dentures were there.

"So I told him that, er . . . ."

"That he must be mad?"

"No, that, er . . . ."

"That you're a lesbian?"

"No! Don't be nasty." She sipped her tea sulkily.

"Come on, then. What did you tell him? The tension's killing me."

"I told him that I'd just got engaged."

The words registered just as a hot stream of tea was sliding down his throat and it seemed to lodge there and he choked and spluttered for air. He managed to find the coffee table and put his cup down without spilling too much. Suddenly Daffy was thumping hell out of his back with her fist.

"I'm all right, I'm all right, honest!" he gasped.

"Are you sure," she asked solicitously. Stopping her thumping and bending to examine his face. "You've gone bright red." She sat on the arm of his chair. It groaned a woody groan, and she began to rub his back in a slow circular motion. She spoke softly, close to his ear: "I had to tell him we were saving up for a ring and that was why I wasn't wearing one. You don't mind, do you, Albie? He was being such a nuisance, it was the only thing I could think of to put him off."

"A swift kick in the knackers probably would have done the trick just as well," murmured Steep.

"You looked funny, just then," she giggled. "I thought your eyes were going to pop out of your head. It didn't sound that awful, did it?" She leaned closer to him and immodestly began to run the tip of her tongue around the edge of his ear. "I'm sorry," she whispered. "I didn't mean to choke you."

He gave off a short, forgiving grunt. He was enjoying the sudden sensation too much to spoil it by speaking: He felt something rapidly swamping his body and clearing his knotted thoughts, something instinctive and natural. It swept up every particle and began to run with him, making him breathless and excited. Her fingers ran brazenly along his inner thigh.

"Come on. On the carpet, in front of the fire. That's it. Now, come here, let me get this undone."

"You don't hang about much, do you?"

"Can't afford to. Aunt Aggie will be back in a couple of hours."

"Kneel up a second, let me get at yours. There you go, is that nice?"

"Oh, it's lovely."

"I'd like to do this to you forever."

"Come on, lie down and take these right off."

"Okay, there they go."

"Leave those on for now, I want to put my hand inside."

"Don't do that, or I'll be all over before we've started."

"I'd like you to do this to me forever, while I'm doing this to you forever."

"How much do you like doing this?"

"Lots and lots."

"Is it better than anything else in the world?"

"No, it's only second best."

"What's the best?"

"I'll show you in a minute."

"You'll never guess what."

"What?"

"Six giant purple ducks and Eddie Waring are spying on us."

"Nosey sods."

"I think they're expecting an up and under.'"

"I don't think they'll be disappointed."

"Reach up and switch them off, please. Then show me

89

what you like doing best."

"Bude were just about to play their joker."

"Show me what you like doing best, please."

"Okay, slip these down, then."

"D'you want me to roll over?"

"Yes, please."

"The carpet's prickly on my bum."

"You're all red down one side. Is the fire too hot?"

"Not as hot as this thing. It's like a poker."

"Good description."

"Shall we put the poker in the fire, now then?"

"All right. Let's give the fire a good poke. We'll soon have it roaring."

"Climb aboard, then. Next stop, ecstasy."

"Excuse me, could you tell me where your first class compartment is, please?"

"You're bonkers."

"There, Okay?"

"Gorgeous."

"Do you want me to stay like this, or shall I go up and down a bit?"

"Yes, please."

"Which?"

"Go up and down a bit."

"Like this?"

"Oh, yes. Do you like doing *this* better than anything else in the world?"

"Yes."

"With me?"

"Yes, with you."

"So do I. Go faster, please."

"Okay."

"I love you. Go faster!"

"Oh, yes, nearly!"

"I love you, my angel!"

"Oh, my God!"

It was hurriedly darkening outside as though the sun had only just realised what time it was. An inquisitive local street

90

lamp illuminated itself, painting the close, boxed walls with its pale amber light, turning to a lurid orange as it met the strong electric red of the fire. They lay silent. Their heavy, sated bodies glowed and ran to impenetrable black pockets like sand dunes against a low but intense sun. They breathed long, deep breaths, as though travelling through a blameless and contented sleep, yet both stared, unblinking, into the strangely coloured room. Only their fingers were touching.

"I love you, Albie," whispered Daffy, as though in a trance. "Do you love me? . . . Do you, Albie?"

Auntie Agnes and Mrs Wilks returned at just after ten o'clock. Mrs Wilks was laughing in the hall and saying: "Oh, Aggie, you'll get us locked up!" As the front room door opened and in came Auntie Agnes wearing a tall, cylindrical pink lamp shade on her head, followed by Mrs Wilks trailing a matching lamp standard. They were supposed to drink tea and Ovaltine at the old age pensioners' club.

"Look what Katie won," announced Auntie Agnes, removing the lamp shade and considering it at arms' length.

"It's nice, isn't it," said Daffy with customary banality.

"That's seven she's won in five months, isn't it, Katie," said Auntie Agnes.

Mrs Wilks nodded modestly: "You'd think they'd change the prizes now and then though, wouldn't you," she said. "Everyone there has got at least three. Gerty Tulley says you can't move in her front room for them. They're costing her a fortune in bulbs and plugs."

"Wayne gets them cheap, you see," explained Auntie Agnes to Steep. He and Daffy moved to the settee. The two old ladies eased themselves into the armchairs.

"That's not Bette Davis, is it?" asked Auntie Agnes squinting doubtfully at the television.

"Yes," confirmed Daffy. "Whatever Happened to Baby Jane."

"Oooo, hasn't she gone old looking, Katie," said Auntie Agnes worriedly.

"She's probably just made up to look old," suggested Mrs Wilks reassuringly.

Steep considered saying, pompously: 'Everybody grows old, you know. Even film stars must endure an ageing process in exactly the same way as the imageless rest of mankind.' But it seemed a churlish and cynical thing to say. Like telling a young child there was no Santa Claus.

They watched in silence until a commercial break came on. Then Daffy announced: "Albert's place is in the paper." She handed the newspaper to Auntie Agnes and pointed where to read. Auntie Agnes began to fumble through her handbag for her spectacles.

"That paper lad nearly knocked us down with his big red Chopper before," put in Mrs Wilks. "Didn't he, Aggie?"

Daffy's eyes widened in sudden astonishment and Steep had to bite his upper lip and push his chin into his chest.

"He can't control it properly," agreed Auntie Agnes absently, still digging into her handbag. "He was obstructing the pavement with it, waving it all over the place, he was. He's not old enough to be out with a big Chopper like that."

Steep had to turn away, a great swelling bubble of laughter pressing against his tightly clamped lips. It leaked out in little puffs and snorts against Daffy's neck.

"Mark my words," opined Mrs Wilks. "They'll be the cause of a nasty accident one of these days, him and his Chopper."

Steep could not help himself. He howled rudely, like a mad man into Daffy's face. She smiled evenly back at him in the manner of a humouring keeper and digged him demurely with her elbow, then glanced, apologetically coy at each of the old ladies.

Auntie Agnes and Mrs Wilks smiled, quizzically at first. "He's got the giggles," observed Mrs Wilks. But they were jolly ladies who found laughter infectious and they quickly began to follow him with some gently rolling chuckles.

"Oh, just ignore him," advised Daffy. "You'll only make him worse."

Steep's throat was beginning to hurt him and his eyes were wet and blurry. He felt two large blobs of tears break in quick succession and trickle down the sides of his nose. "I'm sorry about this," he spluttered eventually, wiping the runaway tears with the back of his hand.

"That's all right, love," chuckled Mrs Wilks. "It's better

than bursting into tears."

Immediately he thought of Mr Samson. He suddenly pictured him sobbing alone through that very night in some cold and empty room, listening enviously to the outside world wrapped in its private proceedings, and wondering where it had all gone wrong. The thoughts drained the laughter from him as though a plug had been pulled from his chest.

The film came on again. Auntie Agnes folded the newspaper and abandoned the search for her spectacles. She squinted briefly at the small headline and commented: "Terrible, isn't it. That's all you ever hear about now, strikes. Are you sure that's Bette Davis?"

Chapter Four

In its endeavours to attain and sustain consistently high production levels, Dram UK had enlisted the services of the Institute of Economic and Productive Efficiency, a part of who's study had concluded that 'a noteworthy proportion of the lack of productivity which, due to poor attendance was more significantly in evidence on Mondays and Tuesdays was due to the absence of financial reward in a tedious and repetitive occupation offering little or no job satisfaction, until quite late in the working week.' So, much the wiser, management persuaded the unions to allow them to change pay-days from Thursdays to Tuesdays, the results being that early week absenteeism dropped and production rose markedly. Now Thursdays and Fridays were the bad days.

"What does he have to come here for," grumbled Cranby. "I never know what the hell to call him."

"How about, Sir?" suggested Fawcett.

"Too deferential, too grovelly," decided Cranby after a moment's thought.

"What did you call him last time he came?"

"Sir," admitted Cranby. "But I'm damned if I'll do it again. He loved every minute of it. You know how bloody arrogant these Germans are."

"You'd think he'd have changed it, wouldn't you. I suppose that's what a lot of them would have done. Was it a common name before the war?"

"I haven't the foggiest, but I've never heard of anyone else with the name before *or* after the war, apart from him and his namesake."

"Do you suppose they're related?" wondered Fawcett, suddenly intrigued.

"I ask you," went on Cranby. "Of all the Germans in Germany why does the only one called Hermann Goring have to be head of Dram's European Operations?"

"Popping over in the old Messerschmitt, is he?"

Cranby did not hear. He seemed to be privately stirring himself to some obstinate resolve. "Well I'm not calling him Sir this time, I mean it," he reaffirmed, then blinking said: "I'm sorry, Cliff, did you say something?"

Fawcett shook his head: "Nothing important," he said, then embarking upon an absently whistled rendering of the 'Dambuster's March'.

The relevance did not immediately occur to Cranby. He allowed Fawcett to whistle on unchecked for some moments, the notes growing louder and more spirited. Then he realised and scowled across the table at the assistant plant manager.

"Sorry," said Fawcett. "Some sort of Freudian slip, I suppose."

"Well, for God's sake don't make any Freudian slips tomorrow," warned Cranby. "We just want to get rid of him as quickly and quietly as possible. Not start the Battle of Britain all over again."

"Is someone knocking on the door?" frowned Fawcett.

"I didn't hear anything."

"Listen, there it is again."

They listened and heard a faint, nervous tapping on the office door.

"You'd better see who it is before they break it down," suggested Fawcett.

Cranby leaned across his desk and spoke into his intercom: "Mrs Spicer . . . Mrs Spicer. That woman," he muttered. "Come in," he called.

At the command the door knob began to turn slowly, agonisingly, with as much spellbinding effect as in the most suspense full thriller. Then the door began to open silently, it seemed unnatural that a door should open so slowly without a creak.

Illogically, considering the violence of her previous entry,

Cranby suddenly thought it might be that awful, frightening woman again. He half considered hiding beneath his desk.

"Sorry to trouble you, Mr Cranby," came the voice from behind the door. It was a man's voice, but very soft, at about the level of a loud whisper and as nervous as a mouse.

Cranby felt a warm hand of foolish but unashamed relief touch his stomach.

It was only George Cubley. The man who had once been a foreman until Joe Miggins had thrown him into the boot of a car and reversed it eight times into a waxing booth wall, inflicting irreversible damage on the car, the wall and George Cubley's nerves.

He was still a tall man — once he had cut a proud and authoritative dash in his royal blue foreman's overall — but he no longer carried himself as he used to. His shoulders sagged now and his head seemed to rest on them directly without any sign of a neck to separate the two. He was no longer a foreman on health grounds. On his return to work after three months in hospital he had been given the specially created position of Head of receiving — Toiletries and Auxiliary Apparatus.

"Hello, Mr Cranby, Mr Fawcett," smiled Cubley like a shy, well-mannered child.

The two men returned the greeting.

"I'm sorry to burst in on you like this," apologised Cubley. "I've just met Mrs Spicer in the corridor, she said she was just popping out for some correcting fluid, she said it would be all right for me to come through. I'll wait outside if . . ."

"No, no, come on in, George," said Cranby amiably. "How's that hobby of yours going?"

"The book-binding, Mr Cranby?"

"That's it, George, the book-binding."

"I've given it up. I dropped this giant encyclopaedia on the cat's head and paralysed it down one side."

"Oh dear, what a shame."

"Its spine was broken."

"Goodness, still it's lucky to be alive, I suppose."

"No, the encyclopaedia's spine was broken, and the cat's skull."

"Oh, I see. How's the wife?"

"She hasn't stopped crying since I dropped the encyclopaedia on the cat. She's been under a lot of strain."

"I'm sorry to hear that, George."

"Thanks, Mr Cranby."

"Now then, what can we do for you?"

"It's not very good news I'm afraid, Mr Cranby," said
Cubley seriously. "This months entire consignment of toilet
paper has gone missing."

"What, just gone?"

"Vanished," confirmed Cubley. "Twelve boxes, six colours.
They must have been delivered here because I got in touch
with the vendors and they sent me these photostats of their
receipts." He waved the photostats briefly. "The receipts
have got a signature on them," he went on, his permanently
worried face forming a supplementary frown.

"Are they legible?" asked Cranby.

"Well, yes, I think so, but er . . . perhaps Mr Fawcett
would give me a second opinion on them."

Fawcett took the photostat, glancing at it casually and
then with honest surprise: "It looks to me like . . . " He
looked up at Cranby. "Angus McShitface."

"That's what I thought," said Cubley keenly. "I suspect
someone has put down an assumed name and made off
with them. The trouble is, there are so many comings and
goings down there in receiving, you see. Lorries and vans
going in and out all the time. And suspicious looking charac-
ters are always wandering about." He took a step closer
and bent towards the two men, dropping his voice even
further so they had to strain to hear him. "Sometimes I spy
on them from my office but I never see any of them take
anything. They just wander about looking highly suspicious.
I don't think they can see me because I always crouch on
top of the filing cabinet and peep through the top corner
of my window. I don't know what you think, Mr Cranby,
Mr Fawcett, but I don't think people can be trusted these
days and I think this just proves it. I mean if your toilet
paper isn't safe, what is?"

"Quite," nodded Cranby.

"Actually, I've been giving the matter some thought,
Mr Cranby," went on Cubley. "And I think it would be a

e

good idea to have 'Property of the Dram Motor Company' printed on each sheet instead of 'Now Wash Your Hands Please."

"It's certainly worth considering, George," said Cranby encouragingly. "I'll bear that in mind. Have you told security about this, yet?"

"Not yet, Mr Cranby."

"Well when you do tell them to keep it under their hats for the minute. We don't want stories like this abroad when Mr Goring gets here tomorrow. God knows what he'd make of it."

Chapter Five

The prospect of the visit by Dram's Head of European Operations, Hermann Goring, had left Cranby irritable and restless and he paced his office in an appropriately downcast manner. He attempted to cheer himself, at least he had been given the opportunity of reminding those that mattered in Stuttgart that he was still here. The thought brightened him only momentarily as he weighed it against a dismayingly gloomy alternative; perhaps he had been walking a promotional-demotional tightrope for the past couple of years; perhaps they were waiting for one spectacular success or one disastrous cock-up to decide his future for him. The most disturbing aspect inherent in that particular theory was that he had no more idea than they which one he was likely to produce first.

Outside, the newly installed, vividly orange and white striped barrier across number three gate caught his eye. For a moment it rested in its closed position, then it began to lift itself up reaching an angle of approximately forty-five degrees before dropping almost to the extremity of its travel only to haul itself up again until proudly vertical. He had noticed its odd gymnastic display just a few minutes earlier when he had arrived but then his irritability had been drowsy and formless. Now it was suitably alert and prickly and needed to be given vent. He moved to his desk and snatched at the telephone.

Halliwell was sitting at the table, that morning's *Daily Mirror* thinly shielding him from one of Worth's steamily threatening mugs of tea when the internal line telephone rang.

"I'll get that, lads," he offered. "Don't you disturb yourselves whatever you do."

The remarks were predictably ignored by Worth and Atkin as they sat at the controls of the electrically operated barrier, gleefully pushing its buttons like large children experimenting with some equally overgrown toy.

"You take it easy as well, table and chairs, and you Geranium Red Express, and you cupboards and walls," said Halliwell loudly as he plodded towards the telephone. He picked up the receiver and held it unguarded only inches from his mouth. "Sorry, what did you say, table?" he said pushing his ear out with a finger. "Thanks very much, did you say? Oh, don't mention it. Hello, security, number three gate," he managed to say despite competition from a gaping, stretching yawn. "Oh hello, Mr Cranby." The yawn fled in terror. "No, I wasn't actually *talking* to the table. It's just a bit of a joke I was having with the lads, that's all." . . . "No, Mr Cranby I don't suppose it would have gone down all that well if you had been Hermann Goring." . . . "Yes I appreciate the fact that Germans have no sense of humour." . . . "Yes I do realise that we are the first employees he sees." . . . "First impressions." . . . "Exactly, Mr Cranby." . . . "Well now you mention it, I suppose it *must* look like a one armed semaphore machine gone berserk." . . . "They're running it in, actually." . . . "Yes, Mr Cranby, I'll tell them right away." . . . "No I won't talk to the table anymore." . . . "Or any of the other furniture." . . . "Right, will do, Mr Cranby." Halliwell replaced the receiver. "Right, table," he snarled at the innocent yellow Formica topped piece of furniture. "That's the last time I'll answer the pigging phone for you!"

Fridays arrived on Bellend's production lines smiling with all the stock, mercenary optimism of a door to door gypsy fortune teller, pedalling her tried, trusted and readily agreeable prophecies for the approaching weekend.

On Fridays the operators performed their dreary duties with perceptibly less resentment, the hours passed a little less sluggishly, the singers sang and the whistlers whistled

100

their tunes garnished with a dash of verve and real cheer, preludes now to the weekend break.

Taking advantage of the intoxicating atmosphere that Fridays brought, most of the plants entrepreneurial element would choose that day to offer their particular lines for sale. Digital watches, tape cassettes, records and countless colours sorts and sizes of clothing all at impressively competitive prices were regularly available. Sometimes one-off sales might offer bottles of spirits, joints of meat, transistor radios or male contraceptives. For the bookmakers however, Friday was a day like any other, as it was for the line side 'shops' run by and for the operators to raise money for their line's childrens' christmas parties.

They sold mainly small items of confectionery, soft drinks and cigarettes, and periodically, when particular 'no questions asked' consignments were diverted in their direction, practically anything else.

The party of sixth formers from the St Monique the Smokeless, Roman Catholic High School for Girls touring the plant as part of their sociology course bore witness to Friday's exuberant nature. Some of the girls looked shell-shocked and dazed by it all; the strange and massive workings of a motor car factory alone being difficult enough for gentlewomanly sensibilities to absorb without being pursued by an unceasing wave of well practiced wolf-whistles, covetous leers and bawled propositions ranging from the harmlessly saucy to the downright obscene. The more worldly-wise and less virtuous though seemed to revel in it, smiling naughtily at the howling operators then falling into giggling little groups: Turning one corner the elderly teacher and the tour guide personnel officer at the head of the procession both frowned, the former in puzzlement, the latter in disapproval of a large hand painted cardboard sign which read: DO NOT FEED THE ANIMALS.

"Albert," said Sammy the way someone does when they want a third party to arbitrate over a matter of contention. "Is a wheel and tyre heavier with or without air in it?"

Sammy and Godfrey stood on either side of the garish

orange three door Khan in which Steep was working, their faces, equally over-bright with the smug knowledge of being irrefutably in the right, shone through the glassless windscreen aperture.

"What are you two up to now?" asked Steep, immediately suspicious.

"Never mind. Which is it?" pressed Godfrey impatiently.

"Well it must be a bit heavier with the air in it, I suppose," shrugged Steep.

"Told you," beamed Sammy exultantly.

"Yeah, but you can't *roll* them properly, flat," countered Godfrey, unimpressed.

"You can't *roll* them up a fucking big hill like that anyway, bollock-brain."

"I know but it must be fifty yards at least from the shed to the bottom of the hill, that's a long way when you've got three of them to carry, *and* we've got to make two journeys."

"Well how are you going to roll them then, clever shite. Three of them, all at once, in the same direction! They'd keep rolling off all over the show. You'd probably end up losing them all. It will be dark, you know."

"Tie them together with a piece of rope or something through the centre," suggested Steep helpfully. Even before he had finished speaking he knew that he would have been wiser to have kept his mouth shut.

"Simple as that," said Godfrey easily, as though the idea had been his from the start and he had been waiting for someone to catch up to him.

"All right, smart arse, we want some rope. Don't forget," grumbled Sammy. He turned to Steep who had finished working on the car and was gathering up his tools. "And I'll thank you to keep your fucking ideas to yourself in future," he said without hostility. "Just look at the state of that now," he added, motioning towards Godfrey as though he were a public convenience that had just been vandalised.

Godfrey beamed uncompromisingly back at them and was about to speak when a voice from the rear of the car interrupted him.

"Okay, you guys, I heard the whole story." It was Spivak.

102

He stepped over the line rail and placed his tool box on the floor and kicked it roughly away from the track, throwing his compressed air gun and its trailing feed line after it. He began to walk slowly towards the front of the car, occasionally hitching his shoulders like an ungainly, waddling James Cagney. "And I'm gonna spill the beans if you don't gimme a piece of the action," he threatened comically.

Steep scrambled out of the car, he had drifted down the line during the conversation and would have to rush the job on the next car, which he should have had half completed by now.

Godfrey moved over to Sammy and Spivak's side of the line.

"Three way split or I sing like a boyd." Was Spivak's rigid ultimatum.

Sammy took Godfrey's shoulder and turned it away from Spivak. "We've got to talk it over," he explained.

"No hurry," conceded Spivak generously. "What number's security?"

The two older men bent together, and they muttered at each other for some seconds. Finally they nodded in apparent agreement and turned back to Spivak, the extortionist. He was smiling nonchalantly at them, and the offer they could not refuse.

"Okay, Spiv, you win," admitted Sammy, closing the few paces between them with open hands of submission.

"You guys aint so dumb after all, huh," gloated Spivak.

Suddenly Sammy grabbed Spivak's arm and Godfrey darted forward grabbing the other, pulling him backwards then lifting his legs from under him.

"Put me down ya stoopid joyks!" squealed Spivak, kicking and squirming between them.

Alongside them now was the conveniently gaping boot of a rich red Kama coupe. With an undignified struggle the two men loaded the flailing arms and legs into it. Three times they tried to close the lid, trapping a leg an arm and a head in their respective efforts to regain freedom. At the fourth attempt the lid slammed shut.

"Let me out, you old bastards!" giggled Spivak. He sounded like a ventriloquist's doll incarcerated in a suitcase.

By this time a group of grinning, animated operators had assembled around the rear of the gleaming red body, occasionally shuffling in tiny steps to keep up with its inexorable movement. Sproat put one of his dim eyes to the petrol tank filler pipe aperture and said: "Hello, Spiv, what you doin' in there? Ha ha ha ha!" Then dodged quickly to one side as a well aimed thirty millimetre nut flew out through the hole like a bullet.

"Let me out, you bastard arse'oles," pleaded Spivak undiplomatically.

"Dear me, where'er your manners?" tutted Sammy. "Say please."

"Please let me out, you bastard arse'oles."

"No, ha ha ha ha!"

Then suddenly, curious little lumps began to rise and fall in the boot lid as though a powerfully beating heart thumped against its cold red skin.

"Quick, have a look at this," waved Kettle, peering with fixed fascination through the gaps in the bulkhead between the boot and the passenger compartment. "He's sendin' the nut in!"

The spectators heads crowded eagerly into the car to view the huddled, embryo-like figure rhythmically smashing his forehead against the inside of the boot lid as though he were some odd, white web-footed chick trying to hatch itself from a particularly unyielding shell.

"Go on, Spiv. Show it who's boss," cheered Godfrey. "Give it the old Kung Fu."

At this Spivak switched his attack to the thin metal pressings that formed the flimsy bulkhead, kicking furiously at them with the soles of his plimsolls. The thin metal began to bend and twist easily, their retaining spot welds barely holding.

"Look out, here's Ted!" someone shouted.

They dispersed like a herd of spooked gnus at a water hole.

"I don't mind staying in here anyway," called Spivak contemptuously. "Some rich blonde tart might buy this car and find me in here and take me home and let me shag her."

As he passed a red Kama coupe Ted Slutswater could have sworn he heard Spivak's voice calling him in a way that seemed distant and yet very close. He stopped and looked about him as though listening for a repeat of some ethereal message. Suspicion and puzzlement combined on his face. "Did I hear Spiv call me then?" he asked Sammy.

Sammy shrugged. "Don't know, Ted. Didn't hear."

The foreman seemed satisfied. "Right, listen," he called to anyone in the area. "We've got some big noise coming over from Germany today so we'll be stopping the lines for an extra quarter of an hour after break for housekeeping, so get your areas tidied up. And don't be working any welts when he comes round either, okay."

" 'ello Ted, you slimey hunchbacked old cunt."

"There it is again!" claimed Slutswater. "You must've heard that. Come on now, own up, where is he?"

"Didn't hear a dicky bird," said Sammy, shaking his head in slow and brilliant bewilderment.

"The little bleeder," laughed the foreman unconvincingly. "He's driving me round the twist." But then immediately the fear returned to his eyes as the spectral voice spoke again.

"I hope you don't mind me asking, Ted," it said. "But when are you gonna take that parachute off?"

The large and lustrous white Kaiser saloon containing Dram's Head of European Operations, Hermann Goring, swept beneath number three gates smartly saluting barrier and curved towards Cranby and Fawcett who stood – trying not to look like subordinate ranks about to be presented to a superior officer and yet maintain an appropriate degree of decorum – on the scrubbed white pavement outside the administration block's main entrance.

"Have you decided what you're going to call him yet?" asked Fawcett quietly.

Cranby pulled a quick face. "I've decided to be spontaneous," he said. "Surprise myself. But I'll tell you one thing," he went on firmly. "Until he's on his way home again the word 'sir' has been expunged from my vocabulary."

Fawcett glanced doubtfully across at the Plant Manager but had no time for further comment as the car came to a halt and the German climbed out.

He was shorter and older than either of his hosts but broader than both. His eyes were classically Germanic ice-blue, his face rough and healthily tanned. It was easy to imagine him in Bavarian shorts and a hat with a white feather in it. Cranby wondered if he had ever performed in one of those silly German dances with all that communal slapping.

"Ah, hello, Mr Cranby," smiled Hermann Goring, offering his hand. Cranby stepped forward and shook the German's hand firmly.

"Good morning, Fritzie, welcome to Belland," he greeted brightly. He bit his tongue so hard that he almost passed out with the pain.

The shop floor's post morning break 'housekeeping' exercise had been of negligible consequence in terms of morale or visual enhancement, most operators confining their efforts to slyly kicking a plastic cup, cigarette packet or discarded but still perfectly serviceable piece of motor car beneath the nearest pallet, quite often causing a chain reaction which would result in a spray of long since similarly concealed debris to come spinning out of the other side. At the end of the period, when the lines restarted, some of the janitors busied their brushes with commendable and uncharacteristic assiduity, which meant that they were almost certainly acting under orders. But the challenge was never one they were likely to equal and soon their innate sense of languor began to re-emerge until, only minutes later, to everyone's relief, it overwhelmed them. There was something reassuring about those untidy and infinitely variable triangles formed by janitors propped up against their brush handles. They somehow fostered the impression that all was well with the world.

"Right, they're on their way," said Slutswater. "Let's have the cards hidden and the newspapers away. Come on, try and look as though you're doing a day's work."

"We will if you will, Ted," returned Spivak, smiling his smile.

The foreman eyed him cautiously, almost nervously for a moment.

"Come on, let's make an effort," he said presently. "Henry, let's have the Hong Kong Echo away now."

Henry Chong lifted his dark, peaceful and inherently wise oriental eyes from his Chinese newspaper. "Okay, Ted," he said obediently. Then adding as an informative afterthought: "It Kowloon Gay News, actually."

"And look at this," complained Slutswater, crouching to pick up two empty crisp packets and a Mars bar wrapper. "Let's try to keep the place tidy just for half an hour longer, eh." He crouched again as he left them to pick up two discarded bumper bolts and an empty Smarties tube, calling over his shoulder as he did so: "This place is like a shithouse."

Spivak commented quite loudly: "What else is it gonna look like when it's got bleedin' big turds like 'im floatin' about in it."

"I don't understand all this," frowned Sammy. "All this tarting the place up and running round like blue-arse flys. I mean someone's being a right hypocritical bastard when you think about it. Any other day no one gives two fucks as long as the lines are moving. But whenever they find out some bosses are on their way, we get all this palaver."

"It's what they expect, isn't it," said Kettle, sounding as though the statement was more profound than any of those hearing it could possibly imagine. "That's why they're bosses. You can't just ignore them, can you? You've got to put on a show." Kettle was now struggling under the weight of his own abstruseness. "To humour them," he finished with some relief.

"And then they look at you as if you were a bleedin' leper or something," went on Sammy. "As if they were doing *us* a favour just to come down here."

"The blue one's your first," said Sproat arriving at the stolen table. He pointed up the line at a car still some seven or eight minutes away. "The one after that snot coloured Kama, ha ha ha ha."

107

Kettle looked up along the line and nodded curtly. "Oh, hang on," he remembered dimly. "No more welts."

Sproat frowned. "What?" he grunted, thickly suspicious.

"Ted said."

"Bollocks."

"The bosses are coming," explained Kettle smugly.

"Fuck them," snarled Sproat. "I've done my ten cars."

Kettle shook his head slowly, as though a more rapid movement might cause it to topple from its shoulders. "One car each," he shrugged. "Ted said. Sorry," he added hollowly.

"I'll let the bastards go then," blustered Sproat. It's forty minutes before I fit another headlight on that line." A finger pecked angrily at the face of his watch.

"Do what you like. Me and Henry are doing one car each, aren't we, Henry."

Henry Chong glanced from one to the other. His expression calm and distainful.

"Right," said Sproat. "No welts now, no welts no more."

"Suits me," countered Kettle.

They spoke with such commitment that a stranger might have considered them to be men of a powerful and unwilting resolve, men who would die before embracing notions of perfidy against their own word. Only their workmates knew better.

"You know, perhaps you light, Sam," said Henry.

"About what?"

"About bosses doing us favour." He waved his rolled up Chinese newspaper across the stolen table towards the verbal combatants intent on their mindless squabble. "Would you come down here and look at that if you not have to?"

Cranby was grateful to see the lines in full flow and hear the healthy, hectic, productive din pressing from right and left like two fat men cramming against him in a lift. Yet, grateful though he was, Cranby had always doubted the authenticity of such intense activity, as a casual observer of a colony of ants might hold doubts against each members apparent frantic aimlessness. He always got the impression that the display was put on merely for effect and suspected that if the operators were removed and the lines allowed to run on their own that the cars would probably build themselves.

The part of Cranby's tongue he had bitten had developed a lump and gone numb and there were some words that he could pronounce only with difficulty. Other than that, and the probability that, by way of over-compensation he was calling the German 'sir' a bit *too* often, things were actually going quite well. Fawcett and Sloan flanked Hermann Goring and Cranby and they chatted cordially and discussed pertinent matters in what Cranby considered a relaxed and businesslike atmosphere. For the first time that day he allowed himself a private, cautious, half smile.

"That line, it has stopped," said Hermann Goring.

"Yes, sir, a touch of congestion at the end, probably," forecast Cranby with brittle assurance. His stomach sank horribly as though suddenly laden with pounds of indigestible cold wet tripe.

"I do not think so, Mr Cranby. It jumped then stopped suddenly. I think perhaps it has broken down."

"Yes, it jumped. I saw it too," confirmed Sloan. He simulated the incident with his hand but nobody bothered to watch.

"Cliff, find out what's happened, would you," said Cranby flapping an impatient hand. "Ask that foreman over there."

The line operators, always prompt to capitalise on the possibility of an enforced stoppage quickly formed themselves into two distinctly polarised groups; those seeking to take immediate advantage of the breakdown blatantly and cold-bloodedly lounged on the wooden benches like slaves before a tyrannical master suddenly stricken and impotent. They smirked and sneered and mocked it and hoped — some even secretly prayed — that its recovery, although ultimately inevitable, would be long and painful: The others, with longer term aims in mind continued to work, scurrying up the paralysed line despite the gamble that if repairs to the line took longer than anticipated, then the outcome at the end of the shift could mean jobs finished anything up to hours away from their official work stations; a state of affairs which was accepted gloatingly and without gratitude by the incoming shift. Should such a disaster appear likely some operators would then actually spend further time frantically taking apart what they had earlier spent time frantically putting together.

Slutswater was bent comically double, his face thrust out only inches from the track rail, his eyes squinting and his lips pouting threateningly at it. His arms dangled like unsynchronised pendulums so that his knuckles brushed the toecaps of his shoes as he inched grotesquely along the line.

"What's the problem?" asked Fawcett.

Slutswater scowled at the questioner's feet, then, seeing who it was, straightened as far as his bent back would let him.

"Just checking for anything untoward, I thought I saw it jump," explained Slutswater, his face an unhealthy red.

"Hmmm, so did Mr Goring."

At this Slutswater's eyes strayed over Fawcett's shoulder to where Hermann Goring stood with Cranby and Sloan. He regarded them for a moment, sniffing inquisitively.

"Find anything?" asked Sloan hopefully.

"No," blinked Slutswater." I didn't really expect to, but I was having a look just in case."

Fawcett nodded. "Maintenance are taking their time, aren't they?" he said looking about him.

"Maintenance?" said Slutswater as though the word was a new one to him.

"It doesn't look very good, does it? Especially with Mr Goring here."

"Er, I haven't actually called them yet," admitted Slutswater, the drifting redness in his face gushed back undammed. "I only *thought* I saw it jump, I wasn't sure and I didn't want to get them out for nothing."

"I think you had better get them out now then, don't you? If they don't mind being disturbed, that is," said Fawcett sternly. "Before Mr Goring begins to think that we're all half asleep."

"Right," nodded Slutswater fawningly. "I'll do that right away." He glanced towards the German, as though hoping that he had not gleaned the gist of the conversation. "By the way, Mr Fawcett, there are three other foremen and a general foreman on this line who haven't phoned maintenance either. I just thought I'd point that out." With that the foreman turned and hurried towards his desk and its telephone.

He stood at the desk and picked up the receiver, dialling the number, then hoisting the receiver to his face. At first it seemed as though the earpiece had somehow begun to melt because it felt soft and slightly warm on his ear. Then he recognised the smell; that black, thick, messy close smell. He snatched the receiver away and glowered at it. The surface of the earpiece was crudely smeared with glue, arranged in choppy, pointed little waves where they had stretched and broken away from their mirror image now nastily malignant about his ear. He cursed beneath his breath and raised his free hand to the ear, tentatively touching it, as though expecting it to hurt. He felt the pinpoints of glue gripping his finger tips and he cursed again. Then someone answered the telephone. He held the receiver six inches from his face and bawled: "Breakdown. Line two. K twelve." Then slammed it down. "I'll have him for this," he hissed, pulling his thumb across the sticky tips of his fingers. "I'll have him. Spivak. The little bleeder."

By now line one's cars, unable to travel any further, queued patiently along its length. Only the lines ahead of line two continued to run, like an accidentally decoupled train, leaving behind it an ever increasing length of embarrassingly empty track.

"Maintenance are on their way," said Fawcett.

"Right," said Cranby. It's something fairly minor I expect," he added, trying to sound confident for the German's benefit.

Hermann Goring began to sniff suspiciously. "Something is burning," he said.

Rex McBean scowled at the operators idle smiles and deliberately dim and rhetorical questions as he strode the long length of his line. He felt their nudging grins crawling over his back, and were it not for the fact that this bleeding German was nosing about somewhere he would occasionally have spun round on them and enjoyed watching their girly giggling shrivel into hangdog embarrassment. He was proud

111

of the way he could do that; it was not every G.F. who could make his operators cringe with one quick, cold glare.

"What's going on?" he demanded on reaching Slutswater. "The fucking janitor's just told me."

"It's only just happened, Rex. Just this minute." Slutswater's voice whined under the pressure. "I've been ringing maintenance." Then he turned around and lifted his eyes up into his head. "Don't look now but Cranby and the German bloke are only over there."

"Why is your ear all covered in glue?"

"Dang-blasted, cotton pickin' con-traption," tutted Harry Melrose as he passed carrying two plastic cups of hot chocolate. "Lemme tell you somethin', Tex," he went on, motioning towards the line. "If that was ma *horse*, I'd shoot it."

Sloan said: "Yes, I can smell it too." He frowned around, scratching the back of his head. "Look, there's smoke coming from that bin."

The others turned towards the large, wheeled square bin, almost as tall as a man, just a few yards away. From over its rim crept a grey cloud, thickening rapidly as though some grubby genie might materialise at its centre at any moment.

"Smells like . . . " began Fawcett. At that instant the bin exploded. The four men reeled away from the sudden deafening violence of it, stunned and panicked and blindly terrified. The Plant Manager looked around him through the spreading black and stinking smoke, gazing uncomprehendingly at the mirrored expressions about him.

Hermann Goring began muttering to himself in bewildered German.

"Just a bit of trouble with one of the bins, sir," assured Cranby stupidly. "It's something fairly minor, I expect."

McBean and Slutswater were first on the scene, clumsily tripping and kicking each other's ankles as they dragged a reeled hose-pipe between them across the line towards the bin and the well-fed flashes of flame now burning quietly within. McBean's right ear was black and gluey as a result of a hastily made telephone call to the internal fire department before Slutswater could warn him.

By this time practically all work within a fifty yard radius of the explosion had stopped, regardless of whether each individual operator's line was still running or not. Fires were not uncommon on the shop floor — although few ever managed such a spectacular overture as this one — and were regarded by the operators merely as an occasional free entertainment.

Those not able to leave their work stations strained necks and eyes and called for and received running commentaries as exciting and professional as in the most thrilling sporting events while the fortunate spectators offered generous vocal appreciation of both flame and foremen.

Dotted among the crowd were foremen from other sections, their faces grappling with various experimental expressions ranging from disciplined restraint to impending dynamism, each attempting to form the expression most compliant to the situation and hence appear the most intelligent. It was a sort of spontaneous, pointless contest without judges or winners or prizes held to celebrate any event which brought salaried personnel together on or about a production line. Sometimes groups of five or six men in smart suits with mysterious objectives would wander about the lines, every now and then gathering around a random car to inspect a particular facet of its build. Such instances proved to be fiercely competitive in this regard, totally out-classing any unfortunate foreman who might have been called to render assistance or advice.

McBean and Slutswater, each awkwardly superfluous to the other's requirements, hauled the hose above the rim of the bin and stood firmly, grimly expectant against the boxed inferno.

"Go and turn the fucking thing on, idiot," growled McBean beneath his breath after several crushingly dry seconds.

The first split second jet of water drilled powerfully through the flames like a gallant lifeboat through angry waves, regrettably however, its helmsman's direction senses had been momentarily aberrant and the jet skimmed the far rim of the bin and sped across the aisle, amply soaking a non-conflagrating fork-lift truck driver and foreman from line one, bringing ecstatic applause and a great roar of laughter from the operators before McBean corrected its trajectory and dipped it into the bin.

The elements tussled privately, evenly matched inside the large metal box for some seconds. Then the flames began to wither, shrinking down into the bin as though in search of cover. Damp black smoke oozed and spread more thickly from its dwindling heart.

The operators drew back from their good views, coughing and complaining. McBean, his face now purple and black speckled seemed certain that he woud choke to death at any moment. Madly he clung on to the hose, as though to do so was all that would save him. Cranby's eyes stung and watered as he turned to Hermann Goring. "Well, sir," he said, half choking from a mouthful of poisoned smoke he had just swallowed. "Is there anything else you'd like to see now?"

Slutswater's right ear was raw and rubbed red, and smelled of the solvent he had used to remove the glue from it. He hung over the stolen table like a precarious precipice, looking down on Steep, Spivak, Sammy, Sproat, Kettle, Harry Melrose and Henry Chong.

A few steps away from them the line was rolling again. It had taken maintenance forty-three minutes to locate, remove and effect necessary repairs caused by two four inch long exhaust bracket bolts wedged deliberately between a track link and the track rail.

"The firemen found two tins of glue in that bin," said Slutswater, his eyes darting from man to man but resting almost imperceptibly longer on Spivak than any of the others. "And they reckon both of them were at least half full."

"Careless, that," said Sammy shaking his head. "Very careless."

"Could've done damage," agreed Sproat. "Even worse, could've woke Spiv up, ha ha ha ha."

Spivak said nothing, just yawned as though by request and dropped his chin back into the propped up palms of his hands.

"Security reckon they might get some fingerprints off the tins," lied Slutswater.

114

"So what?" questioned Kettle aggressively. "They'd have nothing to check them against, would they."

"They could call the coppers in," said Sproat.

"Bollocks," returned Kettle.

"Course they could. It's a fucking criminal offence what's been perpetrated," explained Sproat laboriously.

"He saw Kojak last night," said Sammy quietly.

"Coppers have got no jurisdiction in here," claimed Kettle.

"Fuck me!" breathed Sammy. "So did he!"

"Course they have," countered Sproat. "Suppose someone had got killed or something. Do you think they'd leave it to these silly cunts in security to sort it out, course they wouldn't. Isn't that right, Ted?"

Slutswater nodded soberly. "If they find out who it was they'll probably put him inside."

"Now, terrorism," said Kettle, subtley evasive. "If you're talking about terrorism, that's different."

"Terrorism doesn't enter into it," argued Sproat.

"I don't know about that," put in Harry Melrose. "Those bosses looked pretty fucking terrorised to me, did you see the state of them. I hope they were all carrying a spare pair of undies with them."

"Anyway, how could you get fingerprints off the tins?" asked Kettle. "They would've been washed off."

"I don't know, do I?" shrugged the foreman. "Who do you think I am, Sherlock Bleeding Holmes? I'm only telling you what these guys from security told me."

"Naw, no way," affirmed Kettle confidently. "They're pulling your plonker."

"And they're going to see if they can match any of the prints on those two bolts and the phone," said Slutswater, determinedly pressing on with his yarn.

"That's a fine healthy looking ear you've got there though," commented Harry Melrose admiringly. "Very rural, that ear."

"It looks like it's just come back from its holidays," observed Sammy, suddenly viewing the ear in a new light.

"Lie detectors," suggested Kettle. "They could use lie detectors."

"Arseholes," sneered Sproat. "I'd like to see them try sticking them bits of wire all over me. No chance."

It seemed of little concern or relevance to either man that they had now taken it upon themselves to defend the other's previous argument.

"Well whatever they use," interrupted Slutswater. "When they find the prick his feet won't touch."

They sat in vaguely amused and restrained silence for several seconds, until Slutswater had disappeared along the line. Then the heads began to turn, the eyes looked almost without expression, a few mouths slid into impish smiles.

Spivak opened his eyes after a momentary doze. He eyed the faces unmoved, then closed his eyes again and yawned: "What the fuck's everyone looking at me for?"

Cranby was at home. He had fallen into a semi-reclined garden chair and left himself where he had haphazardly landed.

The garden was pallid and withdrawn at that time of the year, its irregular grassy area holed with empty flower beds like graves without headstones. Cruelly severed rose bushes ran along its borders; in the summer they grew tall and displayed flowers of stunning reds and yellows; now they poked eerily through the soil like deformed skeletal claws.

The coolness of the air and the rapid dulling of the day felt pleasantly soothing against his face. A ripe whiskey radiated its understanding glow inside him: Hermann Goring would be back in Stuttgart by now, he thought, considering the repercussions that the day and its disasters had to offer. Probably at that very moment he would be hacking his way through Cranby's metaphorical tightrope. He closed his eyes to the thoughts and wondered if Elizabeth would mind if he had a second whiskey before dinner.

"How was today?" called Elizabeth from the kitchen, her voice came with hot buttery sizzles and sharp spicy smells.

"Fine," he lied.

"Bit of a bust-up at the Drama Society today," she went on chattily. "Mr, Umtoto, remember, you met him last year.

116

The gynaecologist from Nigeria, very tall, lovely teeth."

"Ah, yes. What's upset him?"

"He says he's fed up always being cast as the black man. He says he wants to broaden his repertoire."

"Tricky," sympathised Cranby.

"We all think he's being very unreasonable about it. Heaven knows Mrs Forsythe and I have bent over backwards to accommodate him in the past."

Cranby frowned unseen at the unintentional double meaning.

"We all agreed to do Porgy and Bess just for him. *And* the Mohammed Ali Story, *and* Roots. That's the last three leading roles he's had in our last three productions. Now he says we're being artistically stagnant because we won't give him the lead in The Sound of Music."

"A black Baron von Trapp," considered Cranby. "Perhaps no one will notice."

"He wants to play Maria," corrected his wife. "He says he wants to . . . " She paused, then spoke as though recalling a line from one of her recent productions. "Transcend the moribund concepts of conventional ostensibility in the theatre and explore the hitherto dumb eloquence inherent in its quintessential incorporeality."

"It'll never work," sniffed Cranby. "Not with those lips."

"Aubrey!" she protested quietly.

"Well, I'm all for conventional ostensibility or whatever he called it," he answered defensively. "For being what we look like we are. God knows, even that's difficult enough."

They were silent for a few moments, then when Elizabeth called his name her voice was closer. Cranby opened his eyes, she was standing in the kitchen doorway, small and neat with a flowered apron tied about the still distinct curvature of her waist, a matching head scarf fastened tidily at the back covered her stiff auburn hair, her fingers were white with flour and she had a smudge under her chin.

"Something's bothering you," she told him.

"Is it?"

"The only time you come over all mysteriously profound like that is when something's bothering you."

"Oh, it's nothing, love," he shrugged and smiled. "Blame

117

Mr Umtoto, he started it."

"The factory?" she guessed confidently. "You're not appreciated in that place. Do they realise where they'd be without you. What is it? Can you tell me?"

"I don't think I could if I wanted to," he said slowly shaking his head.

She came over to him and sat on the edge of the chair.

"Sometimes things get very confused," he said.

She nodded as though she now understood but was equally incapable of defining the problem. She took his hand and they both stared into the same cool empty dimming space in front of them.

"Is is something like Nigerian Gynaecologists wanting to be Julie Andrews?" she asked.

"Yes," he said. "It's something like that."

Chapter Six

The only time of the week capable of out-demoralising the doom and defeat engendered by the start of a shift on Monday morning was that spawned by its older and darker and more vindictive sister, the start of a shift on Monday night. Friday's gypsy fortune teller had collected their confident but unerringly gullible hopes and ran; her prophecies, now without that eternally illusive and alluring sparkle of anticipation had yet again turned out to be worthless trumpery. But they would never learn.

Now an interminable night, nagged with tedium and weariness, both assured of strengthening their grip as the night progressed was all that they had left. For some the very thought, let alone the horrendous reality was more than they could endure without first seeking to soften its brutal edges among the comforting and distracting influences of their local public houses whereupon, once ensconced, those of an undisciplined nature might easily dawdle and drink excessively before heading, inspired to heroism towards his factory and his foreman or inspired to somnolence towards his bed and his wife.

For the rest the night would have to be faced in a state of painful sobriety. The morning and a soft warm bed so far away that such ineffable delights could only be considered in the same fanciful way as they might have considered a jackpot win on the football pools.

By three o'clock the 'lunch' break was over. Limbs were heavy and unresponsive, eyes reddened and dull and still the longest and most arduous stretch of the night lay before them. It would be three hours before the lines would stop

119

again for the final break of the shift.

Steep sat through a fit of yawning across the driveshaft tunnel of a dark blue Kama, his legs either side of it like a jockey in short stirrups. Each operator evolved his own style of performing the same job on the same car over a long period until he found that which was the most comfortable and which enabled him to complete the job in the shortest possible time. Eventually the tasks became automatic to them, they did them unthinkingly leaving their minds free to wander or wonder or worry. Had it been necessary they could literally have worked blindfolded.

Steep reached forward into the dark hole in the car's half assembled fascia, finding almost instantly the connection leading off the main electrical loom to be fitted to the light switch. In the right hand footwell the filling of a half eaten steak and kidney pie had splashed over the pedals and oozed from its pastry casing: Judging the impact with which it had obviously struck the car Steep half wondered whether it had perhaps been discarded due to some sudden loss of temper rather than appetite.

He pulled at the connection but its striped and coloured wires were trapped behind an electrical relay bolted to the bulkhead. This was a common and inexcusably careless result of Graeme Leatherbarrow's almost frenzied anxiety to elongate his nocturnal lunch breaks by as great an amount as possible so that he might spend extra saved minutes with Emlyn, the dessert chef from the east canteen. Steep knew that a sharp hard tug would free the trapped wires; it would bend the relay's bracket a bit but no one bothered about that, and besides, had he left it that would be all the repair men would do when the fault was discovered further down the line, and when the job was finished no one would be able to see it anyway. He pulled at the connection, the bracket bent slightly but the wires remained trapped, he pulled again and they came free, his hand jerked back through the fascia pad and an edge of it slashed open an inch long gash across the back of his hand. Immediately it began to bleed quite spectacularly, rapidly forming several red rivulets hurrying down his arm and fingers. Some of it dripped like sparingly applied tomato ketchup onto the half eaten steak and kidney

120

pie. Curiously, Steep thought how much more appetising it now looked.

Slutswater was seated at his desk, hunched over some papers in a tattered open folder.

"Medical relief, Ted," said Steep displaying the damaged hand.

The foreman looked up with a sort of puzzled disinterest, like a man who had just been roused from a light and comfortable sleep: Once Spivak had daringly tied Slutswater's desk to the moving line while he was sitting at it. As he was now, he was lost and low over his attendance sheets at the time and the desk juddered along with the line for six inches before Slutswater realised what was happening. It scraped along for another six feet with the foreman flung heroically across it in an effort to arrest its tethered wanderings before the rope gave.

Steep held out his hand again. Slutswater glanced at it, then called: "Sammy."

Sammy was fitting boot locks a few yards down the line.

"Any sign of Spiv, yet?" asked the foreman.

Sammy shook his head in mild disgust: "He must have gone for a wank as well," he called tersely.

"Sammy's my only spare utility man," said Slutswater to Steep. "He's giving Spiv a shit relief." He looked at his watch and mumbled: "Quarter of an hour the little get's been gone." He pondered a moment longer then called again: "Sammy, take over from Albert, will you. You'll have to catch those up later."

"Oh, fucking hell!" moaned Sammy extravagantly. "*I'll* have to! Where's Godfrey, the old bastard. Skivin' again somewhere."

"Actually, he's changing all the bulbs in those headlights that you made a cock-up of before," said Slutswater tartly.

"And as for you," went on Sammy, unchecked — he was not a man easily shamed by the integrity of his workmanship being questioned. He nodded at the deep red spider sitting on the back of Steep's hand: "What did you go and do a stupid thing like that for, soft arse?"

"Sorry, Sam," said Steep.

f

The medical room appeared empty. Steep stood at the counter looking for a bell that he might ring and call 'shop'. He tried to ignore the strong smell of disinfectant and the memories of unspeakable embarrassment it triggered in him, but his over deliberate attempt only managed to restore those desperate recollections all the more easily and he tried to shiver them away with a low moaning groan.

"With you in a second," called a friendly woman's voice from behind a partition.

"Right," said Steep, clumsily attempting to clear his throat at a tone similar to that of a low moaning groan. It occurred to him momentarily that his first low moaning groan sounded quite like that of a man due an imminent demise — and he had been told to wait a second! He could be lying there stone dead by now, for all anyone around here cared.

He examined his gashed hand while he waited, first in close-up, then at arm's length, flicking his wrist about for the best light as though admiring a piece of jewellery. It was still bleeding, though less readily than before and it had begun to cake around the wound. He knew the nurse would tell him to wash the blood off before she treated it but it seemed a shame to have bled so impressively without showing it off to someone first.

The door swung open behind him and a small agitated man with darting eyes joined him at the counter.

"This the queue, is it?" he asked restlessly, taking short quick steps under Steep's nose like a bantamweight boxer dodging punches.

"Looks like," said Steep.

"Nurse 'ere, is she, the dark one?"

"Don't know, I've only just got here. They told me to wait."

"Cut your hand, have you?"

No, I think I'm coming down with a touch of bubonic plague, thought Steep. "Yes," he said.

"Looks nasty, how did you do that?"

"Fascia pad on a Kama."

"Looks like stitches, that," forecast the man confidently.

"You reckon?" said Steep becoming worried.

"Definitely." The man confirmed his diagnosis /
tight nods. "Don't let them do it here, though,'
in a sudden whisper. "They're all right with pi₋
bandages and that, but when it comes to sticking neeu.
in you . . . " The man shook his head and sucked in through
his teeth.

At that moment the nurse appeared from behind the
partition. She was a plump woman of around forty with
short black hair and a white crisp uniform filled by the most
splendidly wholesome breasts that he had ever seen. Steep
thought how wonderful it would be to rest his head on them
while she attended to his hand.

"Now then, who's first?" she asked.

"It's burst again, nurse," said the agitated man promptly.
"I just sat down, and . . . squelch," he explained, making
an obscure but probably nauseating gesture with his hands.

"I did tell you not to sit on that side, didn't I?" she said
patiently.

"Well, it's not easy, you know," returned the man
defensively. "Balancing on one cheek. Do you want me to
go in the cubicle?"

"Go on," she sighed, tipping her head towards one of the
two spacious cubicles.

Without another look or word to Steep the man scampered
around the counter and through the curtain into the cubicle.

The nurse turned to Steep and he held up his hand. The
blood had begun to dry and flake and the gash hardly bled
at all now.

She seemed disappointingly unimpressed. "Give it a wash
in the sink, please," she instructed pleasantly. "I won't be
a minute."

Just then the second nurse arrived. She was older and thin
with a narrow, stern face. She carried two plastic cups of
coffee. "That's yours, no sugar," she indicated, placing the
cups on the counter.

"The boil on the bum's in again," said the first nurse. "Do
you want to do him this time?"

"Okay," shrugged the older nurse indifferently. She took
a sip of her coffee then replaced it on the counter and made
for the cubicle.

The first nurse smiled mischievously at Steep's expression as he dried his hands. She motioned him to come around the counter and he found it difficult to pull his eyes from her breasts as he headed directly for them. She took his hand with what seemed to him the tenderness of a lover.

"This is the third time tonight he's been in here," she whispered close to his ear, causing brief shocks of rapture to rebound about his stomach. "Betty'll sort him out."

"Drop your trousers, please," commanded Betty, now behind the curtain.

"Oh, no, it's okay, the other nurse is doing me," said the man timidly.

After a moment's impatient silence came sounds of a short scuffle, a pathetic and surprised cry, and then a zip forcefully unzipping.

"Aw, steady on, nurse. You nearly caught me thingies, then."

"Hmmm, I'll have to cauterise it."

"Er, what's that, nurse?"

"Burn it off," said Betty with a flourish. "Get rid of the nasty thing once and for all."

"Can't you just put another plaster and some cream on it, like the other nurse?" whimpered the man.

"Not much point if you keep sitting on it, is there? I'll just see if that iron's hot enough."

"Iron!" sobbed the man.

"Come on now, don't be such a sissy, it's only like branding sheep," said Betty firmly. "You don't see them making a song and dance about it. Now I'll just get that iron."

It was the man who emerged first, exploding through the curtain like a champion whippet from a trap and dashing towards the door, holding together two fistfuls of his undone trousers about his middle.

Betty came out a moment later, her face as set and stern as before and Steep began to wonder if she had been serious about using a hot iron on the man's boil. But then her face broke into a smile and both nurses began to laugh and Steep smiled with them.

"I think that's the last we'll see of him," laughed Betty.

The door had just stopped swinging when in staggered

Slutswater, his nose and mouth bloody, an eye swollen and forced half shut, his shirt torn and tie twisted around to his shoulder.

"Attacked," he gasped, falling against the counter as though he were the lone survivor from a troop of US Cavalry massacred in some merciless Indian ambush. "Attacked in the shithouse!"

Sammy, Steep and Sproat lolled around the stolen table like drunks after an all night binge; their heads hung low, precariously propped up on insecurely anchored forearms. Steep had a brave white bandage fastened to his injured hand. Between them Godfrey, his nose hovering three inches above a ragged paperback which Sammy had turned upside-down five minutes ago, and Harry Melrose slept like cadavers. A few steps away the cars rolled by in considerate silence. Few operators were still working. The air was drenched with fatigue. The shift had twenty minutes left to run.

"Oh, well," said Sammy.

"Aye. Oh, well," sighed Steep.

"Another one over with, another shift nearer to snuffin' it," said Sammy. The palms of his hands pressed to his cheeks made his mouth move like a glum goldfish.

"Sole purpose of our existence fulfilled for another day."

"Aye, back again tonight. There's only one difference between us and blokes in clink, you know. We have to travel further to get our heads down."

"Where does it all end?" wondered Steep.

"A circle in a spiral, a wheel within a wheel," quoted Sammy, gloomily poetic.

"Never ending or beginning," agreed Steep.

It was a repeat of conversations they had had on countless occasions before, using the same sad clichés and the same heavily hopeless tones that were at the same time light-hearted and secretly serious.

"Oh, what am I doing here?" groaned Sammy as dramatically as his fatigued circumstances would allow.

"Not working, that's for sure, ha ha ha ha," said Sproat.

"Aye, what's it all about?" nodded Steep.

125

"What's it all about, Albieeeee," croaked Sproat. "Is it just for the moment we live . . ."

"Can this be why I was born?" asked Sammy forlornly. "Is this my destiny?"

"A cog," answered Steep. "Of infinite insignificance."

"A cog," echoed Sammy. "Just tell me why I wasn't born rich."

"Would it spoil some vast eternal plan?"

"I don't even want to be significant. Just rich."

"Sounds like an epitaph, that."

"I wouldn't want a lot. I'd be content with a million quid, is that too much to ask?"

"But would it bring you happiness?" probed Steep.

"Fucking right, it would."

"But would it *really*? Bearing in mind that true happiness can only be achieved through careful cultivation of your own self-awareness."

"True happiness," corrected Sammy. "Can only be achieved through having enough money to stay pissed all day."

"That's exactly what I'm *saying*. A cow in a field is *content* because all it wants to do is just stand in its field and eat grass all day. Just like your average drunk is content because all he wants to do is stay pissed all day. But neither of them are *happy* because they don't *know* themselves. Derek Kettle and . . . " He stopped himself before he included Sproat . . "blokes like that are probably *content* but they'll never be *happy* because they don't *know* any better."

"All right then," submitted Sammy. "Supposing someone said to you. You can either have this million quid to be content with for the rest of your life, or you can work for a pittance in a shit hole like this for the rest of your life, but be blessed with the secret of true happiness, which would you choose?"

"That's not a fair question."

"Well," sniffed Sammy. "That puts the kibosh on that theory."

"Hang on," argued Steep, more out of pride now than conviction. "I didn't mean . . ."

"That must be a good book," interrupted Mc Bean, pausing at the table.

"Must be," agreed Sammy, half turning. "He hasn't took his eyes off it for the last ten minutes."

"Harry was reading it before him and he passed out with the excitement, ha ha ha ha."

On another morning McBean might have had the sleeping men wake up, but they could tell by his demeanour that the morning was a rare one and McBean was displaying an unusually pliant side of his character.

"Heard any more about Ted, Rex?" asked Sproat.

"They took him to hospital for X-rays but they reckoned his nose was definitely broken."

"What's going to happen to Spiv?" asked Sammy.

McBean shrugged: "We'll have to wait until we hear both sides of the story. No witnesses, see. Then it's up to management. Now, what did I stop here for? Oh, yes, take a box of handbrake bolts down to the bottom will you, Sam."

"Okay, Rex." Sammy stood up smartly and waited for McBean to carry on up the line, then sat down again, "Broken nose, eh," he said smirking uncontrollably.

"Won't do much for his profile," added Steep.

"Fancy Spiv setting about him like that," put in Sproat. "I blame all those Kung Fu lessons Henry's been giving him. They can make you go funny."

"Ted probably asked for it," surmised Sammy. "You can't go around interrupting people in the middle of a crap, it's just not done."

"That's not what you were saying while you were relieving him on the line," pointed out Steep.

"Ah, but that was before I knew he was going to bust Ted's conk, wasn't it. No, a good long crap is one of the few personal enjoyments left in life. Turds are like cigars, long and brown and you can't rush them."

Sproat howled causing Godfrey to jolt awake. He looked stupidly about the table, his eyelids battling to remain barely open, he gave a tut like an irritable librarian, turned the page of his upside-down paperback and dropped his nose back into it.

"Oh, very elegantly put I must say," winced Steep. "But

it's not really the sort of argument he could use in his defence, is it?"

"Knowing Spiv, defending himself will be the last thing he's bothered about. You know what a loon he is. He'll be tucked up snoring his head off by now. Like a contented cow," he added pushing his tongue into his cheek.

Steep fired a short, harmless sneer back across the table. "And here's a great philosopher like you stuck in this dump, selflessly dedicated to enriching our miserable existences with your sparkling words of wisdom and profundity. I must say I found the analogy between the turd and the cigar particularly stimulating."

"Any time, my son."

"Sam, did I ask you to take a box of handbrake bolts down to the bottom before?" asked McBean, passing again.

"Handbrake bolts? No Rex," lied Sammy unflinchingly.

"Well take a box down then, will you."

"Okay, Rex." Sammy stood up smartly again. "Are you going that way yourself, Rex?" he inquired.

McBean nodded.

"Do me a favour then, take a box of handbrake bolts down there."

"You cheeky bastard!" exclaimed McBean.

"You know where they are, don't you, Rex?" called Sammy after the General Foreman. "Cheers, Rex," he waved.

Both Steep and Sproat gazed at Sammy in dumb admiration.

"Didn't you know?" he said casually. "All we great philosophers are cheeky bastards."

Slutswater had been allowed home from the hospital after treatment. The X-rays had shown nothing else broken other than his nose, though he had required stitches above his right eye and inside his lower lip.

He lay on his back without sleep for the remainder of the night because his nose ached so much and even had he been able to sleep he would not have dared lest he might roll over onto it.

It had been light for more than an hour beyond the

128

curtains and he could hear the milkman's float jangling along the road. Next to him his wife was snoring again. He shook her shoulder: "You're snoring again, Dot," he half whispered as best he could manage with his swollen lip.

"In a minute, dear," she promised, ascending fractionally and briefly from the depths of her slumber.

"Silly bitch," he muttered painfully. "And you've got all the bleeding blankets." He tugged at them but she was lying on them. "Dot, lift up a minute will you, I'm perishing here."

She rolled over to face him making sleepily intimate grunts. Her left arm followed, hurtling over the horizon like a rapidly climbing low level strike aircraft. Slutswater had just regained and arranged his share of the blankets when he noticed the oblivious hand plummeting directly towards his nose.

The scream of pain was so fearful that it caused the milkman to drop both bottles of goldtop on their doorstep.

Chapter Seven

Cranby could smell her approach and feel her dull footsteps through the sole of his left shoe. Then, like a giant wave over a dam her blatant perfume poured over the top of his newspaper.

"Morning, Mr Cranby," she chirped.

"Good morning," said Cranby, still behind the morning's *Guardian*.

She dipped straight legged below his desk and Cranby's eyes slid askance as her beige skirt rose like a curtain at some hurried unveiling ceremony over the thick, pale, muscular legs and the spectacular twin navy blue hills. God! She's got love bites on her thighs! There were five of them, ten pence sized and three more peeping out like bruised eyes from inside the legs of her knickers: Somebody knocked on his door.

"Come in," he blinked, forcing the early morning memories to one side.

It was Sloan. "Morning, Aubrey," he said.

Cranby noticed Gottlieb's left eye latching on to the Head of Personnel and following him with silent scepticism. Cranby suspected that Gottlieb harboured an irrational dislike of Sloan.

"Morning, Nic. Problems?"

"Is it that obvious?" said Sloan without much surprise. He sat opposite Cranby. "Well, at least it's nothing to do with sabotaged production lines and exploding bins, so I suppose that's something to be grateful for."

Cranby did not welcome the reminder. "Did you come in here just to cheer me up?" he asked a little more testily than he had intended. "Or was there another reason?"

"Something and nothing really, but I suppose you had better hear the story, or rather stories. There was a punch-up on the night shift between an operator and his foreman. At least I think there was," reported Sloan uncertainly. "Anyway, the foreman had to be treated in hospital."

"Good grief," muttered Cranby. "How is he?"

"Broken nose, black eyes, that sort of thing. From what I understand the operator who did it is some sort of Kung Fu expert."

Cranby raised a hand and pulled it wearily down the side of his face. "I thought people like that were supposed to exercise restraint when provoked. Presumably he claims he was provoked?"

"That's the funny thing," frowned Sloan. "According to his statement he showed commendable restraint, if you can believe it that is. Actually the whole thing has a distinct touch of the surreal about it. I'm not sure what to make of it."

"Intriguing," said Cranby tiredly.

Sloan removed two sheets of foolscap from a file. "This one is the operator's version. He works on line two of the number two trim system, name of George Spivak." He began to read from the paper: " 'I asked my foreman if it would be all right for me to go to the toilet. He said it would be all right so I went. After about three minutes I just wondered if I could reach the door from where I was sitting, just as a matter of interest. Not that I wasn't doing what I was supposed to be doing as well, I just wanted to see if I could do that at the same time. After I had been trying to reach the door for about a minute I heard someone come in. I heard the person walking up and down for a bit then I saw some shoes under my door and a pair of hands on the top of the door and then the top of a head as though the person was trying to lift himself up. This frightened me because I didn't know what was going on and all I could think about was running away, so I pulled my trousers up — I didn't even use any toilet paper first — and flung open the door. There was a figure standing in the doorway and I tried to run past him but I slipped and fell into him and we both fell over and my forehead landed on his nose. I was absolutely terrified by now and I remember lashing out to try and get free but then someone must have heard the carry-on because some fellows came in and pulled us apart. It wasn't until then that I realised it was Ted, and I said: "Ted! I'm sorry. Are you all right?" and he said: "Fuck off". ' " Sloan looked up from the paper and slid it behind the second sheet. Neither man made comment. "And this is what the foreman had to say." He began to read again: " 'The operator requested a toilet relief and I granted him one. After about fifteen minutes he had not returned to his job and his whereabouts began to concern me and I thought it would be advisable to investigate as unforeseen circumstances had depleted my workforce to a point where his return as soon as possible was important. I went to the operators' toilets and noticed his distinctive white plimsolls beneath the only occupied cubicle. Then, suddenly he lifted them up off the ground as if he was hiding or something so I knocked several times on the door but received no answer. I then began to think something might be wrong with him so I decided to try to look over the top of the door. As I was attempting to do this the door was flung violently open and he charged violently out at me, knocking me to the floor and butting and punching me violently, until some operators came in and dragged him off me.'

"Well, that's it," concluded Sloan, dropping the papers onto the desk. "And not a witness in sight."

"I see what you mean," said Cranby. "What about the men who broke it up?"

"Not much use. They say they just went in and found the pair of them rolling around on the floor. Mind you, I don't think they would have said anything whatever they saw. No operator's going to get one of his own workmates the sack. And I suppose they'd even have qualms about losing a foreman his job, these days."

"So somebody gets away with it."

"More likely both of them get away with it. These incidents are rarely so one-sided that one party is completely innocent, or completely guilty."

"Foremen should have more sense, though," insisted

Cranby. They should be able to see these things coming. That's what we send them to school for, isn't it?"

"Yes," admitted Sloan. "But all the same, it's not a job I'd care for. It's hairy enough being threatened over the phone without having to deal with someone like that face to face."

"Threatened over the phone?" frowned Cranby.

"Yes. A bloke we sacked a couple of years ago rang me asking for a reference, would you believe? When I told him we couldn't give him one he became rather unsociable. As I say, I'm glad it was only over the telephone."

"Good grief, he hasn't been in touch with you since, has he?" inquired Cranby solicitously.

"Oh no, I think he was probably drunk at the time."

"Even so," cautioned Cranby. "You can't be too careful with people like that. I don't know what's happening to this place," he went on, shaking his head in slow bewilderment. "Bins being blown up, assembly lines being sabotaged, you receiving threatening phone calls, foremen brawling with their operators, and me being warned right here in my own office of summary castrations by a hulking great madwoman! Sometimes I wonder if the whole bloody world isn't going completely off its trolley."

Sloan nodded solemnly. "Well, perhaps if we can resolve the problem of the foreman brawling with his operator we can at least claim to have done our bit to keep it sane."

"We can't even do that," pointed out Cranby tiredly. "With everything being so contradictory."

"I suppose not," agreed Sloan. "I suppose the best thing we can do is to play it by ear for the time being. We might as well bring the operator back in because the foreman won't be in again for a couple of weeks, at least. That'll give things a chance to cool down a bit. If we must we could move him to another section when he returns. But other than that there's not a lot we can do whoever you believe."

"I don't think I believe either of them," said Cranby without emphasis. "Are those their files?"

Sloan nodded and took the two files from the larger one on the desk and handed them to Cranby.

"Neither of them have been involved in anything like this

133

before," said Sloan. "The foreman's record is practically unblemished actually, one recorded warning for coming back late from lunch nine years ago, when he was an operator."

"The operator sounds like a bit of a lad, though," remarked Cranby. "Nine recorded warnings and seven disciplinary action reports in five years. Just look at this lot, bad time-keeping, refusing to obey foreman's instructions, involvement in unofficial disputes, persistently inadequate workmanship, unauthorised activities during working hours — what was he doing there? Running a brothel in the car park?"

"Playing football," corrected Sloan. "It tells you further down, along one of the aisles between the lines. There were about a dozen of them involved but Spivak was the one who hit the janitor's foreman in the face with the ball as he came round a corner."

"It follows," said Cranby logically.

"It knocked his wig off," continued Sloan. "I don't suppose he was very pleased about it."

Steep sat next to Kettle and opposite Sproat at the stolen table. Kettle was speaking: "The point I'm making is that, once created, nothing can ever return to the oblivion of non-existence. Decay merely obliges matter to rearrange its molecular structures, which in itself is further creation. I conclude from this that creation is decay, decay is creation. Ergo, accepting that consciousness of one's own existence ceases upon death, that is, returns to the oblivion of non-existence, then surely the very concept of the existence of consciousness itself as a vital entity must be brought into doubt."

"You mean, 'does consciousness exist or is it all in the mind?' ha ha ha ha. A startling hypothesis," continued Sproat more seriously. "But distinctly provincial in its outlook, and quite blatantly flawed. I must say I do find the correlation between the metaphysical processes of consciousness and the purely physiological dimension pertaining to alterations in molecular structures a wholly untenable one. Moreover, its haughty disregard of the

134

theological standpoint is utterly breathtaking in its arrogance."

"Theology," pointed out Kettle. "Is the bastard child of Ignorance the Ragpicker and Superstition the Draggletail. Its invitation to logical debate admits a sinister and divisive interloper. A confidence trickster who quaffs the wine of valid reason and scoffs the cheese of common rationale with an obscene and ruthless voracity that cripples the interlect it starves of sound thought."

"Your argument suggests he is a fellow who keeps you good company," sniffed Sproat. "It contains, if I may say so, many ill-devised and sweeping assumptions."

"Ill-devised only to the mind incapable of de-coupling itself from the well upholstered carriages of conformity. Rigid compartmentalisation is the petty adversary of great thought."

"Forgive me, but I understood that your whole argument was based upon the non-existence of thought, great or otherwise. Or perhaps I am mistaken, perhaps thought is not the plasma of consciousness after all."

"Albie."

"That, sir, is the observation of a myopic cretin, an intellectual dotard."

"Albie."

"At least I may take solace from the fact that I am not an addle-pated dilettante obsessed with my own fatuous fantasies."

"Albie."

"Twat."

"Cunt."

"Albie . . . Albie. It's nearly five o'clock if you're going to look at those motor cars."

"Okay," grunted Steep into his pillow. Then he realised the voice was Daffy's, and she was in the bedroom. He opened his eyes, she was sitting on the edge of the bed. "Hello," she smiled.

"What are you doing here?" he mumbled.

"I'm glad you're so pleased to see me," she said, without taking offence. "I thought I'd better go with you to look at these motors. You know how impulsive you are when you're buying things, you'd probably come back with a great big

Maserati or something."

Steep closed his eyes again. "It's my money," he said like a spoiled child. "I'll buy what I want with it."

"It's silly spending a lot of money on a car," she said earnestly. "You might be sorry in a few months' time. You might want to buy something else then, but you'll still have all that money to pay out every month."

"All right, I won't get a great big Maserati," he promised. "Anyway, I was thinking more along the lines of a Rolls-Royce with a swimming pool in the boot."

She punched the blankets playfully. Then she became silent for several seconds. Even with his eyes closed he recognised it as one of *those* silences.

"And don't get an automatic one," she said finally.

He opened his eyes and looked up at her. "Why not?" he asked, already half suspecting her reply.

"Well, you can't pass your test in an automatic so you wouldn't be able to give me lessons in one."

Steep groaned loudly and pulled the blankets over his head. She seemed prepared for the response. "Well there's no point in giving money to a driving school when you can teach me for nothing, is there?" she reasoned quickly. "I'd be a good driver, I just know I would."

"Well I don't think I'd be a very good instructor," he argued, his voice muffled through the blankets. "Not with my head wedged in the glove compartment praying for deliverance all the time."

"Cuppa tea made," called Auntie Agnes from downstairs.

"Oh, you're really awful," she said sulkily. He felt her rise from the bed.

"Bring my tea up for me, please," he asked without hope.

"Sod off."

"Bring my tea up for me," he repeated, this time as half of a proposition. "And I *might* just consider *thinking* about giving you driving lessons."

After a pause he heard her padding obediently from the bedroom and down the stairs. He knew she would be smiling. A great big 'I knew I'd talk him round eventually', silent secret beam.

She had out-pointed him in another round, at least *she*

136

thought she had. How much longer, he wondered before she dealt him her knock-out punch? And what did she mean by 'you might want to buy something else in a few months' time'? The possibilities were too horrific to consider. Instead, from the warm safe darkness of his hiding place, he muttered: "I wonder what the down payment would be on a nice, clean, low mileage, one owner Chieftain tank?"

The showroom was a large one, as befitting the sign stretched above its expansive plate glass facade, it read:

WALTER WHITTERING WELCOMES YOU TO BRITAIN'S BIGGEST DRAM DEALER

A few people wandered with Steep and Daffy among the second-hand cars; some slowing briefly to dismiss obsequious salesmen. Or to squint into interiors with shading hands and quizzically squashed noses against the windows. Some, more boldly, opened a door to inspect inside, but few could manage this without exhibiting the conspicuous self-consciousness of an inexpert thief.

The second-hand cars stood beneath the hard neon lights in neat ranks on a polished grey tiled floor. At one end of the showroom four steps lead up to a thick red carpeted area upon which a selection of new Drams lounged, gleaming and lavishly embellished by coloured angle-poise lights, exotic potted palms, and, less flatteringly, two bored looking salesmen.

"The second-hand ones are dear enough, aren't they," said Daffy practically. "How people can afford *new* ones I don't know."

She annoyed him because he knew she was right. "What else have I got to spend my money on," he shrugged casually, determined not to go down without a fight. He was glad to see his remark had surprised her.

"We agreed," she bleated.

He stopped to admire a large, hopelessly unaffordable Rover. "I only said I wouldn't get a great big Maserati," he pointed out pedantically.

"Don't be a bloody smart arse," she grumbled, her face falling into a sulk. "It doesn't become you."

He smiled wickedly, enjoying the part while it lasted. "What's wrong with a little bit of extravagance now and then?"

"Extravagance is for people who can easily afford it."

"Ah, but if people could afford it it wouldn't be extravagant, would it?"

"You're a bloody fool if you go into debt for thousands just for a car," she snapped. She half turned away from him and he realised he had upset her more than he had intended. "Leave me out of it," she moped. "Just do what you like."

They became silent for some moments. Unwittingly they seemed to have strayed into a sort of unexplored no-man's-land. And there to have tacitly touched on the other's designs and private plans. They used the cover of silence to scurry back, frightened to their own, safe territory.

"Look out, we've been spotted," warned Steep eventually, catching an approaching salesman in the corner of his eye. His voice was conciliatory. He intoned the words as though they were the elements of an apology.

"Evening, folks," called the salesman, still several strides away. He was a short man, short to an extent where people probably felt justified in making jokes about his lack of physical stature. He wore thick black-rimmed spectacles on a face smitten with curious lump-like features that gave his head the impression of being modelled on a great potato. A circular badge on the lapel of his grey suit read: SALESMAN – LENNY BIDDLESTONE.

"We're just looking for now," said Steep evasively, making to walk away.

"They're a bit pricey, aren't they," added Daffy, nodding a coy smile over Steep's shoulder.

"Well, not really," returned the salesman smartly. Clearly grateful for the toehold that Daffy had given him. "Not when you consider what you're getting for your money." He leaned back on the wing of a tall green Volvo and tried to half sit on it by hooking his leg over the bonnet, but it was too high and he sensibly desisted after the second failed attempt. "If you want to buy a car where the wheels fall off after a week then true enough, we can't help you."

"How about one where the wheels fall off after a fort-night?" inquired Steep.

The salesman gave a token, unamused smile with ugly brown teeth. "How much were you thinking of spending?"

"About a couple of thousand less than the cheapest one I've seen in here." He noticed Daffy glancing up at him. Her eyes like a grateful spaniel's.

The salesman pushed his lips into a comical and predictable pout. "You won't get much for that kind of money, these days," he recited glibly. "In fact, I honestly wouldn't recommend buying a motor in that price bracket, because it's still a lot of money to part with for something that won't be good value. It's false economy. Whereas, as you can see, these jobs are immaculate." He placed the heels of his hands on the Volvo's wing this time, and in an oddly childlike manoeuvre half sprung and half hoisted himself onto it. Immediately he began to teeter perilously, his little legs kicking the air in an effort to maintain his balance. He clutched at the straw that was the car's extended radio aerial. "I mean, if a motor wasn't spot-on we wouldn't try to sell it," he assured them hurriedly while sliding miserably back onto the floor. The grabbed aerial bent thinly at its middle to a right-angle. "After all," he pointed out. "We've got a reputation to think of."

"Oh, I'm sure they're all nice cars," conceded Steep with tactful but strained sobriety. "They're just too expensive, that's all."

"Too expensive," echoed Daffy.

At this the salesman seemed suddenly engulfed by indecision, as though he was struggling with an inner munificence to withhold from them some fabulous secret. "Look," he finally blurted, the inner munificence apparently winning through. "We don't usually offer the older trade-ins to the public, but I'll tell you what I'll do." His voice dropped conspiratorially. "And don't tell my boss, whatever you do." He looked furtively about him like a small spy and then looked again at the angled aerial as though he had just noticed its pronounced departure from the perpendicular for the first time. He half turned and pinched it, close to its

139

bend, like someone about to pick a flower and carefully began to lever it upwards but it snapped cleanly in two after only a brief movement. "We've got a Morris Marina in the compound around the back," he confided, scratching the side of his little lump of a nose with the detached half of the broken aerial. "We took it in part exchange from a couple of old nuns yesterday."

It was dark now but the large enclosed area was brightly lit by high, spying floodlights. A few disorientated sparrows hopped and chattered about their structures. The crammed compound contained mainly new Drams of all models and colours but a number of used cars were segregated into one corner, as though perhaps they ailed with something that might be catching.

"They had it from new," said the salesman. "It's done a few miles, of course, but the engine's just been overhauled and the bodywork's sound."

"Nice colour," said Daffy.

"Have a seat, see how she feels," suggested the salesman, then tugging at the driver's door. "Ah, locked. I'll get the keys, won't be a minute."

"I like purple," admitted Daffy. Then in a whisper: "Wasn't he funny trying to sit on that bonnet. I kept wanting to go and give him a leg-up. And I don't know how I kept my face straight when he slid off and bent the aerial," she giggled. "Still, we shouldn't laugh, I suppose. It must be terrible being that short."

"Oh, I don't know," considered Steep absently, walking slowly around the car pushing down hard on each corner because he had read somewhere that that was what you were supposed to do, although for what purpose he was not quite sure. "He probably only pays half fare on the buses."

"It's got chrome things around the wheels," noticed Daffy.

"How many miles did he say it's done?"

"I don't think he mentioned exactly. Beige seat covers."

"I'm not surprised he didn't mention it," said Steep, squinting through the driver's door window. "Ninety-eight thousand miles."

"They were probably missionaries. I expect they drove it very carefully though. I mean you don't see nuns driving

140

round like Starsky and Hutch, do you?''

"Perhaps they weren't nuns. Perhaps they were Batman and Robin in which case they probably tore the balls out of it."

"Albie! Don't be blasphemous!"

"This side's not locked," announced Steep, opening the passenger door. He leaned across to open the other door, then realised it would give Daffy access to the driving seat so he clambered across and sat there himself.

"It's nice inside, isn't it," said Daffy climbing in.

"Not much room in the back, though," he sniffed fussily. "A certain amount of sexual innovation would be called for to get your end away on that seat."

"Oh, you're awful," she cried, flapping her hand at him. "And in a nun's car, as well."

"I'm not too sure about that, either. If this was a nun's car why is the ashtray full of dog-ends?" He pushed his fingers into the clogged, open ashtray. "Look, there're even a couple of old cigar stubs in there. I suppose they'll have been the Mother Superior's."

"Well it's a nice little car anyway, Albie. I like it."

"I don't like the mileage, though." He peered disapprovingly through the steering wheel at the small white numbers.

Daffy leaned across, the top of her greasy head brushing his ear. She eased it gently onto his shoulder. "Nine hundred and eighty-two thousand, six hundred and seventy-two miles," she read carefully.

"The last one's only tenths of a mile, dumbo."

"Oh, is it?" she giggled. "I don't know what you're complaining about, then," she said, turning her frowning face up to him. "It's only got to do another one thousand seven hundred and odd miles, and they all go back to nought again."

Sproat settled contentedly, like a tired dog on a snug fireside rug, into the rusting steel pallet that would for the next hour — as it had for many previously restful hours — be his private and subtly remote sanctum. It was not large enough for him to stretch out in, its caged dimensions measuring only something like four feet by four, but its base was lined with plastic bags filled with small deliberately shaped pieces of lime-green sponge that nobody knew where to fit on the cars, but which made excellent bedding. He enjoyed the cuddling cosiness and the childish secretiveness of being so close and yet so distant from the running, busy line. It was like being invisible.

The forty-five minute lunch break had fled with its customary haste and he had spent it idly and ineptly losing thirty-two pence at pontoon. He lost regularly at pontoon because he could not add up and he was often still counting the spots on his cards when his turn came to 'stick' or 'twist' and he was pressured into making an instant and usually injudicious decision. To make matters worse he had lost most of his thirty-two pence to the grossly gloating Kettle, a state of affairs which was only partly assuaged by Kettle losing as much in turn to Godfrey.

His next car would reach his work station in approximately one hour. A more accurate estimate had proved difficult due to unspecified problems in the paint shop which restricted the number of bodies it could pass on to the trim lines which therefore ran interspersed with irregular, carless gaps.

The usual selection of rumours were on offer, ranging from 'bad paint' to a mass walk out of the paint shop operators. But Sproat showed little interest in any of them. His next car was an hour away — who cared why?

Foremen would not *always* wake an operator whom they found sleeping on a bench or at a table; but more often than not they would, so it was important to be hidden — but not necessarily sequestered — a half empty pallet of stock right next to the line with cardboard camouflage would usually prove adequate. Personally, however, Sproat no longer slept in pallets next to the line because some bastards had once sealed him in with cardboard and sticky tape and then poked the nozzle of a fire extinguisher in and frozen him in clouds of carbon-dioxide.

But here he was safe. Not that the others didn't know where he was. It was just that his location precluded any similar antics without them assuming the logistical complexities of a minor military operation. He grinned, waved two

142

indiscriminating fingers at the world outside his den, and closed his eyes.

The comparative scarcity of cars on the lines was appreciated by almost everyone. Only some foremen turned sour-faced at the sight of idle operators, and the janitors with their sniffing brushes impaled on their chests complained because they had to sweep the channel between the line rails which accumulated a considerable amount of debris and which, with a full line, was inaccessible.

There was a hint of quiet celebration about the place. The shops traded briskly as operators chewed chocolate bars, crunched favourite flavoured crisps and swigged fizzy lemonade to pass the time. The stolen table looked like the place of a modest, children's party.

Sammy took a rugged gulp from his can of Tizer. "A circle in a spiral," he intoned suddenly after a swallow.

"A wheel within a wheel," answered Steep promptly, as though responding as required to some solemn religious incantation.

"Every gap a Jap, lads, don't forget that," put in Godfrey irrelevantly. The others never seemed entirely certain as to either the object or the implications of their gloomy, tired dialogue, and were careful never to wade too far in towards the centre of their deep doomful exchanges, preferring instead to watch from the shallow edges and occasionally splash at them with some fatuous interjection.

"Sometimes I wonder," mused Steep. "If I'll ever walk out of here and never come back. Just imagine how wonderful it would be clocking off for the last time, ever!"

"I used to think like that once upon a time," reminisced Sammy. "Doesn't do any good, though. The more you think about it the further away it gets. No, I find it's best just to accept the fact that we're here until the end of all eternity."

"Until the Twelfth of Never," said Steep, crunching on a packet of prawn cocktail flavoured crisps.

"Or then," conceded Sammy. "Whichever comes first."

"And until then, what are we?" asked Steep dismally.
"A cog."

"A number."

143

"A nobody."

"A real Nowhere Man."

"Making all his nowhere cars for nobody."

"Guess what, men," announced Melrose. He had just stopped at the stolen table, his rubber headed mallet grasped in his leathery fist and trailing several long rubber weather strips over his shoulder like so much giant liquorice. "There's loads of water just started pissing out of the roof down there. Everywhere's soaked."

The assembled heads turned in the direction indicated. Those who could not see stood up and stretched across the table.

The trouble was fifty yards away down the line and centred around the staircase and walkway leading to the toilet situated on a mezzanine floor slung beneath the paint shop: From there a fairly creditable torrent was hurling itself unchecked over the walkway and down the steel staircase.

"It's the Phantom Sprinkler Fiend. He's come back!" breathed Spivak in the manner of someone re-experiencing some saintly visitation.

"With gaps on?" queried Kettle ungratefully. "Why didn't the soft bastard hang on until the lines were full?"

At that moment the line died.

"That's it, then," forecast Godfrey. "If it's as much as last time it won't go until after break at least."

Grins broke out irrepressibly about the table. Sammy and Steep looked at each other, their moods of carefully fashioned despair shattered now by the sudden excitement.

"O friends, no more these sounds! Let us sing more cheerful songs, more full of joy!" quoted Steep. "There you go, mate," he offered cordially. "Have a prawn cocktail flavoured crisp with your Tizer."

It was the Phantom Sprinkler Fiend's third strike in the last seven months. On this occasion as on the previous two his mission had been successfully accomplished with the swiftness and stealth of an undercover commando. Appropriately his identity was unknown, even to the operators, and among them he was sometimes spoken of in quiet deferential tones.

144

His modus operandi was by now tried and trusted, utilising only a cotton glove and a small helping of slimey black glue. The daubed glove would be put to a match and attached to a sprinkler nozzle in the knowledge that the glove would smoulder reliably, thus allowing him to make good his escape before the smoulder reached the gluey area which would burn with a stink and activate the sprinkler which could not then be turned off until the tank which fed it was drained.

The forced, gushing water had swamped the walkway at the top of the tall staircase and dropped over its edge in a liquid curtain onto the aisle below. As much again raced towards the head of the stairs and tripped and tumbled like a reckless stunt down every steel step.

The early pond soon became a small but ever spreading half-inch deep lake, reaching across and halting two lines due to the affected operators reasonable refusal to continue working. Shortly a third line would be threatened.

All trim assembly janitors were urgently summoned over the public address system to the flooded area. They were about to get their brushes and their feet wet. This had not been their night.

"I suppose someone had better wake Sproaty up," said Sammy. "Rex will probably be round in a minute with steam coming out of his ears wanting a clean up."

Godfrey leaned back on the bench and looked carefully up and down the line. "Go on then," he said. "Here, give him a knock with Harry's mallet."

Sammy climbed up onto the stolen table and wrapped with that familiar rhythm of someone knocking on a door on the underside of the storage rack above him. "Sproaty," he called. "Wake up, you lazy cunt. Sproaty."

"He'd be good on them telephone alarm calls, wouldn't he," observed Steep quietly.

"Sproaty," repeated Sammy. "Derek Kettle's just found a fiver and he thinks it might be yours." He listened for a moment with an attentively cocked ear and then stepped down from the table. "He's dead," he said positively.

"I'll wake him up," offered Kettle, his sneak face wriggling into a reptilian smile. He got up from the table and moved to

g

a nearby storage bin containing half-inch diameter spring washers. He scooped out a fistful and walked with feigned, childish innocence out into the middle of the aisle. He looked about him as furtively as a prospective vandal, then hurled the handful of spring washers up at the underside of the top tier of the rack so that they could rattle like rapid gunfire and rebound down on Sproat's blameless slumbers.

Kettle scurried back to his place on the bench, his dull eyes wide, his scrawny chest heaving with the thrill of it all.

"Who's fuckin' throwin'!" boomed a voice from above, like some wrathful common god.

"We've got a nice little surprise for you," called Sammy as though he were addressing a small child.

"And I've got a nice surprise for whoever threw them fuckin' washers," came the grumpy, godly reply.

"It's the Phantom Sprinkler Fiend," informed Sammy. "He's been at it again."

With that there were sounds of sudden movement from above and a few seconds later Sproat's head hung upside-down, like a fairground target, beneath the rack, his face as early morning bright as a child's who had woken to the first snow of winter. "Has he? Honest?"

"Look for yourself," said Sammy.

Sproat's head disappeared and they could hear him scampering across to the other side of the rack, overlooking the line. He began to whoop like a happy savage. "Just look at it!" he cried excitedly. "It's like Niagara Fucking Falls from up here!"

The spectators to the flood watched in shifts, drifting to and from the fringes of the minor, drenched disaster area with a casual inoccupation poisoned with unseemly smugness: Each shift was a daily defeat for them, victories were only ever modest and occasional, and they found little time for dignity in their celebration.

The massed and muttering ranks of janitors, now grudgingly intent on the squelching task of dispersing the water made several slow but aggressive advances towards the operator's spectating front line; forcing them back with their sodden swilling brushes that drove ankle high waves vigorously before them.

Rex McBean looked like a Shakespearian tragedian. He leaned against a supporting stanchion, the back of his raised fisted hand pressed in formal anguish to his forehead. The bulk of the crowd stood slightly adrift from him; his expression and his stance indicating that their company and their shallow consolation would not be tolerated. Their general reaction to the situation may have been less than discreet but they knew it was seldom prudent to go out of your way to antagonise a general foreman, especially one who was rumoured to have lengthy conversations with fire extinguishers.

"Must be mad, Rex," called Spivak who didn't care and who had just arrived with some of the others.

McBean made no response.

"The bloke that done this," went on Spivak. "The Phantom Sprinkler Fiend. He wants locking up."

"Yeah," agreed Kettle stupidly and too loudly. "For not waitin' until the lines was full."

McBean turned his head to the remark with all the slow mechanical menace of a rotating tank turret. Kettle turned grey. The nearby portion of the crowd became hushed and hopeful. The General Foreman's and the operator's eyes locked together, the one's an icy glare, the other's pitifully bovine and supplemented by a twitching, dim grin.

"Course, you know what'll happen next time he strikes," predicted Spivak easily into McBean's iron face. "Management will take us off pay. Can't blame them, I suppose."

McBean swallowed a large noseful of air then let it all go with a quick snort. He blinked two slow, careful blinks which disengaged his eyes from Kettle's pathetic return. "Aye," he sighed, nodding heavily. "He wants locking up, all right. And I'm sure if any of you lads saw anything suspicious going on you'd be sensible enough to report it to the proper people."

Then Sproat said something that was the most daring thing that many of the operators had ever heard in their lives. "Well I didn't see anything, Rex," he said with jovial frankness. "Mind you, there wasn't much chance of that, really. Not seeing as how I was snoring my arse off at the time, ha ha ha ha!"

Chapter Eight

It was raining on Bellend again. Tiny wet fists made tinny wet clatter on the thin metal roofs of the stored cars. Shallow pools formed and spread over areas normally occupied by nocturnal footballers, tonight they chose to spend their lunch break indoors in favour of sedentary but similarly raucous card games or restless, bone dry sleep. Only the most dedicated joggers ventured outside to splash and squelch around personal and precisely measured circuits: One such enthusiast increased his pace while passing an isolated and unused storeroom, pretending that the bays and howls leaking from within were hungry hounds in his pursuit and not really just the usual paying audience watching paint shop impresario, 'Blue Peters' ' regular Thursday morning double feature pornographic film show: Later on his route he passed a dark corner near the wheel and tyre store and sprinted twenty yards, pretending that the two shadowy figures he thought he had seen were two lurking bogey men. And not really just Sammy and Godfrey.

"Cuppa tea, lads?" inquired Worth.

"Well actually," hesitated Halliwell, rising reluctantly from a comfortable position in his chair. "I was just thinking it's about time we did another quick patrol." He turned to a window and tried to focus beyond his own reflection into the miserable night.

"It's pissing down," frowned Worth.

"Oh, that's a fine attitude, that is," put in Atkin phlegmatically. He slowly turned a curled page of a 1978 Christmas

148

edition of *Mayfair.* "Real Empire builders sentiments, those are." He went on quickly before Worth could speak. "What do you suppose Christopher Columbus said when he woke up on the day that he was going off to discover America? And Edmund Hilary from the bijou comfort of his little tent before his final assault on Everest? 'I'm not goin' cos it's pissin' down'?"

"They would have done if they'd been standing here," grumbled Worth.

"It's not too bad, now," said Halliwell patiently, pulling on his uniform mackintosh. "At least it will keep me awake. I'm going anyway. Who's coming with me? . . . Well don't trample me down in the rush will you?"

"Oh, I'll go, then," shrugged Worth.

"Right. I'll hold the fort then," said Atkin shamelessly. He gasped silently at the lady sprawled provocatively across the centrefold. "Promise me you won't get too wet, now."

"What time is it?" asked Sammy, his voice barely raised above a whisper.

"Can't see," answered Godfrey.

"He's due at a quarter past two, isn't he?" said Sammy impatiently. "It must be that by now."

They stood midway along the shortest side of a damp, densely shadowed triangle, their stiff cold backs pressed anxiously against the wall as though stranded on some high ledge — a position adopted as much to offer some hope of shelter as concealment. A gust of wind helped some blind rain onto their faces, for a moment the chilled droplets fingered them suspiciously then fell away as the wind let go.

"Isn't night-time dark," commented Godfrey thoughtfully.

Sammy swore beneath his breath.

"I mean you don't realise with street lights and all that. I wonder what they did before they had lights?"

"Probably bumped into things and tripped over a lot," muttered Sammy.

"Hmmm," agreed Godfrey pensively. "They must've

had forehead like mallets in them days." Godfrey shivered. "Hope no more joggers go past," he said. "I'm sure that last one saw us."

"I can't even see you, never mind bleedin' joggers."

"Well why did he sprint off like that when he passed us?"

"That's the way they do it, I suppose. Sprint a bit, jog a bit," reasoned Sammy.

"He might have thought we were two queers," realised Godfrey, suddenly distraught.

"Fuck off."

"He might have," protested Godfrey. "Two queers, 'avin' a go."

"In the pissin' down rain?"

"Two kinky queers!"

"Fuck off."

"Well what would you think if you saw two blokes hangin' around in the dark outside the wheel and tyre store?"

"I'd think they were gonna pinch some wheels and tyres."

"Oh yeah," considered Godfrey more easily. "I never thought of that."

"What time is it now?"

"Can't see," said Godfrey, then puzzledly. "Where does rain come from?"

"The sky," grunted Sammy unhelpfully.

"Yes, but I mean, how does it get up there?"

"It's the moisture in the atmosphere, isn't it," explained Sammy uncertainly. "It makes clouds."

"And then the rain falls out of the clouds?"

"That's right."

"Well why isn't it raining every time it's cloudy?"

"What is this, a bleeding nature study lesson? Look, you've got your rain clouds and your dry clouds, haven't you?" said Sammy inconclusively.

A surprise rush of wind sent the rain slanting icily against their faces.

"Another thing I can't understand," shivered Godfrey after a pause, "is why does it come down in all those separate little drops. Why doesn't it come down in one big cloudful, like emptying a bucket?"

"I thought it was," observed Sammy sourly.

"I'm glad it doesn't, though. Just imagine it. You're just walking along and next minute, splosh! And you're piss wet through from having about a couple of million gallons of water landing on you."

"Are you sure this bloke knows where to wait?"

"Course he does. And all we've got to do is shove the wheels through the hole in the fence and that's that, mission complete and fifty quid each in our pockets."

"It's not much for pneu-pigging-monia," muttered Sammy.

"It's safest in the rain," reasoned Godfrey. "Security never come out of their huts in the rain, everybody knows that, and anyway, you didn't *have* to come in on this, you know," he reminded.

"It seemed like an adventure in broad daylight," moaned Sammy, suddenly miserable. "Just *talking* about it. I was bored and it sounded exciting. My missus would kill me if she knew what I was up to."

"Well you're in on it now. Both of us are. Wheels are in motion."

"Very funny."

"What?"

"Forget it."

"No, we couldn't let Kneecaps down now," said Godfrey. "He wouldn't like it."

"Kneecaps! Oh Jesus! You said it was for some bloke you knew in your local. You didn't say it was for the sodding Mafia!"

"He's not in the Mafia," assured Godfrey excessively. "He just drinks in our boozer, like I said. They just call him that on account of when he doesn't like someone, sometimes he bites their kneecaps off."

"What have you done to me?" groaned Sammy. "What the fuck have you done to me?"

"I had to, mate, honest. I only happened to mention in conversation that there was this bloke in our wheel and tyre store who let you have cheap swag as long as you got it out yourself and that was that. I couldn't have done it myself, could I? You don't know him, he's not a nice person. I don't want to end up walking like a Flowerpot Man."

"That's right, I don't know him," realised Sammy quietly.

"And he doesn't know me. Does he?" he added threateningly.

"No, no," insisted Godfrey. "It was all no questions asked."

Sammy sighed hugely. "Right, that'll do me, I'm off."

"Wait, you can't," pleaded Godfrey, snatching at the darkness and finding Sammy's wet arm. "I'll never make it up that hill four times, not at my age." His voice cracked with real fear. "You can't just leave me!"

Sammy fell back against the cold wet brick. "You mad bastard," he muttered. "You crazy mad bastard." It was not clear for whom the remark was intended. "Just don't get me involved in anything like this again, right."

"Okay, Sam," promised Godfrey wretchedly.

"Kneecaps," breathed Sammy, shaking his head to himself. "Christ, you pick some lovely mates, don't you?"

"He's not . . . " began Godfrey.

Sammy shushed him abruptly.

They listened. The hard clanking clatter of an electric trolley approached, its fat, solid tyres hissing over the wet concrete.

"That's him," said Sammy.

The noise of the trolley grew louder. After a few seconds the splash of light from its single weak headlamp skidded obliviously past them along the ground like some bribed or blinkered scout. Moments later the trolley trundled by, only inches from the black corner in which the two men hid, then it pulled up leaving its towed wheel and tyre laden carriage directly level with them. They watched the driver fixedly through the rear perspex window of his cab. He took a cigarette from a packet and wedged it in a corner of his mouth, then the small bright flare of a match briefly lit the side of his face. That was the signal. The all clear.

A sopping wet jogger plodded inelegantly through the rain towards Halliwell and Worth.

"And he's not even getting paid for it," pointed out Halliwell quietly.

"Must be mental," sniffed Worth. "Stark raving . . . "

"Morning," nodded Halliwell. Stepping aside so the

jogger might squeeze between him and the line of overflow cars from the storage areas parked along the kerbside.

"Morning." The jogger waved a bedraggled but amiable sleeve.

". . . mental," finished Worth fussily.

Behind them they heard the jogger grunt with a suddenly redoubled effort, as though perhaps suspecting that the security guards were really two vicious, night wandering murderers in disguise.

They continued along the narrow tarmac path between the inner perimeter road and the precipitous grassy bank, at that point rising thirty feet to the fence at the top. They were approaching an area unlit by a tall dead lamp post. Darkness seemed to hang from it like black canvas from a tent pole.

"Fred Atkin was right about you," remarked Halliwell.

"That bloke was soaking wet," argued Worth. "He didn't look as though he was having much fun to me."

"It's not a question of *looking* as though you're having fun, is it? It's all about peace and inner tranquillity, like those Guru blokes who kip with their big toes jammed in their ear-holes," bluffed Halliwell.

"You what? It's all about bloody great blisters and inner double pneumonia, more like."

"Personal challenges," countered Halliwell easily. "Pushing yourself to your limits, forging new frontiers . . . exploring strange new worlds . . . boldly going where no man has gone before . . ."

"Just a minute, Mister Intrepid Explorer," interrupted Worth in sudden realisation. "When did you last . . ." He struggled for a while to find a suitable example " . . . negotiate the treacherous rapids of the Upper Limbloodypopo?"

"Did you hear something then?" said Halliwell stopping suddenly. By now they had travelled deeply into the area left unlit by the snuffed light.

"Come on, now, never mind changing the subject," pressed Worth.

"Someone whispering," interrupted Halliwell. "Up there somewhere."

Both men listened, trying to concentrate beyond the

153

constant soft pattering of the rain on their caps. Halliwell could sense his partners uncertainty, as though he suspected or hoped that the whole thing was a joke.

"Nothing," said Worth shortly, blatantly relieved. "Not a dicky bird."

Halliwell waved an arm to quieten him, freezing it in mid-wave as he listened harder against the rain, his eyes fixed on the barely glistening grass half way up the bank.

He heard and saw it at almost the same time. On the periphery of his vision it moved towards him down the bank; extra black against the darkness, whispering little splashes that became louder as it gathered pace.

Crudely Halliwell thumped his arm into Worth's chest knocking him several staggered steps backwards. An instant later the shape bounced heavily on the path in front of them, its momentum almost carrying it over the bonnet of a parked Kama but its lower edge tripped on the top of the wing and it fell back onto the path.

The security guards approached it cautiously, like people forced to approach a wounded and therefore unpredictable animal.

"Wheels," said Halliwell, crouching and running his gloved fingers across the tyre treads and pulling at the thin rope holding them together.

Both men had their backs to the bank now and could not hear the other wheels bowling towards them, like another of the species racing to defend its mate.

"Someone's been trying to pinch them," said Worth uneasily. Neither man found the statement as grossly obvious as they might have done; as only now did the sinister and unnerving probability of black-cloaked human involvement occur to them.

The second set of wheels had taken a course slightly right of perpendicular; approaching the bottom of the bank they struck an obstruction and leapt clear of it.

"They're still up there," realised Halliwell.

At that instant the wheels smashed into the same Kama's roof like a fist into a sheet of tin foil, buckling it with an almighty metallic crack. Halliwell toppled from his crouching position onto his back with the sudden bite of the shock and Worth cringed and froze, pushing his head down tortoise-like into his shoulders as though about to be struck.

It was Worth, with the psychological advantage of withstanding the ordeal on his feet who showed the first outward signs of recomposing himself.

"Fucking hell," he gasped. "That bastard could've killed us!"

Halliwell scrambled indignantly to his feet. The palms of his gloves were wet and embedded with grit. He began to rub them slowly and ineffectually against the sides of his already dripping mackintosh and turned to look along the bank, his face burning now despite the cold rain, his heart thumping as though it filled his entire chest: Forty yards away two figures half scrambled, half fell down the greasy slope.

"Come on," snarled Halliwell. "Let's get the bastards."

Sammy was grateful to reach firm ground at the bottom of the bank. The backs of his trousers clung nastily to his legs and backside from the mud and the soaking grass. He paused for an instant, glancing fearfully back along the footpath; the security guards were barely thirty yards away.

"Over here," he hissed at Godfrey, hard on his shoulder.

They squeezed between two cars and ran across the road to where several hundred more stood in cold, silent ranks.

"Get down!" ordered Sammy, once they had reached the cover of the cars.

"They slipped, Sam, I couldn't hold them, the rope was wet," explained Godfrey pitifully.

Sammy was peering diagonally through two windows. The guards were still coming. "Come on," he said. "And keep your head down."

They set off along the narrow channels, crouched comically like men pretending to be monkeys, turning sharp rights and lefts and rights.

"It's makin' me dizzy, Sam. Where're we goin'?"

"To Walton if you don't shut up," snapped Sammy.

They paused, both men gulping in the cold, wet air. All around them raindrops tapped on cars like a million impatient fingers. Sammy raised his head slowly above the glistening roofs. The guards had reached their point of entry and were exchanging words and pointing. Then one of them cut in among the cars and the other began to stalk back along the perimeter.

"What are we gonna do?" gasped Godfrey. "We could hide under a car," he suggested hopefully.

"And hope they get fed up looking for us and go away by the end of dinner break," rasped Sammy.

"Well can't we run in a straight line for a bit? I'm all dizzy."

"What time is it?"

"Twenty-five to."

"Shit, we've only got ten minutes to get back."

"We could do with a getaway car," put in Godfrey absently.

"Well, fuck me!" breathed Sammy after a moment's thought. "And what are we surrounded by?" Godfrey looked at him uncertainly. "About three fucking million getaway cars, that's what!" explained Sammy joyfully. "Come on, quick!"

They hurried on between the cars, moving in a straight line now at the approximate centre of a giant rectangle, parallel with its longest sides and in the opposite direction to the security guard who was scouting along the perimeter. Some of the cars were parked bumper to bumper and they had to scramble over them, sometimes slipping and cracking knees and shins and elbows. Godfrey was bent more from his exertions now than anything else, his breaths piled on top of each other and rattled in his throat like someone about to die. His posture was akin to that of a miserable, undernourished gorilla.

Suddenly Sammy stopped without warning and Godfrey, blinded by the rain and the tiredness ploughed his shoulder into Sammy's backside and sent him thudding into the side of a car. He turned and swung his fist in aimless temper. "Get down," he mouthed, roughly dragging Godfrey down to below the level of the car's windows.

They squatted silently and still for a few seconds. Some spent rain gurgled down a nearby grid. Sammy's voice was thin and breathless: "Let's see where they are," he whispered.

Both men began to haul themselves up, their finger tips

156

balancing them against the car, their noses close to its cold, wet body. As their eyes reached window level their hearts almost stopped simultaneously because there was a face staring back at them from inside the car, just the width of the glass away. Only because they had no spare breath did they not cry out from the shock.

The window wound down and the face squinted out into the dark and the rain. It was Graeme Leatherbarrow. "Oh it's Sammy," he blinked, with an equal measure of surprise and relief. "Who else is there?" he frowned. "Oh, it's Godfrey. You two just scared the cack out of us," he said without heat.

"Graeme, will you keep your voice down," hissed Sammy.

"You're saturated, the pair of you," went on Graeme, unoffended but dropping his voice compliantly. "You look like a couple of escaped convicts. Come and have a dekko at these two, Em, they're like a couple of escaped convicts."

A second face crammed intimately into the window. It was the runtish, ferret-faced Welsh dessert chef. He peered anxiously out at them like someone summoned to observe the aftermath of a nasty accident.

"This is Emlyn, by the way," introduced Graeme. His cheek brushed easily against Emlyn's. "That one's Sammy, and that one's Godfrey," he pointed.

"Pleased to meet you," said Emlyn coyly.

"The feeling's mutual, I'm sure," returned Godfrey stiffly.

"How do," grunted Sammy absently, lifting his head fractionally over the roof of the car. Neither guard was in sight now — which worried him. They could be anywhere. They might have caught their voices and be sneaking up on them. They might be hiding behind the next car.

"Listen, Graeme, you haven't seen us, right?"

"Cross our hearts," promised Graeme genuinely.

"And I'd stay in there for a while if I were you. Wind the window up and lie low."

"We don't need telling to do that twice," grinned Graeme saucily. Emlyn blushed.

"Come on, bollocks, let's get a move on," urged Sammy to Godfrey. "Oh, and another thing, Graeme," said Sammy. "Make sure Emlyn washes his hands before he makes any more custard."

Graeme laughed, but carefully quiet. "Bye, lads," he waved from the dry side of the closing window. "Good luck."

"Where are we gonna drive to?" asked Godfrey, his question directed squarely at Sammy's backside as they hurried off again at their odd, ape-like angles, now zig-zagging again towards the outer edge of cars.

"Anywhere," answered Sammy. "Anywhere that gets these bastards off our backs."

They arrived at the end of a passage where two, three door Khan's sat; they could have been blue or red or green in colour but both looked black in the artificial light.

"This one," nodded Sammy. A second later he heard a shout from behind him. He squinted back along the tight channel. A security guard was charging towards them, waving and shouting directions to his partner. "Quick, get in!" ordered Sammy. He pulled open the driver's door as far as the close proximity of the next car would allow. Then, for some precious moments there ensued an untidy and uncompromising struggle as both endeavoured to gain entry through the same door.

"The other side, the other side, stupid!" snarled Sammy, elbowing and kicking at his mate.

"No, why me? Why me?" argued Godfrey, fisting and kneeing in return.

"Cos you can't fuckin' drive, loon!"

The realisation stunned Godfrey just long enough for Sammy to push him clear and squeeze a leg and shoulder into the car. "Now get in the other side, quick."

Godfrey conceded and swung the door out of his way, trapping Sammy's windpipe and shin in the process causing a cry of strangulated agony to stagger and die somewhere in the dripping night.

Hundreds of safe yards away the startled jogger was too weary to inject any further urgency into his pace. Soon he would reach the plant's main entrance, therein there would be warmth and good light and a population. He was glad his night's jogging was almost over. He was glad he was not out there with the darkness and the cry of strangulated agony.

158

The keys were in the ignition. Sammy slammed the door and locked it and began to turn the engine. For three seconds it churned but did not fire. Godfrey clambered in through the passenger door. "They're nearly here," he sobbed.

"Lock your door," croaked Sammy. "Come on, start you bitch!"

He glanced in the door mirror, the guard was only a couple of car lengths away. The engine coughed and fired into life. The guard stretched for the door handle. The tyres screeched in surprise. From the corner of his eye Sammy saw the guards straining fingers lunge for the door handle. Then disappear.

"Did he see us?" asked Godfrey fretfully. He sat hunched and twisted in his seat, peering anxiously over the backrest and through the rear window. "Did he get a proper look?"

The engine screamed. Sammy realised that he was still in first gear and crunched clumsily through second and into third, then snapped on the windscreen wipers. "He didn't see us," he said unconvincingly.

They were approaching the end of the storage area now, ahead lay the inner perimeter road.

"Sam," said Godfrey feebly, still staring fixedly through the rear window.

"What," snapped Sammy impatiently.

"They're coming after us."

Sammy looked up to the rear view mirror; they were a hundred yards behind, headlamps blazing like enraged, glaring eyes.

In a few seconds a right-angled turn would be required to get them heading one way or another along the perimeter road. For most of those seconds Sammy gazed into the mirror as though hypnotised. He was alerted to the impending change of direction by a sudden horror stricken grip biting painfully into his thigh.

"We're going too fast!" howled Godfrey.

The turn was almost upon them. Sammy stamped on the brakes, the tyres screeched madly and the hunched Godfrey flew from his seat and smashed his head against the fascia. Sammy spun the steering wheel to the left and the car began to heave and slew sideways, its nearside wheels rearing and spinning a foot above the ground. Then it thumped back onto all fours; and the inner perimeter road stretched ahead of them.

Godfrey scrambled back onto his seat and began to fumble with the seat belt.

"Take that frigger off!" exploded Sammy.

Godfrey was ashen. "I wanna give meself up," he moaned.

The security guard's car was coming up fast, its blazing headlamps pushing their dazzling yellow beams into his face. Sammy slammed the car into gear and accelerated away, constantly glancing up at the mirror, waiting for their pursuers to turn the corner.

"Where are we goin' now, Sam?" murmured Godfrey. "Do we have to go so fast?"

Security Guard Atkin raised his languid head from his *Mayfair* magazine and embarked upon a long and luxurious stretch. He heard a car approaching at speed and turned with unoccupied interest towards the window. He began to yawn as an unlit Khan flew past the lodge. He shook his head wearily and bent his arms into his body like a large ungainly bird folding its wings. Barely five seconds later another Khan flashed by, this one with its lights blazing. He continued shaking his head and complemented it with a few lazily disgusted tuts. "Mad swines," he muttered, and fell back into his magazine.

They were coming up to a sharp right turn, a brief straight then a sharp left as the road edged around a protruding corner of the press shop. The chasing car was back now, its headlamps burning into the mirror.

"Can't we get out and make a run for it?" pleaded Godfrey. "We could go through the press shop and . . ."

"Will you shut up!" snapped Sammy. "And what did you do that to my friggin' leg for. It's hurtin' like fuck now, yer daft bastard."

"Mind this bend!" screamed Godfrey.

"I can see it! I can see it!" shouted Sammy. "And let go of me bleedin' leg, will yer!"

The car screeched and staggered inexpertly around the corner, along the short straight and around the second bend. There was a long straight ahead of them now running the

160

entire length of the press shop. Sammy flicked his eyes up to the mirror; any second the headlamps would be back. He looked again a hundred yards further on. Then a hundred and fifty. Two hundred. There was no sign of them.

"They're not coming," he said quietly, as though to say it any louder would make it untrue.

"What?" asked Godfrey suspiciously.

"They're not coming," repeated Sammy, this time with more confidence. "They should be around the bend by now."

"Oh, hello, men," yawned Atkin. He had discarded his magazine and strewn himself across two chairs in the manner of one of its featured ladies. He yawned again and began to scratch behind his ear. "Still raining, is it?"

Neither man responded. They took off their caps and began to remove their soaking mackintoshes. Halliwell shook his mackintosh accidentally on purpose in the direction of the inquiry.

Atkin sniffed. "Did those two cars pass you before?" he asked conversationally. "They came through here like something from a cops'n'robbers show."

"We know, we know," grunted Halliwell irritably. "Z Victor One's just pissing well ran out of petrol."

Sammy and Godfrey walked back through the press shop. It was a vast and frightening place with every inch of its vastness a tiny but madly exploding cacophony. The presses were as big as houses built in endless streets, and their massively powerful jaws, fed by imitatively mechanical operators, chewed insatiably on sheet metal that they spat out as wings and boot lids and doors.

Sammy and Godfrey were silent through the press shop because they were miserable and wet and they did not have the energy to make themselves heard above the din. It was not until they left it behind and came upon the body assembly area which was still having its lunch break that Sammy said: "It's just as well I've got some overalls to change into. "His discomfort materialised on his face. "My undies are all stuck to my arse."

"I've got this idea," said Godfrey thoughtfully. "About getting Kneecaps off our backs."

"*Our* backs?"

"All right, all right. *My* back. It came to me in a flash when we were in the car."

"You mean while you weren't being hysterical and wanting to give yourself up and clawing chunks out of my leg."

"I don't know why I didn't think of it in the first place. It would have saved all this bother, I suppose."

"You mean you could have got us out of this?" exploded Sammy incredulously. "You put me through all that and you didn't have to!"

"But I hadn't *thought* of it then, had I? It only came to me after I banged my head in the car."

They had reached the trim lines by now. The hooter sounded and the lines around them jumped smartly into action.

"Cover for me, will you?" said Godfrey. "I won't be long." He winked confidently. "I've just got to go and make a phone call."

Chapter Nine

Since pay days had been switched to Tuesdays it was quite unusual for both systems to pull thirty cars an hour on a Thursday night; but tonight Bellend had managed it, which gave rise to some immodest celebration among its foremen, superintendents and managers. The operators were less euphoric.

There were only minutes remaining before lunch break. The lines had been bulging full without a sign of a gap all night and those massed and undisciplined assaults on their cars were turning to sweaty retreats.

Derek Kettle was crouched inside the as yet engineless engine bay of a white Kama, his experienced hands moving swiftly but with little care as they pressed together final loom connections and tightened final bolts on the final car of his stint. He was a half an hour up the line from his work station which meant that, taking the welt into account, it would be almost an hour and a half before he would have to start work on his next car. The thought pleased him and his mouth made the effort of a smile, but it did not take naturally to any form of joyous manifestation and looked only as though it was registering the discomfort of indigestion: For some operators, those who did not read or do crossword puzzles or find safe and secret places to sleep the thought of so much free time did not particularly appeal, especially during a night shift when the hours were slow and somnolent; but with Kettle it was an instinctive thing. The line — like everything else according to his puzzled and puzzling philosophy — was something to be dominated, something to outsmart, to keep one step ahead of. He did not so much regard these aims as a challenge because his dimly belligerent nature was incapable of any such noble aspirations. It was a futile, private battle, more like. A battle that he knew he would never win because the line kept coming; like time or God it had no beginning and it had no end. He had no answer to its grinding perpetuity but he had to fight it and be ultimately beaten by it every day anyway. And that was why he hated it.

"Come on, Derek, dinner time," called Spivak. "They're dealing the cards in a minute." As he strode by he absently thumped the wing of the car with his fist, neither he nor Kettle being aware that the bonnet stay had not been located into its retaining slot but merely rested against the bonnet's leading edge. It began to slip.

Kettle had four more screws to fit, the first became tight after only a couple of turns, why, he neither knew nor cared, he left it projecting a half an inch from the metal panel and fixed the second onto his screwdriver. The thin stay slipped a fraction further.

At the stolen table Sammy and Harry Melrose attacked bags of steaming canteen chips, engrossed in their greasy succulence, while Steep and Godfrey chewed without relish on bland homemade sandwiches. Godfrey sniffed miserably between bites in acknowledgement of his newly acquired cold.

"My youngest lad was breaking his heart crying when I got home this morning," said Harry Melrose through a mouthful of four or five chips. "His hermit crabs had had a punch-up during the night and they'd all bitten each other's legs off. They only had about three left between nine of them."

"I wonder what started it," pondered Sammy, grinning broadly.

"Could have been anything," shrugged Steep. "Booze, football, politics, lady hermit crabs."

"We had a bit of bother around our way as well yesterday morning," put in Godfrey, only half listening. He chewed on his sandwich with as much apparent savour as a cow with its cud. "One of our local villains had his house raided by the police — something about having two million knocked-

164

off cigarettes in his garden shed, I believe."

"Somebody must have had it in for him," said Steep.

"Half of our district had it in for him for one reason or another. And our coppers have been after him for years, they'll put him away now for definite."

"Let's hope so. Otherwise someone's going to be in the shit, all right," sniffed Sammy. "Right up to their knee-caps in it."

"He used to paint their shells," went on Melrose doggedly. "Four red and four blue. He was trying to train them to play football with a Maltesa so he could have matches between Liverpool and Everton."

"That's only eight," pointed out Steep. "What was the other one, ballboy?"

"Referee," corrected Melrose. "He used to paint that one black and spend ages explaining offsides and indirect free kicks to it."

"Looks like he's going to have to delve into the transfer market, then," said Sammy.

"He'll be lucky," said Steep doubtfully. "You can't get your hands on a quality mid-field hermit crab for love nor money, these days."

"Frogs," declared Godfrey, just catching some sagging snot and snatching it back up his nostril with a short, sharp sniff. The others looked to him in puzzlement. "We used to have frogs when I was a lad," he explained.

"What, for playing football?" inquired Melrose.

"No, we used to shove straws up their arses and blow their guts out of their mouths."

"Aye aye, Godfrey," complained Steep mildly. "I'm trying to eat my butties, here."

Godfrey was about to speak again but his face was suddenly seized by a violently exploding sneeze that sent a fine spray of mucus jetting across the table. Steep and Melrose snatched their respective meals away from the area of settling fallout and Sammy began flapping his arms frantically over his chips. "Why didn't you stay off with that, stupid," he snapped.

"It's only a cold," countered Godfrey easily. He dabbed his tender red nostrils with a damp, grey handkerchief.

165

"Anyone who stays off work with a cold must have something wrong with them," he went on casually. "If it turns into pneumonia, I'll think about it."

"What about all these bleeding germs you're spreading," complained Sammy, still defensively flapping over his chips. "We might all have foot and bleeding mouth disease by then, mightn't we, Sproaty."

Sproat dumped his toolbox and trailing air line near the table. He seemed lost in some secret but apparently wonderful reverie. He turned towards them and there were tears brimming in his dull eyes; tears of a rapture which could not be contained in laughter.

"What's wrong with you?" frowned Sammy.

"Derek Kettle," sobbed Sproat joyously. "I was just walking past his car and he said something about fancying a kip for the next couple of hours, next thing the bonnet went fuck off, right on top of his head!"

They made a ragged assembly, like unmanaged mourners around the snow white car in which the senseless Kettle slumped. Somebody had opened the bonnet and fastened it securely so that everyone could have a look at him but nobody had ventured to touch him or move him. There was some joking and sniggering but much of it was nervous because nobody was absolutely certain as to whether or not he was dead. Around them the plant had adopted the appropriate graveyard silence that it always did with the coming of lunch break and the initial crowds had thinned and drifted quickly, for although such incidents proved extremely popular during working hours most operators were not prepared to allow their morbid fascinations to encroach into time for which they were not being paid.

"Shouldn't somebody go and give him a poke or something?" wondered Steep. "See if he groans or something."

Sammy sucked in through his teeth and shook his head. "Poking him is a job for a trained medical finger. I've phoned the medical centre and Rex is on his way up. All we can do now is wait," he concluded with mock drama.

"Funny thing," said Steep absently. "I've never seen one

single dead person in real life, if you see what I mean. Every single person I've ever seen has had all their vital bits and pieces working away inside them. All those millions of hearts and lungs and brains all doing their bit."

Sammy nudged Steep and nodded furtively towards Sproat who was relating his eye-witness report to Fishwick the barber. Steep took the point. "Well, all those hearts and lungs, anyway," he conceded. "But, I mean, when you consider how complicated it all is, and how it all keeps going for three score years and ten. It just makes you think, that's all."

"Isn't nature wonderful," recited Sammy. Steep nudged him and nodded furtively towards Sproat who was still relating his eye-witness report to Fishwick who now seemed to be trying to edge away from him in the direction of the canteen. Sammy shrugged. "Even nature can make a cock-up now and again," he admitted.

"And then there are all those dead people," went on Steep. "Thousands more of them every day and I've never seen a single one of them. It's as if they just vanish, once they've snuffed it."

"They do," confirmed Sammy. "Into little urns and holes in the ground."

"I don't mean like that. It's just funny, that's all."

"All right, all right, stand back now," came McBean's officious, organising voice from behind them. They turned, regarding him as they might have regarded a loud mouthed bore at a quiet party. "Where is he? Let's have a look at him."

Kettle was slumped forward in the engine bay, his shoulder resting against one side, his forehead flat against the bulkhead which had made it difficult for the operators to see if he was still breathing. His toolbox had toppled to the ground and spilled hundreds of screws and washers and little black plastic clips; McBean kicked them from under his feet as he approached Kettle and leaned across the opposite wing, bending down and looking up close to Kettle's face as though trying to identify who it was. Making no indication as to whether the exercise had been of any value he straightened and moved away. "Anybody see what happened?" he asked around.

"I did, Rex," piped Sproat, breaking off from his conversation with Fishwick who grasped the opportunity and hurried away towards the canteen. McBean closed his eyes for two regretful seconds, as if sorry he had asked.

"The bonnet bumped his crust," testified Sproat keenly. He held his hands out at a stiff arms length and slapped his palms together like a clapperboard. "Just like that."

The whirr of the small electric ambulance came into earshot. McBean looked blatantly relieved. "All right, make room for the nurses now. Let them get at him."

"I hope it's the friendly one with the glorious knockers," commented Steep quietly. "I could make room for her any time."

"Yeah," nodded Sammy. "I wouldn't mind tearing the back out of that one myself."

Steep pulled a face. "My God, you've got a lovely turn of phrase, you have, I must say."

The miniature open ambulance stopped as close as the barrier of mechanical and constructional metalware that ran the length of the line would allow. The two nurses hopped out purposefully, one of them fetching a full sized stretcher from the back, and headed towards the small crowd. They were indeed the same two that Steep had visited earlier in the week and immediately he could sense that suddenly tensed and sharpened atmosphere that even a plain woman kindles upon entering an all male territory: It was the older one who carried the stretcher. She placed it next to the car while the younger one spoke briefly to McBean. Both nurses then examined the unconscious Kettle, reaching for his hand and carefully touching parts of his head whilst conferring quietly with each other.

Each assembled eye ran lecherously over the younger nurse's whispering white uniform. At one point she stretched across the car so that her big breasts pressed against the wing and her uniform tightened around the marvellous endless sweep of her backside and the smooth sturdy trunks of her thighs. The sparking of obscene thoughts was almost audible.

They enlisted McBean's assistance and cautiously eased the light-weight operator from the car's yawning white

168

mouth, then arranged him fussily on the nearby stretcher. He lay lifeless and pale. It seemed strange, almost unnatural to see him so quiescent, so peaceful. Everyone imagined that even in a state of deepest unconsciousness he should at least growl or snarl occasionally.

"He's dead. I bet you he's dead," affirmed Spivak.

"No he's not," countered Melrose. "Look, his belly's going up and down."

For a moment they each closely studied the stricken operator's small paunch of a stomach. "No, I can't see anything," insisted Spivak as though convinced that the scrutiny had no point.

"Yes, look, there it goes!" declared Sammy. "Look. Up . . . down . . . up."

"He's right, I can see it too," confirmed Steep.

Spivak scowled both claims away. "All right then," he postulated cunningly. "If he's still alive, how come he isn't arguing with anyone?"

They could not find an answer.

The nurses declined McBean's offer of further assistance and between them hoisted the sagging stretcher and, long-armed, made off with quick, heavy steps towards the ambulance.

"How is he, love?" inquired Sammy of the younger nurse who was the trailing member of the trio.

"He'll be all right," she puffed good-naturedly. "He's got a lovely big lump on his head, though."

"I reckon he was conning us," accused Sproat maliciously. They sat around the stolen table, Spivak was dealing the cards. Sproat went on: "It's just the sort of trick that bastard would pull to get off the job."

"The bonnet must have hit him," reasoned Godfrey. "The nurse said he had a lump on his head."

"Oh, it hit him all right, I *saw* that. But it doesn't mean he was unconscious, does it?" persisted Sproat. "Think of how much compo he'll get if he says it knocked him out."

"Oh, so that's it, is it?" realised Sammy. "You're only crying because you're his witness and he hasn't cut you in

169

for your ten per cent."

"Bollocks," denied Sproat.

"He'll get a few bob for that," surmised Godfrey.

"He can stick his ten per cent, the swindling bastard," growled Sproat.

"You can't fool trained medical minds," said Sammy easily. "They'd know if he was trying to con them."

"What, that lot!" scoffed Sproat. "What about that bloke from the waxing booths who went down there saying he had pains in his chest and they gave him some Milk of Magnesia and told him it was indigestion. He snuffed it the next day from a fucking heart attack!"

"A mistake anyone could have made," sniffed Sammy. "Anyway, if anyone's got a right to moan it's me. *I'm* the one who's got to take over from the silly bleeder." Sammy frowned at his own statement, realising for the first time that he would indeed have to fill Kettle's vacated position. "Where is the ugly, bollock-brained gobshite's first car, anyway?" he scowled.

"An hour and a half away," said Sproat. "*And* all his stock's made up," he added, brightening visibly at the thought of his workmate's wasted efforts which now fell into the hands of his replacement.

Silently Sammy picked up and began to fan out his cards. "Good old Derek," he remarked quietly. "I do hope he's not too badly hurt."

"What're you making, Spiv?" inquired Steep. He had just finished for the shift with half an hour of it remaining. His hands were scrubbed clean and still stung from where the soap had wriggled into the tiny bloodless cuts.

Spivak had been finished some time longer and was seated at the stolen table absorbed in fashioning a familiar if boastfully oversized sculpture from a large lump of grey sealant. The sealant was a good medium for modelling because it had the approximate consistency of Plasticine and his thinly skilless but extravagantly working fingers had pulled and stretched it into its crude but recognisable form. The tip of his tongue poked with childish concentration from a

170

corner of his mouth.

"It's a big dick," he replied simply, without looking up. "Can't you tell?"

"Well I thought it was, but I didn't like to say." Steep propped his chin on his palms and watched for a few moments in puzzled fascination. "What's it for?" he eventually asked.

"It's a surprise."

"I'm sure it will be for somebody."

Spivak looked up and smiled in that madly polite way of his across the table. "Now, if you'll excuse me," he said as though he was about to leave. "I've just got to organise my testicles."

"What're you making, Spiv?" inquired Sammy some minutes later, then without waiting for a response: "What's he making, Albie?"

"Guess."

"It looks like a big dick."

"Wrong," said Steep. "It's a fully working scale model of the Flying Scotsman."

Spivak held up the sculptured member, now fully equipped with a set of roughly formed and equally ambitious testicles, between two fingers and carefully lowered it onto the fulcrum finger of his other hand, sliding it minutely back and forth and studying each movement with a scientific squint until the whole assembly balanced perfectly. This accomplished he took one end of a long length of thick string and tied it firmly about the mentally noted point, then hoisted it for display on a short length above the table, smiling with the jaunty achievement of an angler who had just hooked a large fish. "How's that, then?" he beamed proudly. The suspended phallus spun slowly to face them, as though it too was eager for their opinions.

"Very nice," blinked Sammy. "Isn't it Albie?"

"A belter," agreed Steep. "But what's it *for*?"

"I'm going to have a wizard wheeze," announced Spivak, narrowing his eyes mysteriously. With that he stood up and looked carefully all about him. Then he tied his weighty creation around his neck so that it hung like some powerful pagan fertility symbol in the middle of his narrow chest and, surprisingly, began a clambering assault on the overhead

171

storage racks' metalwork supports. He was three or four feet off the ground when he paused and leaned in towards their bemused expressions. "Give me a shout when the tarts from the soft trim show up," he grinned, hanging long armed like an impish chimp.

Steep and Sammy looked at each other with mirrored, open faces. Spivak resumed his ascent and quickly disappeared above them.

Shortly they heard some ferocious warning snorts then almost instantly subsiding in the wake of a gale of dirty laughter from the suddenly disturbed Sproat at rest in his private, padded pallet.

"He's mad, of course," stated Steep, adopting the professionally aggrieved and ominous tones of a psychiatrist who had been forced to allow a blatantly lunatic patient back onto the streets.

"Definitely coming in on three engines," concurred Sammy.

"Mind you," pondered Steep. "If it wasn't for the likes of him and the Phantom Sprinkler Fiend, things would get pretty boring around here."

They appeared as four tiny but brightly bundled figures at the far end of the line. They were always punctual and Sammy had confidently forecast their imminent arrival less than a minute earlier.

Most operators had comfortably finished now with only ten minutes of the shift remaining. Steep and Sammy had been joined by Harry Melrose, Godfrey and Henry Chong who had unusually fallen asleep but the act was more difficult to detect with him because his narrow oriental eyes were good camouflage, and provided he kept himself reasonably upright and did not snore he could easily get away with it.

The four women faced the long and largely unacknowledged traipse along the lines each working morning because the soft trim sewing room — where they stitched together the fabric seat coverings — was situated in a detached building on the opposite side of the plant from where the corporation bus deposited them: Their presence brought none of

172

the rowdy reactions from the operators in the way that some of their fresher, more comely colleagues would have done because they were dry women, each lost to the disruptions of a neglected middle-age. They proceeded in a solid line abreast, taking short, fussy biting steps like unsynchronised soldiers with bad feet, their heads drawn magnetically into a blunt triangle of wonted gossip.

"They're on their way, Spiv," reported Sammy up towards the racks.

"They're on their way, Spiv," repeated Sproat in the first tier, like a ship's officer repeating an order from a superior. "Prepare to dangle, ha ha ha ha."

"Preparing to dangle," responded Spivak, fainter in the top tier.

Melrose and Godfrey frowned but grinned expectantly. They had been told that Spivak was up to *something* but had resisted a fuller brief in the interests of spontaneity and dramatic tension.

"I think this might get fairly embarrassing," said Steep worriedly. "In fact, I don't think I'll be able to watch."

"Shut up, will you," moaned Godfrey without heat. "You'll spoil it."

"How far away are they?" asked Steep. He held his hands over his eyes like that particular wise monkey. He half laughed, half groaned: "I don't want to watch. Tell me when it's all over." Then peeped compulsively through his fingers.

"Fifty yards and closing," said Sammy, his observation hidden in a stretching leaning yawn. "Forty-five . . . Forty." Sammy grinned teasingly at Steep's apprehension. Godfrey and Melrose began to fidget excitedly. "Thirty-five, thirty-four . . ."

"All right, bleeding mission control," grumbled Steep. "We don't need a count-down." He dragged his fingers away from his eyes and dug them fretfully into his cheeks. "I mean, he might get the sack if any of them complain."

"He got away with duffing up his foreman, didn't he?" reminded Sammy. "If he can get away with that, what harm can a little bit of . . . er."

"Flashing by proxy?" suggested Steep.

"Yeah, what harm can a little bit of that do? And anyway,

he doesn't give a shite. He's mad, remember?"

"A little bit of *what?* Shut up, will you," giggled Godfrey.

"Dangle at will!" came Sproat's suddenly barked overhead command.

"Dangling commenced!" responded Spivak, fainter and higher.

All eyes swivelled upwards. They stared in speechless wonderment as though some strange alien spacecraft was about to descend on them. What actually descended on them looked considerably more strange, even than that. Spivak had slung the freakish grey genitalia across the back of one of the high neon lights in the middle of the aisle and now it slid into view, lowering itself smoothly and slowly on its thick coarse string, the thick elephantine trunk of its penis, unwaveringly horizontal due to the substantial weight of its counterbalancing testicles, suggested an obscene yet almost balletic poise. Godfrey and Melrose swore in quiet, grinning harmony. Godfrey nudged Henry Chong awake. The man from Hong Kong opened his eyes without annoyance and blinked placidly at the grinning Godfrey. "Look at that, Henry," he enthused.

Henry Chong looked. Not a trace of surprise touched the natural inscrutability of his round cinnamon face. He returned to his previous position of sleep and shrugged. "Big gley cock hanging flom loof. You see one, you see them all."

The four women did not notice the hanging thing for some time, intent as they were on their gossip. They were hardly half a dozen paces away before one of them screamed, and then not full-bloodedly so, more in the manner of a woman frightened by a surprise mouse or spider. In the communal, contagious way of women the others each gave little panicked jumps and released small emulative squeals and made instinctive grabs at their chests. The frightening thing hung motionless, like the head of some angry, rearing cobra staring squarely, mesmerically into their faces. They stared back for some seconds, their faces clouded with looks of vague familiarity, as though attempting to recall where they had seen such a device before.

The audience at the stolen table grinned and smothered

174

laughter behind masking hands. Other operators stopped and watched, sniggering and pointing with distant enjoyment. Steep's face burnt red hot with embarrassment; his head turned away but his eyes pulled it irresistibly back towards the surreal tableau. Above him he could hear Sproat choking himself on his own gagged, hysterical laughter.

It was the woman who was taller and thinner than the others who first broke free of the dangling organ's apparently hypnotic spell. She separated dynamically from the others and began a wide, wary semi-circle, keeping a cautiously distanced eye locked on it as she edged by.

Somehow Spivak managed to manoeuvre the suspending string so that the thing spun and followed her as she went, its own crudely cut vertical eye regarding her in turn with a quite vivid menace.

A second woman, short and squat with jowls like a bulldog, seeing the audience of smirking operators became promptly, primly tight-lipped and marched off along the same extensive arc as her friend. The remaining two stopped to study the phallus like unhopeful physicians. They seemed less concerned by, or less aware of the operators and the looks of miscalculated puzzlement that were spreading among them. Desperately Spivak joggled it about so that it bobbed and bounced for attention in front of them.

"Like I was saying, Doris," confided one to the other in the secret way of women. "My Ron's done his best since my operation, God love him."

Doris understood as only another woman who is both a confidante and a gossip could about such things. She nodded her scarfed head, quietly sympathetic.

"But I'm telling you, Doris. Even *that* thing wouldn't touch the sides now."

Doris shook her head with a minutely sombre movement and mouthed some silent tuts. But her friend sighed and smiled as though recalling a good joke and suddenly resumed her journey, avoiding the great hanging cock but without the exaggerated detours of the others. Spivak's joggling had loosened its string and lost its balance and now it took on a forlorn and impotent droop. Doris trotted after her friend like a dog expecting a large juicy bone.

"Sometimes he makes me laugh, though," said Doris' friend still smiling. "Sometimes he says its like waving a Woodbine about in the bleeding Mersey Tunnel."

Chapter Ten

Sloan's telephone was ringing dully through his front door as he arrived home. He fumbled his key into the lock and turned it, then hurried to the telephone on the small table in the hall.

"Hello, 2424."

"Hello, Nic."

It was Helen. The sound of her voice drove a sudden shock through his stomach. At once he was nervous and apprehensive and excited and hollow down to his deepest insides.

"Hello, Helen," he said brightly. He found himself shaking. "How are you?"

"I'm fine, Nic. You?"

"Fine, fine."

"Listen, Nic." He could tell she was trying to be deliberately distant. "My sewing machine is still down there. Is it okay if I come and collect it?"

"Sewing machine? Oh, yes, it's in the spare room. Come over whenever you like."

"It's kid sister's birthday in a fortnight, twenty-one, would you believe. She wants me to create something devastating for her party."

"I'll send her something. Still breaking hearts, is she?"

"New one's daily, by all accounts."

He wanted to say something about them being two of a kind, but knew she would think he was feeling sorry for himself, which he was.

"How's the Ferrari?" he asked.

"Fine."

"And Douglas?"

"Fine, both fine."

"Good, good. What time can I expect you, then?"

"Nic. You don't mind me calling round, do you?"

He made to speak but she interrupted him. "You know I'll know if you're telling fibs."

"Of course I don't mind. Don't be daft. What time?"

"In an hour. About six if that's okay."

"Fine. Six it is. I'll look forward to it."

"Nic."

"Yes, love?"

"Don't look forward to it. Please."

He heard a car pull up outside shortly after six. He moved to the window. She was driving Douglas' Ferrari. She climbed out from its lean low body into the cool drab evening, her shoulder length auburn hair and golden brown tanned skin glowing in warm exotic contrast against the car and her loose white sleeveless dress. He made for the door, then stopped himself. Better to let her ring the bell, he thought. Don't appear too eager. But what did it matter? She had left him and she did not love him anymore. Now she loved something in sanitaryware called Douglas. She was here to collect a sewing machine, that was all. But she was here, that was the main thing. Surely it was worth a try. What did he have to lose? The thoughts collided inside his head like reckless dodgems. He felt confused, uncertain, almost dazed. The doorbell rang.

"Hi," she smiled. It was not her special smile. Not the smile she had once reserved for him. Not the smile with her eyes that were the deepest brown he had ever seen. It was a polite but insignificant smile, the kind she might give to a tradesman or a shop assistant.

"Hello. Don't stand there, come on in."

He closed the door behind her. He felt somehow sordid and grubby.

"You're looking well. Been away?" he asked.

"Hawaii," she said. "We got back last weekend."

Immediately he sensed the point of a wedge of silence beginning to force its way between them.

178

"You always did suit a tan," he managed. She smiled, slightly uneasily, he thought, at the compliment. "Remember the way I used to turn as red as a lobster?" He recalled one year in the Seychelles and how they had laughed, him in wonderful agony, at his blistered, fiery crimson stiffness and how it had incapacitated him and made him walk like a decrepit Frankenstein's monster. He recalled how she had gently massaged his tender burning body with cool, soothing creams. And how he had giggled with the ticklish pain each time she set about a different peeling part of him. He recalled how happy they had been: Now, with her standing there as though she were waiting for a bus it was hard to believe that there was ever such fun and such ingenuous love between them. It seemed to have happened to him in another life, which in a way, it had.

"Douglas turns as brown as a berry." Helen went on. "We stopped off and spent a couple of days at Disneyland on the way home. That was amazing. We could have done with a month to get round it all."

She was speaking to him as though he were a queueing casual acquaintance waiting for the same bus.

"Did you meet Mickey Mouse?"

"Oh, yes," she smiled stiffly. "And Donald Duck and Pluto. We shook hands with all of them. And Douglas got a kiss from Snow White."

"Have you ever noticed the way Mickey Mouse's ears are always perfectly round no matter what angle you see them from?" he asked in an effort to be conversational.

She frowned. "Can't say I have to be honest."

"Strictly speaking he's got cannon balls for ears."

She laughed thinly, then said: "No, he definitely had normal mouse-type ears when I met him."

"I expect he's paid to have them fixed."

Their smiles strained uncomfortably at each other. Then she raised a slender brown arm to her mouth and gave a little dry cough and looked expectantly away as though hoping she had caught the sound of an approaching bus.

For the first time he noticed that she was not wearing her wedding ring. Unreasonably he felt a stab of hurt cut deep inside him, turning quickly to an emptiness he had not

179

known since the early days.

"Does Douglas know you're in his car?" he found himself asking.

"Of course he does," she replied without heat. She was still being distinctly cool towards him, but she played along with the patter. "He's had me included in his insurance. Anyway, I'm a *good* driver."

"Good driver," he repeated. "I wouldn't let *Fangio* within fifty yards of it if it were mine."

"Well, Douglas is like that," she said simply.

They fell uncomfortably silent. Unspoken and unconfirmed inferences raced like poisoned gossip from one to the other. He wondered whether he should blunder his way through some sort of apology and was grateful when she caused the opportunity for him to do so to pass.

"He's in Harrogate until Sunday," she said finally. "Some seminar thing."

His heart surged and he realised that they were still standing in the hall. "What am I doing keeping you standing out here," he said with the sudden apologetic hospitality of a previously remiss host. "Come on through."

She followed him, reluctantly, he thought, into the lounge. They stood, six feet apart, like strangers both to each other and to the room that they had once joyfully furnished and decorated and lived in together.

"Take a seat," he offered. "Can I get you something." He was beginning to notice a certain uneasiness edging into his voice.

"Oh, I don't want to be a nuisance," she said politely. "Really, Nic, if you could just get the machine, I'll be off."

"It's no trouble," he assured her. "Actually I haven't had dinner yet if you . . . " He knew that was a mistake.

"No thanks, Nic," she said firmly. "I don't think that would be a good idea."

"Perhaps you're right," he conceded. "It's only fish fingers."

The quip fell flat between them. For some moments they stared awkwardly at the same cushion on the same armchair. He considered another apology but he knew that it would only serve to demonstrate the desperate inadequateness he felt. It was not the time for a feeble apology. He suddenly sensed he had reached a point of no return. Something forthright was called for. Something unequivocal. His heart thumped as though it were trying to force its way through his chest. He turned his eyes up from the cushion and into hers, so soft and warm even when they were trying not to be. His mouth was as dry as dust and he had to swallow hard before he spoke.

"Right, the sewing machine," he said. "I'll just go upstairs and get it."

"You'd think they'd have emptied the ashtray, wouldn't you?" complained Daffy in her ineffectual way.

"You'd think the tight-fisted swines would have put a cupful of petrol in the tank, as well," grumbled Steep, glancing at the appropriate gauge.

"Oh, haven't we got any petrol. Which one's the petrol thing?"

"The one pointing to the little red square with its tongue hanging out. Now if you'd like to get your big head out of the way I might be able to see where we're going."

"We'd better get some at the next garage," advised Daffy solicitously.

"Good idea."

"It's quite quiet, isn't it," observed Daffy after a while.

"That's because the engine fell out half a mile ago."

She laughed and turned to the window. "Can we go somewhere nice over the weekend?" she asked, still looking out at the lifeless early evening and the flow of dumb, drab council houses.

"This weekend?" he queried. "After a week of nights. You know I'll be like death warmed up."

"Well, when you're on days, then?"

"Okay, when I'm on days, then."

"Promise?"

"Promise," he promised. "If the weather's nice," he added, pushing his tongue into his cheek and glancing at her askance.

"Oh, don't be mean. We could go to the countryside," she suggested as though there was a specific place so named.

"It would be best to take it for a good run before the guarantee runs out. So we've only got fourteen days. That's not much of a guarantee, is it?"

"It's not much of a car," pointed out Steep.

"It's a nice car," she pouted, running her fingers through the beige seat cover's flattened woolly pile. "It's better than a great big Maserati, any day. And look how much we've saved compared with the ones in the showroom."

"It's not much of a bird puller, though," he said deliberately, because she was starting to irritate him and because she had said: 'Look how much *we've* saved.'

She made a face and turned towards him. "It's pulled me," she said, taking his remark as a joke.

A half formulated reply came to him, the words 'two old bangers together' being its nucleus. But he considered such a response to be excessively unkind and he did not pursue its construction any further. Instead he said: "If I'd come away with a second-hand pogo stick it would have pulled you. It's just as well they're not in vogue with nuns at the moment."

She made her face of laboured amusement. Then said thoughtfully: "We've never been anywhere really nice together, have we?"

"We went to Rhyl for the day last year," he said, being deliberately obtuse.

"I mean on our own," she pressed. "Not with Auntie Aggie and Mrs Wilks trailing along."

"Trailing along!" he exclaimed. "I was knackered after that day out with those two. They made a mob of Hell's Angels look like a bunch of fairies! Remember that big cylinder thing that spun round and made you stick to the wall and then the floor dropped away and left you hanging there. I wouldn't go on it because it looked scary. But we couldn't get them *off*."

"Now we've got a car we can go to nice places on our own."

"*We've* got a car?" he questioned. "I didn't see you making much of a financial contribution towards its purchase." He sounded heavily pompous, even to himself. He had not really meant to say it but she was still irritating

182

him.

"I'll pay for your petrol," she offered.

He pressed his lips into a tight contrite smile and turned to her briefly. "No, that's all right," he said. "We'll go somewhere nice soon. On our own."

"And you don't have to do all the driving if you don't want to," she said in her predictably probing way.

He knew that silence was his only defence, inadequate and easily breachable though it was.

"Albie," she continued after a pause of some calculating seconds.

"No," he said without conviction, instantly recognising the tone.

She pressed on regardless. "When are you going to give me my first lesson?"

He felt himself physically shrivelling in his seat. "Give me a chance to get the thing home first!" he protested, hoping but doubting that she would leave it at that. "Anyway, we haven't got any L plates," he remembered gratefully.

"Well when we've got some L plates will you?"

"Yes, all right," he muttered.

As though given her cue she dipped into her bag and pulled out two new cellophane wrapped L plates. She held them either side of her head, in the manner of an ice-skating judge displaying her marks. Steep glanced miserably at them, and at her smug and smirking expression. Nonchalantly disgusted he changed gear but his foot slipped off the clutch and the gearbox screeched in protest.

Daffy began to giggle. "Failed!" she proclaimed triumphantly.

He listened as the Ferrari's engine fired and moved away, its rich, deep burble fading down the road. He sat on the edge of an armchair, his hands cupped over his nose and mouth like an oxygen mask. The room around him was desolate, its contents strangely cold and sombre. She had not even let him carry the heavy sewing machine out to the car for her, he reflected. She had just left him on the doorstep and said: "Bye," as though he were a tradesman or a shop assistant and gone back to Douglas' house, where the rooms would be sunny and bright and blithe.

His stomach grumbled rudely. He had not eaten but had no appetite. He pulled his fingers over his nose and mouth and stopped them below his lower lip, working the tips against the stubble on his chin. The evening sprayed its thinning light more sparingly now about the room. Early shadows formed. In an hour or so they would grow to fill the room with a great hanging emptiness. How appropriate.

He could get drunk, he considered. Get pissed out of his head and see if that made any difference. He went to the drinks cabinet and took out a glass and an unopened bottle of Teacher's.

It never took him to tears or anger or lust or any of the other normally shuttered emotional outposts to which others journey with drink. It just softened everything inside his head, made things gradually more hazy until he could no longer make them out and they became unrecognisable for what they were. Spirit induced drunkenness always came quickly to him; along with a snug, woolly blandness, frequent snorts of flatulence, and a ferocious appetite.

He was in the kitchen, aproned and pedantically busy among bubbling pots and spiced, steamy smells. A whole, fresh salmon lay at his mercy on the worktop, its dead eye staring pathetically up at him.

"Aw, don't look at me like that," he said with a conciliatory wrinkling of his nose. "It wasn't me who swiped you from your peaceful little river, you know. I bet you were just swimming along minding your own business, thinking what a nice day you were having when you saw this little worm wriggling about and thought, 'yum yum, that looks like a tasty morsel', so you stroll over to it and take a bite and, whoosh! Next minute you're snatched out of the water into an alien ambience and some bastard's battering your head in on a big stone. And what are you thinking by this time? I'll tell you what you're thinking. You're thinking, 'well fuck me, some days life can be really shit'."

The doorbell rang. He made to answer it, then stopped to tear a paper towel from the roll. He folded it and placed it solemnly over the salmon's head. The doorbell rang again, a long, impatient burst.

"Excuse me," he said to the salmon, wiping his hands on his shiny plastic Snoopy apron, then lifting the towel with a diffident forefinger and thumb and peeking comically at it. "Someone is ringing the doorbell."

It was a tattily dressed man, almost as tall as himself but broader and stronger looking. His face was gaunt and unshaven and his eyes were instantly, instinctively recognisable as those of a fellow drunkard.

For several seconds they stood swapping silent expressions of puzzlement and drunken pouts and swaying like twin skyscrapers in a hurricane.

"Did you want something?" asked Sloan eventually. "Only I'm about to prepare a cruelly bludgeoned dead salmon for dinner."

The man raised his left hand to his narrow forehead and dug his fingers hard into the skin, dragging them across and back as though relieving a slow deep itch. Sloan noticed that all his fingernails were grimy and chewed in half and he winced and drew back from their ugliness.

"Your name Sloan?" the man finally questioned. His voice was thick and blunt and had Sloan been sober he would have recalled where he had heard it before, and been frightened again by its menacing tone.

"That is correct. Nicholas Ronald Louis, to be exact." He leaned secretively towards the man, their strong breaths collided like two hot spiced winds. "But I'd rather not discuss that, if you don't mind."

"Don't suppose you remember me, do you?"

Sloan frowned a comical drunken frown. There *was* something familiar about him, but it was only the vaguest of vague recollections. "Do you want to give me a clue?" suggested Sloan with a dim smile.

The man fumbled an empty green wine bottle from a pocket and held it like a club by its neck.

"You're my wine merchant?" guessed Sloan.

"Name's Miggins." Suddenly, curiously, he was snarling. His upper lip tightened, baring broken yellow teeth, and his drunken eyes became narrow and malicious.

Sloan's face crumpled again into its obtuse frown. Then, in one blurred movement the bottle smashed against the wall and its vicious jagged neck lunged at his face.

Although he was slow to react, Miggins' aim had not been accurate and the razored glass only caught the side of his cheek, just below his eye. Immediately he felt a warm dampness begin to spread down his face.

With his lunge, Miggins half tripped over the doorstep. Sloan slammed the door against him, pinning him somewhere about his middle and holding him there. Their faces were barely a foot apart; Sloan's held nothing but stupid shock; but Miggins' was a crazed wild animal, spitting and snarling. And then he got an arm through and grabbed at Sloan's forearm. He managed to shake him off but in doing so allowed Miggins to push open the door. Sloan found himself retreating into the lounge. There was nowhere else to go except up the stairs which seemed instinctively inappropriate, or the kitchen, and even in his state of drunken confusion he knew that a kitchen full of boiling pots was no place to be trapped with a madman.

There was no electric light on in there and the shadows were older and darker, but enough evening light remained to see about the room quite clearly. Miggins ploughed in after him, sending the door straining against its hinges and springing shut. He still held his broken bottle and he blundered forward, his arm outstretched like an inept, charging cavalryman. Sloan sidestepped him and swung a fist that caught the side of Miggins' head, just behind the ear. Sloan's knuckles cracked painfully but the blow and the weight of his attacker's momentum was sufficient to fell Miggins and he flew across a long low, glass topped table and thumped heavily onto the couch.

For the first time Sloan had split seconds to take in what was happening. He was in his own lounge, dripping blood from a gash in his cheek and fighting with a man who apparently seemed bent on ripping the rest of his face apart with a broken bottle. Or was he? Was it all a nightmare? Had Helen really gone?

In a rage the sprawled Miggins kicked a wild boot at the table. He connected with the underside of the glass top and it gave a loud fracturing crack and then spectacularly erupted like a glacier being dynamited from inside. The shards and fragments flew about the room and before they had all landed Miggins was up again. He had dropped his broken bottle and came at Sloan with his fists, pounding like pistons against Sloan's shoulders and protective forearms. He backed away, pieces of glass snapping and grinding beneath his feet until the knob on the door of the drinks cabinet jabbed into his back like a traitor's gun.

The punches kept coming, his arms were aching and tired from them, and there were brutish kicks as well, sharp and stinging about his shins and knees. Behind his shielding, battered arms he noticed steady drips of blood from his face bouncing and skidding off his shiny plastic apron. He felt his strength being drawn from him with each new blow and each new drip. He had to do something. He was sure his legs were about to give. He had to break out.

He chose to run directly at Miggins, head down like a rugby player going into a tackle. It must have been the suddenness and the surprising force of the run that broke through Miggins' attack; then the top of Sloan's head smashed into Miggins' face. He felt the features, the nose, the mouth and teeth giving under the impact. Both men crashed to the floor, they seemed to have a dozen limbs between the two of them now, all flailing and lashing like blind spiders.

Sloan's face fell flat against the carpet and from nowhere his mind snatched and momentarily held a memory of how Helen had laughed when he told her in the shop that they simply had to have that carpet because the colour matched her eyes. Had she really gone?

Miggins caught the back of Sloan's head with a punch, then, realising that he had at last struck a solid target, began to bombard the area with both fists. Sloan was held between Miggins' strongly encasing arms and he struggled to haul his head clear of the blows. The blood from his cheek had gone black on the brown carpet, and it smeared over his face as each accurate punch pushed it back into the spreading damp patch. Blindly he managed to grasp an arm and hold it at bay long enough to roll free. For the first time since he had butted Miggins he caught sight of his face. His nose had burst open and blood covered his lower face like a deep red mask, it splashed over his throat and spread into neat round blotches on his clothing.

Both men began to drag themselves to their feet, each needing to be first to gain the advantage. Sloan's head was only at waist height by the time Miggins was upright. He lashed his boot at Sloan's face, catching him under the chin and jarring his head so it felt as though it might tear from its shoulders. He fell back against the stone hearth while Miggins half turned away, swaying and squinting over the couch for his broken bottle.

Sloan had no strength to move. He was in agony with his jaw and it did not seem to fit properly into its hinges any more.

Miggins picked out his broken bottle half hidden beneath a cushion. He kicked the frame of the smashed table out of his way and leaned clumsily to grasp it, then he turned and came towards Sloan, a frightening, lumbering silhouette against the window.

Within easy reach, poised in its stand, stood a heavy, brass ornamental poker. He reached out an aching arm and grabbed and swung it in one action at the advancing Miggins. Through pure, blind luck it struck his thrusting forearm and sent the broken bottle somersaulting away. He tried to follow it up with a return swipe but the movement was a hasty and exhausted one and the poker struck the fleshy part of Miggins' thigh and spun away out of his hand. Miggins' boot thudded into Sloan's chest. Suddenly he could not breathe. He felt as though his chest had collapsed onto his lungs. He tried to haul himself to his feet. He fumbled for the mantelpiece by which he could pull himself up. One hand found it and sent a carriage clock and some small china ornaments spinning and smashing onto the hearth. But now his legs had no strength to hold him, they kept buckling on him like a new born foal's.

Miggins came at him once more and smashed his fist into Sloan's open and unguarded face. His legs gave easily and he fell to his knees, then his crumpled torso toppled and thudded like a dead man onto the carpet. His jaw felt hideously twisted and the full weight of his head seemed to be pressing on it. He gasped to find some air, each shallow breath accompanied now by a thin consumptive wheeze. But he could still think straight enough to know that whatever Miggins' maniac intentions were, he could no longer do anything to stop him.

He lay and waited, closing his eyes on the pain and the utter exhaustion, and whatever else was to come. Suddenly he could see Helen smiling at him, the way she used to, with her specially reserved smile. The smile with her eyes that were the deepest brown he had ever seen, and he began to sob. Instant tears swamped his swelling, sweating eyes. Miggins' boot thumped into his ribs and he thought he felt something give inside his chest. Why didn't she love him any more? Oh, God, why?

There was a huge and hideous woman sitting at the stolen table when Steep arrived for the Friday night shift. She sat alone clad in a brown tent of a coat, her large grey face set and smouldering. Her thick arms gripped the table like wide supports for the main hulking structure of her body. In front of her on the table was a small crumpled piece of paper with what looked like some roughly drawn variety of map and some writing on it, which she examined periodically as though for confirmation of her whereabouts.

The operators regarded her with frowns and curiosity, firing peeks and glances around, through and over cars from the other side of the line. None of them, not even Spivak would dare to speak or sit with her because she looked as though she would just as soon pull your arms off as look at you.

"Who is she?" muttered Steep. "What does she want?"

"She was already here when I arrived," shrugged Sammy. "She's just sat there and hasn't moved except every now and then she has a look at that piece of paper in front of her, as if she's reminding herself of something."

"Hasn't Rex seen her?"

Sammy grinned. "Oh, yeah. Rex has seen her all right. Somebody went and told him she was there so he had to go and ask her what she was doing here. I don't know what she said to him but he went the colour of boiled shite and practically *ran* back to the clock."

"Why hasn't he phoned security?"

"Perhaps she told him not to. *I* certainly wouldn't argue with her. I should think when she tells you something, you stay told."

"More likely he did and they all went and hid in the bog," sniffed Steep.

"She's only blinked *twice* in the last five minutes!" disclosed Godfrey who had been spying on her with fixed fascination for some time. He was slightly crouched and squinting around the windscreen pillar of a yellow Kama. His straining eyes did not deflect towards them when he spoke for fear of missing blink number three. "She just sits and *stares*," he breathed.

"Perhaps if we *all* went over to her," suggested Steep. "And if we all smiled and asked her nicely what she wanted. I mean, even if she won't say she couldn't eat more than two or three of us in one go."

"You go first, then," challenged Sammy.

"Listen, I don't have to go over there at all," pointed out Steep. "That hooter's going to go at any second and the same instant that line is going to start. May I remind you that you're the one who's standing in for Derek Kettle, so you're the one who's going to have to start fitting headlights. Now it may have escaped your attention but the aforementioned headlights are stored in the pallet which is situated right next to the table which is currently home for Mrs Grizzly over there. So you can either go first with all of us behind you, or you can go first on your own."

"No, I think I'll let Sproaty or Henry go first," decided Sammy as though modestly declaring himself unworthy of some small honour. "Let's face it. I'm basically one of life's back-room boys. Not for me the glory."

Steep regarded him disdainfully. "You mean you're chicken."

"Well, that is another way of putting it."

They both looked again at the massive woman. "What *does* she want?" wondered Steep. "Maybe she's come to

190

the wrong place. Maybe she's waiting for the bingo to start."

At that moment the hooter sounded and immediately the line kicked into its endless nightly crawl. It seemed to be what the woman had been waiting for because she stood up, pushing the juddering table away from her, and rolled out from behind it. She held the piece of paper in her big paw and she examined it once more with a short-sighted squint, then lumbered like a medium sized bear towards the line.

Some of the operators openly winced at the sight and others hurried off, quite out of character, to collect their tools.

She stopped at the side of the line and scowled across at those who foolishly remained. The cars trickled by between them and her like a narrow, torpid river. Then she spoke, her voice every inch as large as her frame. "I want to know who's called Derek Kettle." It was a straight demand, not a request.

A tentative relief ran through them all. Derek Kettle was in a hospital bed undergoing precautionary observation. Thank God it was none of them she wanted.

Unnoticed, Sproat cracked open one of his dangerously vacuous grins. Suddenly, horrifically, he was pointing at Steep. "He is, ha ha ha ha!"

For seconds no one moved. The big woman glared at Steep, her black eyes as chillingly hostile as anything he had ever seen. He could only stare back at her, open-faced, his expression a mixture of disbelief and innocent, dumb denial. Then his jaw began to work and attempted to refute the accusation but each word was snatched and disjointed. Suddenly the woman lunged across the line at him. The speed of the movement caught and shocked everyone except Steep who reacted instantly and instinctively by sprinting to the back of the car and leaping across the line to the other side. The mountainous woman chased after him, bounding across the line with an incongruous agility but by now Steep had already reached the front end of the car and jumped back so that they were again on opposite sides.

191

He was unaware of everything around him now, except the giant woman and the need to maintain a healthy distance from her. But somewhere he heard Sammy comment: "She can't half shift for a big girl." And then Spivak call heroically: "Have no fear, Albie. I'll save you."

He blinked around to find the madly gallant Spivak close to his shoulder. "Next time around," he winked confidently. "I'll see her off, mate."

Steep had no time to refuse the help because she was already coming back at him across the line. He gave a frightened yelp and ran. Spivak courageously stood his ground. Formally readying himself for his task he arranged his wiry arms into angles of prepared defence, and began to bounce on his oversized white plimsolls.

Steep watched, fearful for Spivak as the huge woman bore down on his prancing mad minder and then cringed as she flattened and trampled across him as though he was not there.

Steep began to run up the line. He figured Rex McBean ought to know that a giant lunatic woman was chasing him. He imagined a General Foreman would know what to do in the circumstances: Frozen faces flew past him as he ran. The line was running but cars were slipping away unattended by the operators because all interest was in the chase.

McBean was standing at the tall, foreman's desk. Steep almost ran into it in his fearful haste. "Rex. That woman's after me!" he gasped. "Tell her who I am. Tell her I'm not Derek Kettle!"

The General Foreman offered neither hope nor help. He looked anxiously down the line. The woman was pounding towards them like an angry bear in full flight. "Fuck that," he muttered, and then bent and crawled in beneath the desk.

"Rex!" implored Steep. "She's a bleeding maniac! She'll kill me!"

McBean remained silent in his hiding place. Steep looked again. She was too close for him to delay any longer. He ran back across the line and out into the wide aisle. The main security office was directly ahead of him, three hundred yards away and hazy with the distance. He began to run for it.

He ran for fifty yards before he turned his head. Crushingly she was still after him, perhaps twenty yards behind. He had no idea whether he was pulling away from her or whether she was gaining on him: He suggested to himself that he was ensnared by one of his odd dreams — indeed the valley, walled with blurring, sometimes shouting faces, through which he ran seemed to corroborate the suggestion. But against that, he was puffing too hard and seized by too real a fear to properly convince himself: Sometimes when he was certain he was dreaming he would deliberately confront the danger or the challenge that his subconscious had set against him — if it *was* a dream and he turned and confronted this one, he might never wake up to find out.

Two hundred yards to go. He looked back again. The woman had definitely lost some ground on him. She was trailing by maybe twenty-five or thirty yards now. Irrationally he began to doubt that he would make it to the yet remote security office. He would trip and fall, or develop a sudden cramp. Or he would tire and slow allowing the giant, rabid woman to gain inexorably and eventually overhaul him.

He ran past a staircase, then skidded and spun back and began to climb it, jumping three steps at a time. It was a high, straight staircase and he could feel his pumping thigh muscles hardening into knots. She would be slower up the stairs, he thought. He could lose her in the paint shop and then find his way down again and get to the security office.

Suddenly the whole structure began to shudder. He was only three jumps from the top. He paused and looked back, gripping the cool steel handrail and breathing hard. She had begun to climb after him — incredibly, employing the same devouring strides as himself. Her arms spanned its width and hauled her along. The staircase bounced with each nearing, climbing stride.

"Listen. I'm not Derek Kettle, honest!" shouted Steep desperately. "He was only joking, that bloke. My name's Albert. Really it is!"

The big woman was predictably unmoved. He turned miserably and took the last three jumps and burst through the swing door at the top.

193

j

There was a short, narrow walkway beyond the door that turned once to the right and then expanded into some toilets: Two operators, hung thoughtfully over the urinal, viewed the speeding Steep with no great interest and shortly dropped their heads back towards the playfully gurgling gutter. They were disturbed again just a few seconds later. This time the whole mezzanine floor began to tremble to a rhythm like that of a moderately rapid bass drumbeat. They turned quizzically towards the entrance in time to catch the shocking and frightening arrival of the mountainous woman. One of them peed unsociably all over his companion's shoes as he spun and then dried up. In their sudden fear and bemusement it did not occur to them to cover or put themselves away and they stood and stared almost full on to the woman, their sickly willies cradled delicately between two fingers, poking limp and pale from their trousers like condemned sausages.

The woman regarded each operator ferociously, but only long enough to determine that neither was the object of her pursuit. Then she jutted her bear's head towards the cubicles and seeing that they were all unoccupied, charged heavily out through the opposite doorway: Both operators frowned uncertainly at each other. Then down at the one's quietly steaming shoes.

Through the toilets was another walkway which led back down onto the lines or up to the paint shop. Steep climbed the short flight upwards.

Nobody noticed him as he pushed through into the paint shop. It was sparsely populated compared with the hectic production lines down below and much quieter, but the smells of paint and primer were distastefully strong. He searched briefly for some local concealment from where he might observe his pursuer's next actions but the prospect of a helplessly cornered discovery made him think again. He began to run without any specific plan or direction. He would lose the woman first, then he could worry about where he was.

He heard the swing door blow open and lever damagingly on its hinges behind him. He did not bother to look back. He realised quickly that it would be more difficult to shake her off up here than he had thought. The place was all long straights ranked alternately with lines of freshly painted or dull steel bodyshells. Moreover, he was unfamiliar with the floors vast layout. It occurred to him alarmingly that the next corner he turned might be a dead end.

He was fighting hard for breath now, his throat was burning and dry, his legs were heavy. He had to find a way to get out of her sight. It was too easy for her here. He had to disappear — The roof! Outside on the roof it would be pitch dark; she would never find him. He looked around for the nearest outside wall, somewhere in it there would be a door marked 'Fire Exit'.

It was over on the right, the red door standing out against the cream painted brickwork. He veered towards it, clambering across two deserted static lines full of bodies and then one which moved almost as fast as a walking pace. He cracked his ankle sickeningly on one of the body's cradling skids as he jumped across it. He almost stumbled over as he landed and then the sudden bite of pain and the rawness in his lungs made him want to throw up. He fought against it. Now the door was right in front of him. He pulled at the bar and pushed it open.

It was black outside and for five seconds he was blind. He could only feel the cold, damp, lofty wind slicing through his thin shirt. Then, gradually, roof-top shapes began to emerge; broad square ventilation inlets, the sawblade roof of the body assembly area, shady brickwork corners and sly angles, and some abandoned moulded chairs that had not borne a backside since the last of the summer sunbathers had deserted them six months ago.

He could briefly see his breath in front of him before the express wind snatched it away, and there was a weak band of light sticking nervously to the wall from the dilute spillage through the high and narrow milky windows. There was a ventilation inlet which he could only guess was about fifteen or twenty yards away. He decided it would make good cover; he could watch the door from there and see if she came through, and if she did he would still have a good distance on her if she came his way.

The damp gravel crunched under his feet so he lifted

himself onto his toes and hurried for it at a classic sneak. His ankle was hurting and he hoped he would still be able to run on it should the need arise.

The inlet was wide and as tall as he was. Through it he could hear oblivious, warm working echoes. He wished he was down there, oblivious and warm.

They would all be talking about him now. Having a good laugh. He wondered if anyone had contacted security, and if Rex McBean had come out from underneath his desk yet. The important question of why the woman should want to inflict such clearly heinous injuries upon Derek Kettle came to him almost as an afterthought, and although he could not imagine, frankly, it did not surprise him that anyone should want to.

He did not watch the door for long before it rattled open and the woman stood like a boulder filling its aperture. His stomach tightened as though gripped in a fist. The thin fluorescent light from inside squeezed past then stretched and threw her shadow so that it fell just a couple of yards short and pointed directly at him like a tell-tale finger. She hesitated there for a full ten seconds. He could see her big head making sweeping scans through the darkness. Once her head froze in mid scan and he was sure she was staring directly at him: Finally she stepped clear of the door and it clattered shut behind her, thankfully painting out the pointing finger. He watched her as she began to follow the path of the jaundiced light that ran close to the wall. She was moving away from him with every lumbering step. He shifted around the ventilation inlet to watch her go. The fisted grip on his stomach began to ease, suddenly it was a warm, tickling hand of relief. Another five seconds and he would creep off in the opposite direction . . . Well, after the next five, then . . . Definitely five seconds from now.

She was moving slowly and uncertainly. She seemed to be taking ages to establish a healthy distance from him. Suddenly she turned away from the wall, paused, then stepped unsteadily off the lighted path and into the consuming blackness. Worriedly Steep strained his eyes to try and follow her but the merging colour of her coat made it impossible. Now the hand in his stomach stopped its tickling and began to prod him with its finger.

He listened hard above the wind's cold, flat dirge for some sounds of her movement — faintly he could hear footsteps on gravel. He could not determine the direction of their movement because the wind picked up the sounds and tossed them deceitfully around the dark roof-top. Then the footsteps stopped. He listened for their resumption. For one long, cold minute he listened and heard nothing of them.

He peeped carefully around the ventilation inlet, first one side, then the other, but the harder he looked the blacker the night became. He was very frightened now, more frightened than he had had time to be since the whole mad thing started. Suddenly every impenetrable shadow, every breath of the stalking wind wanted to hurt him. He felt a strong blind urge just to run, and had he not been so frightened he might have congratulated himself for recognising the urge as a ranting panic and sensibly resisting it.

He *would* have to make a move, though, and running seemed to be the best way of making it. But which way? Where was she? Oh shit, but she might be lurking and waiting for him to do just that. His only alternative was to strike out into the darkness and hope that it was in a safe direction and that she would not be able to follow him. Wasn't that his reasoning for coming out here in the first place? God, what an arsehole of an idea that was!

It seemed ridiculous that just twenty paces away was a door through which there was light and warmth and people and normality. For a desperate moment he considered shouting for help at it. He was cold and he was frightened. Surely somebody had told security by now.

There was a staircase running down to ground level about equidistant from him as the door. If he could reach that and get down it without being seen he would surely be safe. However, such a mission could be risky because he would have to cut across part of the black area in which the giant mad woman had last been heard. He looked longingly for some seconds at the dimly visible yellow handrail, then he made the decision, quickly, before he had time to consider any more of its potentially dire consequences.

Suddenly he was clear of the ventilation inlet and hurrying

at a tip-toed crouch across the wide open roof-top towards the staircase. Despite the darkness he could not have felt more frighteningly and helplessly conspicuous had he suddenly been captured in the beam of a brilliant searchlight.

He could hardly believe it when he reached the top of the staircase unchallenged. He paused incautiously, a sudden bolt of ill-timed over-sureness firing through him and half turned to search the cold, dark windswept roof. There was no movement and no following sound. Strangely he felt a tingle of daring excitement with the rashness of his delay. Then he gripped the cold handrail and descended carefully but quickly, one step at a time, always expecting the sudden shuddering to start up which meant she was after him again. But he reached the bottom and it did not come.

He was at the back of the main assembly building, in a wide valley, its other wall being formed by the soft trim building. It was sporadically lit by weak, wall-hung lights and its neglected concrete surface was cracked and holed with small grubby ponds. He could feel the active hum from both sides of the valley and he felt bouyant, almost heroic in himself.

He paused at the foot of the staircase and considered what he should best do now. The nearest security lodge was beyond the soft trim building at the end of the dingy valley. He decided it would be best to report there.

His story would give the guards a laugh, he imagined as he walked. They might not even believe him and he would coolly tell them to phone the cowardly Rex McBean for verification.

There were rusting stacked pallets parked against the walls at odd intervals. Twenty yards ahead a large shapeless bulk lay a few feet from one of them. Steep was almost on top of it before he saw that the bulk had a large lifeless head protruding from it and sickeningly contorted arms and legs. The sight and the sudden realisation immediately blew all the shock from him and left him strangely hollowed and numb. With an empty, impassive calmness he knelt at the side of the giant mad dead woman. One knee sank two inches into an icy puddle but he did not feel it. He bent closer until his face was only inches from the woman's and he squinted curiously into it. The head lay on its side, palely lit by the thin incandescence of a nearby lamp and the eyes stared with aghast frozen stupefaction at his submerged, numbed knee. A slender worm of blood wriggled from a nostril and ran away like half of a pencil moustache to meet a creeping patch of red beneath her. Her skin was the colour of the concrete and her slightly opened mouth seemed to suggest that it at least, was only faintly surprised.

Steep reached out cautiously to touch the dead face, as though he thought it might try to bite him. He carefully touched the grey cheek, it was soft but cold. Fancy all this being a dream, after all, he thought with great relief.

He heard the harsh unpliant clatter of a towing electric trolley somewhere behind him. He looked back and began to wave amiably at it until it was close to him and it stopped with its Cyclops headlamp beaming into his face. Steep held up his hand against the light and watched the driver climb down from his cab. He approached slowly and with a heavily circumspect frown as though fearful that he had stumbled upon a freshly perpetrated murder.

"Evening," smiled Steep. "She's dead. She fell off the roof," he explained with childish simplicity.

"Fucking hell," breathed the trolley driver.

Steep looked again into the woman's face and impulsively gave her dead, bloody nose of his dreams a playful tweak. "This is the first dead person I've ever seen in real life," he explained with a grin. "If you see what I mean."

Chapter Eleven

It was a notable Monday morning for Halliwell. Notable
because for once he could perform his external duties with
the dignity that he considered proper to his position because,
surprisingly, Bellend's air was light and mild. The sky was
still grey, but at least it had gone to the trouble of not
raining on him.

He strolled up and down random aisles of the vast South
Two car park, like a slightly bored officer inspecting a
motley parade of soldiers.

On average three employees' cars a week were totally or
partially stolen. Normally the theft was fairly regulation,
but Halliwell had known of doors, wheels, seats, bonnets,
boot lids and bumpers being stolen in his time. Thankfully
such incidents seldom took place at half past ten on mild
Monday mornings. Even if they did, Halliwell told himself,
it was such a nice day that he might just hold their spanner
for them.

He glanced at his watch. The wages van would be arriving
in five minutes. He began to make his way back to the lodge.

Along both sides of the perimeter road abutting South
Two stood a solid line of cars, left there by owners who
preferred to forgo the Le Mans type exodus from the car
parks at finishing time. The road in these areas was marked
with double yellow lines but so many cars parked so
frequently on them that they had been almost completely
erased. Once, Halliwell recalled with somewhat barbarous
satisfaction, a heavily laden container lorry had skidded
and lost control one night when the road was icy, badly
damaging seventeen cars, and killing a man who was inno-

cently trying to steal a radio from one of them.

As he crossed the lifeless road Halliwell noticed a green van moving slowly then stopping a hundred yards away, half way down the shallow incline. Whatever they're selling they won't do much business at this hour, he thought. He wondered if he should go up and tell them to move it but the pleasant air made him lazy and the trudge up the hill did not greatly appeal. Instead he veered off in the direction of the lodge.

Inside the lodge a tuneless duet of Worth and Atkin swamped the wireless' more melodic rendition of *Tie a Yellow Ribbon Round the Old Oak Tree*.

"Hell's bell's," complained Halliwell, wincing at the din. "Turn it down a bit, you're frightening the horses."

"That's the trouble with you, Robert," said Atkin, breaking off from his inharmony with Worth. "Uncultured ear-holes."

"I've heard better noises coming from uncultured arse-holes," returned Halliwell dismissively.

Atkin sniffed and returned, unperturbed to his heinous union with his colleague, but the song had almost run its course and the disc jockey began to prattle over its dwindling notes.

"Anything exciting happen in the car park?" asked Worth absently, habitually fussing with his tea making equipment.

"Nothing I couldn't handle," yawned Halliwell, taking a seat opposite Atkin at the table. "This weather's knackered me," he said wearily, resting his elbows on the table and pushing his face into his palms.

"I know what you mean," said Atkin. "It's got me shagged out as well."

Halliwell slid his hands around to the side of his face. He regarded Atkin with silent disdain. "*All* weather shags you out," he said pointedly. "Heatwaves, blizzards, monsoons, they're all the bloody same to you."

"Yes I know," admitted Atkin. "Sometimes I try to worry about it but if there's any weather going on outside I can never work up enough energy to."

Halliwell closed his hands over his face again. "I could do with a nice quiet snooze," he mumbled.

"Right, Sidney," said Atkin. "A quick chorus of 'Rockaby Baby' for our sleepy old chum."

Halliwell eyed Atkin through the bars of his fingers and muttered an obscenity into his palms.

He felt himself drifting surprisingly quickly and had to check himself to keep from going under. But he kept his eyes closed and began drifting again. The conversation between Worth and Atkin and the incoherent rambling of the unheeded disc jockey began to soften and blur, becoming respectfully distant and subtly merging into one gently lulling tone. He was a second away from sleep when he heard the door open. An exquisitely cool breeze slid between his fingers and brushed against his closed face. But something was wrong. He could sense it even before he opened his eyes. There was suddenly something strange in the silence between Atkin and Worth. Only the crass chatter from the disc jockey rippled the uneasy atmosphere.

He opened his eyes and turned his head slowly towards the door. As he turned he caught a glimpse of Atkin sitting across the table from him. His face was drained, his eyes were frightened and fixed and his whole body was as still as a statue. Halliwell turned until his chin touched his shoulder: Four feet away from him, pointing straight back into his face was the evil piggish snout of a sawn-off shotgun.

His heart seemed to miss and then gallop inside his chest and his head. He felt as though he wanted to be sick. Ridiculously at a time like this, the disc jockey suggested he send in a dedication for the Golden Oldies Hour.

The man holding the gun said something but it came out croaky and muffled behind the bright red motor cycle helmet that completely covered his face. The whites of his eyes were barely visible through the closed dark visor and they were everywhere, darting back and forth as though trapped and searching for an escape.

He coughed and swallowed. "You, over there with those two," he ordered with over-rehearsed hardness. His voice was young and frightened and nervous. Too nervous to be carrying a gun, thought Halliwell. He stared in rigid fear at the young man's right hand clamped tight about the butt and the trigger. It was sucked pale because he held it so tightly, and the pad of his trigger finger was, horrifically, slightly flattened from the pressure he exerted on the lever.

202

Please God, don't let it be loaded.

He poked the gun awkwardly at Worth who had still been attending to his tea making apparatus. Worth glanced back fleetingly at his precious brewing things with the look of a father fearful for the safety of his children, then moved slowly across the room, sticking close to the opposite wall as though on the edge of a precipice. For a few steps he half raised his hands in that classic television manner always adopted by such persons similarly embarrassed, always unbidden and strangely devoid of self-consciousness, but Worth could not emulate their prompt familiarity with the action and abjectly and carefully lowered them again.

"Now sit down," he told Worth. "Listen, the three of you. Just do as you're told. Right." His voice cracked on the last word and he swallowed hard again.

The three security guards sat awkward and hollow with fear, their eyes fixed with the blank intensity of blind men: Atkin's fingers began a drumming action, but silently, their tips barely brushing the table. He looked down at them briefly but did not seem to notice their agitated movement. He looked hurriedly elsewhere and left them busily at it: Worth was next to him, a half an inch of his tongue projecting and wriggling like a trapped pink fish between his clamped teeth. Halliwell found them oddly and almost unbearably irritating and he wanted to scream at Atkin's fingers and Worth's tongue to keep still, unaware of his own foot tapping to a strong and racing beat below the table.

Suddenly Halliwell could imagine the young man as a child, probably little more than ten years ago, playing innocent war games with his mates, flourishing his plastic machine gun with childish ease and daring and making staccatoed machine gun noises through his teeth and saying jaunty things like: 'You, over there with those two,' and 'Listen, the three of you. Just do as you're told. Right?'.

Now he was grown up and doing it for real. Now only the ease and the daring were plastic. If that thing was loaded then somebody was going to get hurt, Halliwell knew that. He wondered how many baddies the young man had machine gunned to death when he was a child, and all for the sake of freedom and righteousness and John Wayne. What

203

happened?

"Next a biggy from Sonny and Cher," announced the disc jockey. "Right after the break."

The young man was looking over their heads now and through the window beyond them. His large bright red helmeted head moved in tiny, worriedly searching jumps and he gulped a swallow loud enough for them all to hear. He was holding the shotgun low with its butt pressed hard against his stomach. If he fired it like that he'd rupture himself, thought Halliwell.

It took barely ten seconds for the wages van to arrive. During which time a voice on the wireless yelled at them to rush out and buy a half price broadloom Axminster carpet. Halliwell thought it sounded like a good idea.

"Look normal," the young man demanded unreasonably. His voice was stretched taut. "Don't do anything stupid." He stepped back against the concealing strip of wall between the door and the window as the armoured van approached and stopped at the gate. The green van that Halliwell had noticed earlier crept up and stopped close behind it.

"You," ordered the young man. He snatched the shotgun up to his shoulder and tipped its black eyed barrels terrifyingly at Halliwell. "Get up and go to the door, just like normal. I'm telling you again. Don't do anything stupid."

Halliwell stood up with some little difficulty because his legs had become suddenly boneless and somehow no longer completely under his control, and moved as normally as his estranged legs would permit towards the door.

Five feet nine inches, he estimated, gauging the young man's height against his own, slim build, local accent, late teens or early twenties, denim jacket and jeans, bright red crash helmet: The shotgun's suspicious, close, deadly eyes followed him unerringly towards the door causing each mental entry to be pushed into oblivion by the subsequent one. He was wearing a bright red crash helmet. That was all that stuck.

Halliwell reached out for the door handle when there was a sudden screech of tyres outside, then a crunch of colliding metal as the wages van smashed its heavy rear bumper into the green van pushing it easily backwards up the road.

Halliwell froze in mid-reach. Worth and Atkin spun in their seats to see what had happened. Then the shotgun went off.

Its deafening, exploding report instantly crammed itself into every cranny of the small room until it reached bursting point and a window gave way and Worth's chest tore open as he was sucked backwards out of his seat towards it, until he collided with Atkin.

For a full five seconds no one moved. Their eyes stared but did not comprehend because the bang from the shotgun still fogged and filled their heads.

Atkin sat like an uncomfortable and embarrassed ventriloquist with Worth sprawled across his lap in the manner of a large, unruly dummy. His upper chest and neck gaped and pumped thick, real blood.

Outside, a million miles away, the two vans neared a result in their brief and mis-matched push of war. The wages van was heavier and had more muscle. It left the green van standing sideways across the perimeter road and ran.

"Move!" the young man suddenly bawled. There were definite tears in the voice. Locked together inside the bright red helmet with the shock and the fear and the frustration.

Halliwell still stood close to the door. He did not move because he could not move and he did not hear, so the young man ran at him and smashed the butt of the shotgun into the side of his head. He staggered sideways, the lodge began to spin around him and it tried to go black and his legs tried to buckle under him but he fought it and kept on his feet. The side of his head went numb but his ear felt as though it was on fire.

The young man was out and running towards the green van now. Angry rods of steam hissed from its punched in radiator as it bad temperedly manoeuvred itself.

He dropped the shotgun half way and left it where it fell in the road. Voices in the van yelled at him to go back for it but he just kept running while the voices kept yelling at him to go back for the gun. He reached the van and tugged frantically at the door but instead of it opening, two large fists came through the window and began to drum comically against the hard, bright red crash helmet, and then a thick wooden shaft from some implement came through and began to bash and prod it too and all the time the voices screamed at him to go back for the gun: Eventually he did, running so fast that he was continuously almost falling headlong. He snatched up the shotgun and turned in one movement, dropped it and snatched it up again. This time the door was open and ready for him. Beckoning arms reached out and wrenched him off his feet and the van made off, noisey and blustering, its door flapping like an elephant's green ear. The young man's feet were sticking out and thrashing crazily in the air. They were still running.

It was as though some violent and freakish whirlwind had sprung up right there inside the lodge and then, satisfied that it had caused sufficient destruction, whirled away.

Halliwell could hear a baby gurgling in his one good ear. He turned towards the sound and the movement made him stagger like a drunk. It came from Worth. Blood bubbled from his open throat and chest. Atkin was bent over him, holding him gently in his arms and rocking him minutely like a comforting mother. Must phone, thought Halliwell. Must phone. But he had forgotten where the phone was and he thought if he moved again he might fall over. Worth just lay there and gurgled from his throat and chest and stared fixedly up Atkin's nostrils as though he had discovered something terrible up there. Then the gurgling stopped. Atkin's white, helpless, blood spattered face turned up towards Halliwell.

As promised, the disc jockey came back right after the break. "It's exactly ten forty-five," he informed them brightly.

Suddenly a violent pain shot through Halliwell's head as though it were a hammer driven steel spike.

"How's your Monday morning going so far?" inquired the disc jockey. "Not too fed up I hope."

"When can I have a go in the car? . . . When can I have a go in the car, Albie?"

"What? I don't know. Tomorrow maybe."

"Pardon."

"Tomorrow. Later in the week. I don't know."

206

"You'll be in bed all day tomorrow. Why can't you take me out now? Just around the block . . . Albie?"

"Listen. Can you just drop it for now. I'm not in the mood."

"Sorry. Is it that woman? Is it still bothering you?"

"I'm all right. Just don't go on, eh."

"Sorry. I just thought it might take your mind off it. We'll leave it for now then, until you feel more like it. D'you want to test me on the Highway Code?"

"No."

"Okay . . . The price of things in this catalogue."

"How come you can never manage to make more than half a statement in any one sentence?"

"Pardon."

"Nothing."

"Honestly, at these prices it would cost a fortune if you were furnishing a house or something."

"It's just as well you're not then, isn't it?"

"Pardon."

"Nothing."

"You're not half mumbling a lot lately, Albie. Auntie Aggie's been gone a long time. I should have gone with her. All that shopping will be heavy."

"She'll be nattering. She'll come back with a box of matches and a toilet roll."

"And a plug."

"What?"

"A plug for that other lamp standard she won at the bingo. I reminded her to get one for it before she went."

"Oh."

"She said she'll have more than Gerty Tulley soon, at this rate. She said they call her Gerty Tulley, The Lamp Standard Queen down at the bingo. She's even got one in her outside toilet, so I believe."

"How positively decadent."

"It's been good practise for you really, hasn't it. Living with Auntie Aggie, I mean. With her being a widow and that."

"Daf."

"You've always been the man of the house, putting plugs

on and that. It's been good practise for when you get your own place."

"Daf, listen. What do you say we pack it in?"

"Pardon."

"I said, perhaps we should stop seeing each other."

"Is it me going deaf or are you mumbling again?"

"I said I think we should stop seeing each other."

"What? How d'you mean?"

"Christ, I can't make it much plainer."

"Don't make jokes like that, Albie. And you're shouting now. Mumbling then shouting."

"I'm not joking. I've been thinking, that's all. I think we should."

"Why?"

"Oh, don't start crying, please."

"You're shouting. Stop shouting."

"Sorry. I've stopped shouting now so stop crying."

"Tell me why."

"I just think it's best, that's all."

"And that's supposed to be a good enough reason, is it?"

"I can't explain. It's just the way I feel."

"There must be a *reason*."

"There's someone else."

"When? How long? . . . Tell me."

"I don't know. A few months."

"When have you been seeing her? Where did you meet her?"

"Oh, does it matter?"

"Tell me."

"I met her on the bus. We get the same bus in the morning when I'm on days. I've been seeing her . . . when I haven't been seeing you."

"What's her name?"

"Daf, this isn't . . ."

"I want to know her name."

"It's Sarah."

"Why? Is she prettier than me? That wouldn't take much, would it? Has she got a nice body? Is that it? Bigger tits than me?"

"Don't be . . ."

"Has she?"

"Yes she has, and her bloody ears don't stick out, either. Sorry, there was no need for that. Come on now, stop crying. Auntie Aggie will be back soon."

"There's more to it than just having a nice body, you know."

"I know, I'm sorry, forget I said that. Come on now, stop crying. You don't want Auntie Aggie to see you like this. It'll only upset her."

"You mean *you* don't want her to see me like this. And what about *me?* What am I *supposed* to do? Aren't *I* entitled to be upset?"

"I'm sorry, Daf. I'm *really* sorry . . . Look, perhaps it would be best if you went home, I can get you a taxi if . . ."

"What about *my* mother. She's got eyes too, you know."

"I'll take you home if you like. You'll be all right by the time we get there. I'll still teach you to drive if you like."

"Christ, you can't wait to get rid of me, can you? This new bit of stuff waiting outside, is she?"

"Do you want to go home or not?"

"No, I don't."

Her head dropped and she cried quietly into her hands. Steep pushed his own hands into his face and worked them as though he was trying to rub the skin off. Then he pulled his hands away and looked at her across the dim little room with all her simple, spotless female dreams crumbling about her wretched sticky-out ears. He turned away and gave a long, thin, helpless sigh; the out rushing air making way for a frightening displacing loneliness in his chest.

He wanted to go over to her and put his arms around her and kiss her greasy hair and her sticky-out ears and tell her he was really sorry and please not to cry. Instead he stood up and paced aimlessly to the small window.

His eyes were unaccustomed to the street's sudden brimming daylight and he squinted out, close to the grey hanging net curtains. They smelled dry and dusty.

A fatally early fly lay on its back on the window frame, all its legs arranged and smartly pointing upwards as though it were a trained fly performing a trick.

Everything seemed so unreal; the posed dead fly, the full day outside, the dim little room around him sad with Daffy's sobs and his lies. It all belonged in the same half-lit world as the dead woman who had turned out to be Andrew Bright's mother, mad with vengeance. He tried hard to think himself out of it but his head was full of fog. What did he want? What *did* he *really* want?

Auntie Aggie was coming along the street and he wanted to run away and hide somewhere. He felt drained and miserable. And he felt a powerful and, he told himself, unjustified guilt.

"Auntie Aggie's coming," he said, not turning. His voice was strangely flat because he did not know what tone it should properly be.

Auntie Aggie was on the other side of the street, walking and talking with another elderly woman who lived over there. They stopped almost directly opposite where Steep was standing and briefly wound up their conversation. They waved and Steep heard them laugh across the narrow street at something Auntie Aggie said in parting.

Daffy sniffed and sobbed behind him. "Oh, come on, Daf," he pleaded emptily, turning this time. She looked up at him for the first time in what seemed like an age. Her eyes looked sore and red and they seemed to have sunk back into her head. She found a handkerchief somewhere and she mopped her wet cheeks and her raw eyes.

"Come on, don't cry," he said awkwardly.

They heard the front door rattle open and shut and Auntie Aggie call to herself: "Oh, bloody hell. I forgot the pigging light bulb."

Steep stood helplessly still. He felt like a burglar who knew he was about to be caught red-handed. Even Daffy made some token dabbing and shifting attempts to compose herself but it was much too late by now. They listened to Auntie Aggie going through to the kitchen.

"You could go now," he said desperately, hating himself for saying it. "I'll say you had to leave in a hurry."

Daffy's red eyes looked blankly at him. There should have been anger or bitterness in them, he thought. But there was none of that.

He heard Auntie Aggie shuffling back up the hall and again he desperately wanted not to be there. She stopped outside the door and called in: "Anyone want tea?"

"Yes, all right then, please," said Steep automatically. Then he looked helplessly to Daffy like the guilty party in an identity parade about to be given away.

She sniffed and swallowed and took a careful breath. "Yes, me too, please," she said steadily. Auntie Aggie went back to the kitchen. "She'll have to know," said Daffy, her voice becoming rough and cracked again. She turned her red stained face up to him. "She's going to find out what's happened." She looked at him steadily and they were silent for some seconds. Then her eyes compressed and squeezed out two more tears. Suddenly she was studying him, regarding him carefully with a strange and worrying curiosity; as though she had detected something in his look that he had not intended to be there. He hid it by spinning away to the window.

Auntie Aggie came in balancing a tray with three tea-cups steaming like power station cooling towers. Steep hurried and pulled the door open wide for her and then closed it. She was being careful with the tray and she did not notice Daffy's smeary face until she was well into the room and close to her. She bent slightly, like a solicitous old waitress about to receive a complaint. "What's the matter, love?" she whispered as though Steep was not meant to hear.

Daffy tilted her face up to him. She studied him as she had before, but this time more briefly, as though only for confirmation. His look was still there. It was stuck to him and it was whispering something at her and he could not shut it up.

Daffy took one of the steaming teacups from the tray. "Thanks, Auntie Aggie," she smiled, dabbing at her tears. "Nothing's the matter, really."